CAPTURED BY
THE WIZARD

Steve struggled vainly against the ropes that held him. He could smell the moist leaves rotting on the forest floor and the smell of wood burned long ago. He was naked, bound hand and foot to stakes driven into the ground. How had he gotten here? He thrashed madly—he *must* get free!

"Do not bother to struggle, Master Wilkinson," a familiar, rasping voice said. "You are mine now."

Steve looked up into the red, burning eyes of Belevairn. At least, he *thought* it was Belevairn— that was who the voice belonged to. But Belevairn looked . . . different. He wore no gold mask and, instead of the mummified corpse Steve knew him to be, he looked like . . . *Steve* . . .

Steve saw the wizard smile as the realization hit him. Oh, God. Oh, dear God, this couldn't be happening.

"But it is, Master Wilkinson," Belevairn said, sensing his thoughts. "I defeated you at Quarin and now I have defeated you here, in your own mind. I have always been your better. You have lost."

Steve screamed . . .

Ace Books by Thomas K. Martin

A TWO-EDGED SWORD
A MATTER OF HONOR

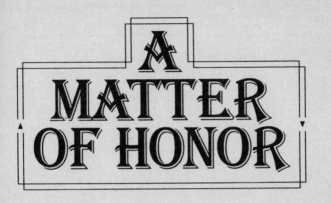

A MATTER OF HONOR

THOMAS K. MARTIN

ACE BOOKS, NEW YORK

This book is an Ace original edition,
and has never been previously published.

A MATTER OF HONOR

An Ace Book / published by arrangement with
the author

PRINTING HISTORY
Ace edition / October 1994

All rights reserved.
Copyright © 1994 by Thomas K. Martin.
Cover art by Donato.
This book may not be reproduced in whole or in part,
by mimeograph or any other means, without permission.
For information address: The Berkley Publishing Group,
200 Madison Avenue, New York, NY 10016.

ISBN: 0-441-00107-6

ACE®
Ace Books are published by The Berkley Publishing Group,
200 Madison Avenue, New York, NY 10016.
ACE and the "A" design are trademarks
belonging to Charter Communications, Inc.

PRINTED IN THE UNITED STATES OF AMERICA

10 9 8 7 6 5 4 3 2 1

Chapter
-------- One -------------

STEVE WILKINSON WALKED from the track to the men's locker room. He stripped out of his sweaty clothes and stuffed them into his gym bag. The shower was going to be a welcome relief after this afternoon's mile.

He sighed as he stepped into the shower, allowing the hot water to relax the muscles of his legs. It had been a long recovery from his month-long coma. Thanks to a couple of months of physical therapy and his own follow-up exercise program, he had bounced back.

His mind wandered back to the dream experiment that had placed him into the coma in the first place. What nobody knew, and what Steve dared not tell anyone, was that the coma had *not* been the fault of that experiment.

No one would believe him if he told them that he had fallen into the coma because a sorcerer on another world had accidentally conjured his soul away to clothe it in another body. All that would accomplish would be to get him locked up in a funny farm somewhere. It certainly wouldn't get Doctor Engelman's tenure restored.

With another relaxed sigh, he turned off the shower. He had to hit the books for that calculus test tomorrow. He paused to examine himself in the mirror as he dried off. The face that looked back at him he had known all his life—short brown hair, brown eyes, clean-shaven.

The body had changed, however. Instead of the scrawny bookworm he'd been since childhood, some definition was beginning to show. Not too bad, he decided. He wasn't in the condition that he'd been in back in Quarin, for certain,

1

but the last five months had made him a far cry from the bookworm he'd started out as.

It took a lot longer here than it had in Quarin, though. Now he understood why—one had to take the time to heal between sessions. Theron and Caradoc had eliminated that with their healing arts. There he could accomplish in one day what it now took him two or three weeks to manage. Of course, the average person in Quarin didn't have access to healers, either. Steve had been a . . . special case.

He threw the wet towel into the gym hamper on the way to his locker. He had to quit living in Quarin. The year he had spent there, while his body lay comatose for a month back here, had marked him for life. That he couldn't change, nor would he want to, but it was time to pick up and go on with his life here. Quarin, and Aerilynn, were gone forever.

His new dorm mate, and old friend, Frank Caldwell, was a big help. He was determined to make certain that Steve got out, rather than letting him spend all his time hitting the books. There was even talk of Frank fixing him up with a couple of girls that he knew, but Steve wasn't sure he was interested in anything like that quite yet.

Steve stood up from the bench and got his wallet and comb to put back in his pants. Frank had mentioned a party tonight, in fact. Hopefully he would already be out so Steve could crack the books instead. . . .

"Hey, look who's here," Steve heard a familiar voice say behind him. "It's Wimpy Wilkinson!"

And then, of course, there was Bruce. Steve had blissfully forgotten him during his year in Quarin. He reached into the locker and pulled out his belt before turning to face Bruce. The jock had a couple of his football friends with him, of course. Steve smiled wryly.

"This is the men's locker room, Wilkinson," Bruce said. "The girls' is across the hall."

"Hey, man," one of the other guys said. "Lay off. I heard he's been sick."

"Thank you," Steve said to his nameless defender. "But you apparently don't know Bruce. That just makes it better, you see, because that way he *knows* I won't hurt him. After all, he really *is* a coward."

Bruce's mouth fell open in surprise as his face began to turn purple. After a few inarticulate, strangling sounds he finally got his voice under control.

"You little bastard!" he said, starting forward. "I'll . . ."

Whatever Bruce was about to threaten was cut off by a cry of pain as Steve's belt buckle sliced open his cheek. Bruce recoiled, raising his hand to the wound. His shocked expression as he looked down at the blood on his hand was almost comical. Almost.

Bruce looked up angrily, just as Steve's foot landed in his abdomen, sending him over the bench behind him to slam into the lockers. He slid down between the lockers and the bench, apparently unconscious.

One of the others reached toward Steve. That was why Bruce never went anywhere alone—he liked to have backup.

Steve grabbed the extended wrist and slammed his other hand into the elbow. There was the sound of breaking bone as the arm bent the wrong way. His opponent's face paled and his eyes rolled back into his head before he fell.

Steve turned to the one who had spoken in his defense when this mess started.

"Hey, man," the guy said, retreating, "I don't want no trouble."

Kill them whispered through his mind. *They deserve it.*

Shut up, Steve thought back firmly. The voice in his mind silenced after sending a wave of anger at him.

"Then I suggest," Steve said, flatly and evenly, "that you go over to that pay phone and call an ambulance for these two jerks." He fought to ignore the thought that had passed through his mind. It was not his—it was Belevairn's.

"Yeah—right."

Steve turned and left, once the other was a safe distance away. Hopefully Frank hadn't left the dorm yet . . .

Belevairn cowered on the steps to the throne as Daryna glared down at him. Her angry green eyes pierced him from a face hidden in shadow.

"Why do they still live?" she demanded. "No one may shame a member of the Twelve and live to speak of it. No one!"

"M-Mistress . . ." he began hesitantly.

"Silence!" she commanded. "You shall lay their heads at my feet on the morrow."

"Mistress, I . . . I cannot . . ."

"And why not?"

He could not answer. There was some reason, but it eluded him. Why could he not kill them? Then he remembered.

"I w-would be . . . expelled?" The answer did not seem right.

"I . . . I mean imprisoned," he corrected. But who could imprison him—one of the Twelve?

"Who *are* you?" Daryna asked. The question confused him even more. He was Belevairn, commander of the *kaivir* and one of the Twelve Dread Lords of Delgroth.

"Who are you, impostor?"

His gaze rose to meet hers. She had risen from the golden throne and was descending the marble steps toward him. He trembled but could not move as she approached him, although a part of him longed to run . . . to flee . . .

She cupped her hand underneath his chin, her green eyes staring into his. Without warning, she ripped away the golden mask. He gasped, but did not crumble into dust as he had feared. Then he heard the tinkling sound of her laughter.

"Why Dreamer," she said sweetly. "You have come to me at last."

She bent her face toward his, to kiss him. As her lips parted Steve saw the fangs they concealed. He began to scream . . .

"Steve!" someone shouted, shaking him by the shoulders. "Steve! Wake up, man!"

Steve blinked and looked around at the familiar surroundings. Frank's face slowly came into focus in the bright light.

Steve was sitting up in his bed at the dorm.

"Frank?" he said.

"Yeah, it's me. That must have been *some* nightmare," Steve's dorm mate said.

Steve fell back onto the bed, throwing his arm over his eyes to block the light from the ceiling fixture. He let out his breath in a ragged sigh. It had all seemed so real—the stone steps, the gilded throne, all of it. And all through Belevairn's eyes . . .

"You were really acting weird," Frank said after a moment. "Babbling, tossing and turning. Then you just sat up and screamed. I almost hit the ceiling."

"Sorry, Frank," Steve replied.

"Wanna talk about it?"

"No. It was just a nightmare. It's over. What time is it?"

"Just after four-thirty," Frank replied.

He would be getting up in two hours. The way he felt right now, it would be at least that long before he got back to sleep. Steve threw his feet over the side of the bed.

"What are you doing?" Frank asked as Steve began to dress.

"Getting up," Steve replied, tucking his shirt into his jeans. "After that I won't be able to get back to sleep—at least not for a while."

"Are you sure you don't . . . What are you going to do with that?" Frank's gaze fell on the sword Steve took out of the closet.

"Going to work out a little bit," Steve replied, buckling the sword belt around his waist. "Unwind a little."

The mail-order replica had been the closest thing he could find to the sword he'd used in Quarin. He was not overly impressed with the blade, but the balance was good enough for practice . . .

"Be back in a bit," he said before closing the door to the dorm room. Frank just nodded at him.

The courtyard of the dorm was deserted. Natural enough at this hour. The early morning air, this early in the summer, was still crisp and fresh.

You are *me*, Belevairn's voice whispered in his mind. *We are one.*

Never! Steve shouted back silently. He was answered with only a malicious chuckle.

Steve trembled in anger. The ritual that had culminated in Steve's death in the forest outside Quarin had passed his and Belevairn's minds through one another. The memories of each were indelibly written into the mind of the other. Before Steve, however, no one had ever survived the ritual to learn that the transfer went both ways.

It was made worse by the fact that Steve had not had the benefit of the magic that normally prevented the alien memories from becoming a separate and distinct person within his own mind. Now he was cursed with Belevairn's constant presence in his mind. Steve took a deep, shuddering breath and assumed the stance Erelvar had taught him.

The ring of the sword as it flew out of its scabbard into a flat arc broke the stillness of the sleeping campus. Steve listened as the echoes rang back, savoring the weight of the blade in his hand.

He stepped, left foot forward, bringing the sword down in an overhand smash that would shatter the shoulder of an opponent. *Step again; complete the arc; bring the sword around into the backhand shoulder strike . . .*

This night's dream had been the worst in weeks. No doubt his encounter with Bruce had stimulated it. That, and the alcohol he had drunk later. *Step again; bring the sword to the left in a flat arc. Again—bringing the sword backhand to the right, the blade horizontal . . .*

It would probably be best not to drink again for some time. The alcohol weakened his will—allowed Belevairn's memories and personality to gain too much power. *Arrest the arc; step; thrust forward. Pull the sword back; thrust up, over and down behind the enemy's shield . . .*

But the exercise, the physical training—those were alien to Belevairn's experience. Those things strengthened Steve's hold on his mind. *Step; thrust backhand; up, over and down—hold position; complete the arc; swing around in a backhand smash to the head . . .*

The worst part was knowing that, just as Steve was possessed of all Belevairn's knowledge, Belevairn knew everything that Steve had ever been taught. *Step; swing the blade back, down and up to the opponent's left knee. Complete the arc; step; bring the blade up against the right knee . . .*

He had seen what even incomplete knowledge could do in the hands of a sorcerer when he had taught Artemas about lightning. What could Belevairn, with a thorough understanding of basic physics, accomplish? *Step; swing down in an overhand smash to the head. Arrest the arc; step; swing back, forward and up between the opponent's legs . . .*

The possibilities were horrifying. Steve resheathed the sword, glancing up at the window to the dorm room he shared with Frank. No matter what Belevairn did, it no longer concerned Steve—it was time to get on with his own life. . . .

Chapter
------- Two -------------

BELEVAIRN WAITED, IMPATIENTLY, as his mount probed the mists of the Gray Plain for an entrance to the physical world. The Power was so weak here that conditions must be perfect for any one location to be able to receive him— he never knew where he would emerge . . .

A familiar, twisting sensation heralded his departure from the Gray Plain. The mists parted and they emerged into absolute darkness. Even as he noted the musty smell of dry earth surrounding him, he felt the flesh of the demon-steed beneath him dissolve into nothingness. He cried out in surprise as the saddle, left behind by the fleeing demon, fell out from beneath him.

He landed amid the falling tack and harness. The impact with the compacted earthen floor would have been painful had he still been mortal. As it was, nothing more than his pride was injured. What had caused his mount to flee so? If he had lost it here . . .

No . . . he was able to feel it nearby. Angrily, he summoned it to him, his mind wrapping about the demon's will. The *goremka* attempted to comply, but met resistance—painful resistance. Belevairn released his hold on the mount, curiosity replacing anger. Where had they arrived? The darkness was absolute, and the echoes of his movement confirmed that he was underground.

Belevairn tried to call forth what meager Power lay in this place to fashion a light and was rewarded with immediate, searing pain. He hastily released the Power before it could injure him.

Idiot! He should have realized when the *goremka* could not come to him that they had emerged on sacred ground. Weak as it was, and filtered through the barrier to the Gray Plain, the Power had been neutral. Here on the actual soil that contained it, it was unusable, even dangerous to him.

That left him in something of a predicament. Belevairn knelt down and fumbled in the darkness until he found his saddlebags. After a few more moments of fumbling, his hand closed on the object he sought. Hopefully it had not been damaged in the fall.

The bright beam of the flashlight showed him a large, octagonal room. Very primitive—Stone Age, perhaps. More distressing, however, was the fact that he could discern no exits. Was this some type of sealed tomb?

No; in the ceiling he saw what must have once been the entrance—an earth-choked, square hole in the stone roof. Still, if he could not clear it, this might as well be a sealed tomb—his.

Reaching that hole was going to be a problem. The entrance, if such it was, was a good ten or twelve feet overhead. Belevairn shone the light around the room. There was possibly enough rubble to build a pile high enough for him to reach the roof. He leaned the flashlight against a pillar and set to work.

Several hours later, Belevairn had finally excavated the entrance enough to reach the surface. He carried his tack up the mound of rubble and pushed them through before pulling himself out of his would-be tomb. He rose to his feet, brushing the dirt from his clothing as he looked around in the full moonlight.

He was in a desert—it looked like the American Southwest, but he couldn't be certain without checking. He hoisted the saddle onto his shoulder and walked over to where the *goremka* waited, safely off the consecrated ground of the ancient temple. As he saddled his mount, the first light of dawn began to glow on the horizon. He pulled a small radio out of the saddlebags. Hopefully it had fared as well in the fall as the flashlight.

It had. A drawling disc jockey on some country music station soon confirmed his location. Belevairn had emerged in Colorado. That wasn't good enough for his purposes, however. Again Belevairn rummaged through his saddlebags, removing a sextant and compass. In order to contact and coordinate with the *kaivir* awaiting him in Nicaragua, Belevairn would have to determine his exact location.

Soon he had it—one hundred and nine degrees west longitude. According to his maps that should put him near, or maybe even in, Mesa Verde National Park. Pueblo country—that temple he had arrived in was probably Pueblo in origin.

The cellular telephone *had* been damaged in the fall. Now Belevairn would have to wait for local noon before he had enough Power to contact Nicaragua. Damn! A quarter-day here would be almost three days back in Delgroth. Because of that time difference, his activities here on Earth had consumed over five years while only a little over five months had passed in Nicaragua.

Still, it did little good to mourn his fortune. He should scout the area to ensure that he was in no danger of being seen. Demons mounted on flying horses would be much harder to explain away here in the United States than in Central America.

The local terrain, now illuminated by the growing daylight, fit what little his stolen memories knew of Colorado. He was atop a deep canyon—one of many that wound its way through the countryside, intersecting with others to create the flat-topped mesa he stood upon. Belevairn mounted and led his mount out over the canyon, beginning a slow tour of the perimeter of the mesa.

Apparently this site was deep in the Colorado desert, reasonably far from habitation and, currently, not plagued by sightseers. Belevairn smiled. Much better than the time he had arrived at Stonehenge and had been forced to spend almost half a day hiding from tourists.

Mike Daniels snapped several photographs as the sun rose over the opposite mesa. A few more shots of the sun rising amid the juniper, and he would go back to camp for breakfast. He scanned the opposite mesa through his telephoto lens—this trip to Mesa Verde was sure to have netted him some prize-winning photos.

He almost fell from the edge of the mesa when he spotted the horse through his camera. It trotted through the air of Soda Canyon, sparks striking from its hooves. Mike ducked behind the shadows of Cedar Tree Tower, hardly believing his eyes.

Smoke and fire snorted from the monster's nostrils, but the rider was even worse than the mount. It was wearing some kind of black robe and baggy trousers. Its black cloak flapped behind it. The rider's face turned toward him, looking over the top of the mesa. Mike tried to press himself flatter against the side of the tower, praying that the thing did not see him.

Sunlight flashed off the golden mask it wore. Or was that its face? Mike's fingers frantically worked the action of his camera. *Nobody* was going to believe this . . .

"We just need to pick up some beer for the party, tonight," Frank was saying. "It won't take long."

"Sure, Frank," Steve replied, pulling into the shopping center's parking lot. In this instance, Steve knew that "some" beer meant at least two or three cases.

"You can just wait in the car, if you like," Frank said.

"No," Steve said. "I need to pick up something for me to drink tonight."

"Oh, yeah. Are you still having those nightmares?"

"You should know," Steve replied. "Have I woken up screaming since I stopped drinking?"

"No . . . you haven't," Frank said after a moment.

"Case closed."

They walked into the coolness of the convenience store. Steve had missed the spring semester during his coma and following convalescence. He had barely gotten released in time to register for the summer semester.

Frank headed straight for the beer coolers like a dog on a scent. Steve turned down another aisle toward the soft drink coolers. That damn stuff probably wasn't much better for him than the beer. Maybe he would get some fruit juice instead.

He absently glanced at the magazine rack. He always got a laugh from the title pages on the pulps. He smiled at the nonsense headlines about alien and Elvis sightings. What was the difference, after all?

Steve stopped in the aisle at the sight of one weekly magazine's full-color cover. A man in black robes with a black cloak rode on the back of a horse in mid-air. Steve's smile vanished and a chill passed over him as he stared at the cover photograph. For several moments he could not tear his gaze from the picture to read the outrageous headline.

GHOST RIDER HAUNTS THE COLORADO PUEBLOS!

"Belevairn," Steve whispered. It could not be true. How could the Dread Lord cross the gulf between worlds to Earth?

Even as he wondered, Steve knew the answer—the demon-horse, the *goremka*. And there was no doubting the identity of the . . . being in the photograph. The bearing, the dress and the golden mask left no room for doubt.

But why? Why would Daryna send Belevairn to Earth? Was he after Steve? At that thought, a lump formed in Steve's throat.

If he was after us, he would already have found us, Belevairn's voice replied contemptuously in his mind.

That was true. The real Belevairn would know exactly how to find Steve.

Then why is he here? Steve asked reluctantly. He did not enjoy conversing with the person who now shared his mind.

I do not know, Belevairn replied. *I have been a bit out of touch lately.*

Steve frowned. There was only one person on Earth who *would* know the answer to that question—Belevairn himself. . . .

"Hey . . ." someone said, behind him. Steve's elbow snapped back at the unexpected sound, almost hitting Frank in the stomach before Steve could stop it.

"Whoa!" Frank said, stepping away from Steve, his eyes wide with surprise.

"Sorry, Frank," Steve said. "You . . . startled me."

"I guess! Have you been taking karate or something?"

"Uh . . . yeah. Yes, I have. Part of my physical therapy." It was a better explanation than the truth. It was nice of Frank to provide it for him . . .

"You need to lighten up, man," Frank said. "You almost nailed me!"

"Sorry."

"Are you ready to go?"

"Almost. Let me grab some Pepsi."

"Sure."

Steve left the magazine rack and grabbed a six-pack of Pepsi. On the way back to the counter he paused at the magazine rack again. Finally, he took a copy of the magazine and walked up to the checkout.

"Don't tell me you believe that shit," Frank said, gesturing at the tabloid Steve laid on the counter. "Just look at the phony picture on the cover!"

"Of course not," Steve lied. "They're good for a laugh, though."

What else could he say? Hey, I know the guy the cover story's about? Not likely. Frank would think he was completely insane—and rightly so.

Why *was* Belevairn on Earth? The story inside was probably pure garbage, but it might give him some leads.

It wasn't until much later that night that Steve was able to get away from the party and read his magazine. He had excused himself early, claiming fatigue. It was amazing how much mileage one could get out of having been seriously ill six months ago.

He settled into the dorm lobby's only stuffed chair and began flipping through the magazine, searching for the cover story. Why the hell didn't they put a table of contents in these things, anyway? He finally found the story more than halfway through the magazine.

A few more pictures adorned the article. Steve spared only the slightest of glances for them—he was already certain it was Belevairn. He was more interested in whatever facts he could glean from the article . . .

GHOST RIDER HAUNTS COLORADO'S DESERT SKIES
by Richard Alexander

Cortez, Colorado

Amateur photographer Mike Daniels almost fell to his death when a horseman from Hell surprised him during a vacation near Cortez, Colorado.

"All I wanted were a few shots of the desert sunrise," Daniels said when questioned by reporters. "The last thing I expected was to come face to face with the Devil himself."

Daniels, an accountant from Columbus, Ohio, was vacationing with friends in Mesa Verde National Park where the incident occurred. On the last day of their vacation Daniels left the group to get some pictures of the sun rising over the Colorado desert.

Daniels had taken several photographs just after dawn. Afterwards, the amateur nature photographer was about to start back when he saw the demonic horseman.

"I was so shocked I almost fell into the canyon," Daniels explained. "When that horse came trotting around the side of the mesa in mid-air, I almost had a heart attack. I don't even remember taking the pictures."

Daniels said that the horse's hooves were striking sparks as the monster trotted through the air. Smoke and fire puffed from its nostrils, and Daniels said that its eyes glowed like embers.

Even more terrifying than the nightmarish steed, however, was its rider. Daniels remembers a feeling of great evil that emanated from the horseman and said that "looking into his eyes was like looking into Hell itself."

Authorities were at a loss to explain either the bizarre encounter or the photographs taken by Daniels. "We've never had anything like this happen before," said Mesa Verde park officials. "There's no doubt that Mr. Daniels saw something—we just don't know what."

Steve glanced at the next page. Surely that couldn't be the entire article? It was the cover story, for cryin' out loud!

That was, indeed, the entire article. All he had learned was that Belevairn had been sighted in Mesa Verde National Park. There was a little more information, however. A small, black-and-white map showed some place called Cedar Tree Tower as well as the positions of Mr. Daniels and the "monster" in relation to it.

But no date had been given and the time had only been indirectly mentioned. Still, it must have occurred less than, say, two or three weeks ago—this magazine was a weekly publication.

The big question facing Steve was what was *he* going to do about it? The name of some national park and a few photographs weren't much to start on.

Steve sighed. It was still early enough in the semester to drop his classes. What would he tell people? Especially his parents? That he was going to go hunting for "Ghost Riders From Hell?"

Why go at all? Belevairn asked.

I have to, Steve replied. *No one else knows what must be done.*

You'll get us both killed, fool.

Shut up. With an effort of will, Steve forced Belevairn's presence to the back of his mind. Steve, himself, might never be free of the sorcerer, but perhaps he could at least rid two worlds of him . . .

Chapter
-------- **Three** ------------

THE OLD, LIGHT blue pickup truck bounced along the narrow road. Steve glanced down at the map on the passenger seat next to him. It had been eight days since he had first seen Belevairn's photograph in that pulp magazine. There had been no follow-up story in the next issue he'd bought in Denver.

He had wanted to get out here sooner, but it had taken several days to wrap up his affairs in Albany. Steve glanced up in the rear-view mirror at the twelve-gauge, pump shotgun in the gun rack behind him. Selling his Firebird had given him enough to buy this old truck and the shotgun, as well as a little operating cash. *Very* little operating cash.

Hopefully he would find some clue to Belevairn's whereabouts at Mesa Verde before his capital ran out. Unfortunately, this would be the height of the tourist season. On the one hand, that would help conceal his activities, but it could also hinder him.

It was too much to hope that Belevairn might still be in the vicinity—a national park hardly seemed an out-of-the-way spot to conduct his business, whatever that might be. Still, if the sorcerer *had* decided to stick around, the combination of buckshot and magnesium flares loaded into the shotgun ought to give him a nasty surprise.

At that thought, Steve pulled over to the side of the road. That shotgun might give *him* a nasty surprise if he didn't get it out of sight before he tried to enter the park. He carefully placed it behind the seat before going on.

A few miles later he arrived at the park entrance. Two small booths guarded the entrance into the park. Steve pulled up to the one on the right and paid his entrance fee for the day. The female ranger in the booth handed him a stack of brochures and information in exchange before passing him through.

Two or three miles past the entrance, Steve came to Morefield Village. The "village" consisted of a small ranger station, a gas station, a cafe and store. Nothing exciting. Still, it was a place to stop and look over the pamphlets he'd been given at the entrance. Besides, he could use a bite to eat.

Dick Alexander glanced up from the newspaper he was not reading when the faded blue pickup pulled into the parking lot. Another tourist to join the hundreds that had come through here since the sighting, three weeks ago. He reflexively glanced at the license plate—New York.

He was about to go back to not reading the paper when the kid got out of the car. Something about him just didn't match the average tourist. He was just too . . . cautious. That was it—he looked around the parking lot as if he half expected someone to jump him.

Alexander took a closer look. The young man was in his early twenties, around a hundred and seventy pounds, brown-haired and clean-shaven. He locked and closed the driver's door and headed into the cafe. With any luck the kid would sit in the outside section where he was.

As usual, Lady Luck was not quite so cooperative. Naturally—the kid wasn't trying to watch all of the cars coming into the park, so why not sit in the air conditioning? Alexander got up and wandered into the cafe proper.

The kid was sitting in the nonsmoking section, going over the map of the park with a seriousness that further convinced Alexander he was no ordinary tourist. There was no interest or fascination at all in his expression—he was looking for something.

It's probably nothing, Dick, he thought. He knew better than that, though. More accurately, it might not be related to what he was working on now, but it was definitely *something*. If it proved to be interesting enough, it wouldn't matter that it wasn't exactly what he was looking for.

The kid had bought a full meal, so it was safe to assume
that he would be staying put for a while. It might be
interesting to see what was lying on the seats in his truck.
Alexander wandered out into the parking lot.

The truck itself, an old Chevrolet, was about as nondescript as they came. Except for the New York plates, it
wouldn't be given a second glance around here. What was
inside was much more interesting.

An empty gun rack hung in the rear window. Alexander
wondered where the rifle that normally hung there was
right now. Laying on the passenger seat was the issue
of the *Clarion* with Alexander's article about the sighting.
His eyes widened in surprise as he looked at the familiar
cover photo.

Well, well, he thought. *Looks like there was more of a
connection here than I thought*. He would have to devote a
little time to investigating Mesa Verde's latest visitor. . . .

Steve found Cedar Tree Tower on the map the ranger at
the entrance had given him. The opposite mesa was Park
Mesa. It was roughly five miles from the only road that
touched Park Mesa to a point opposite Cedar Tree Tower.
That would be a *rough* hike, in this terrain.

Also, the brochures were happy to inform him, if he
were caught taking an unauthorized hike or entering a
site without a ranger present he could be fined up to one
hundred thousand dollars and spend up to twenty years in
jail. He would have to be *very* careful to avoid getting
caught. Twenty years here would be about two hundred
back at Quarin. God only knew what Belevairn would be
able to accomplish with that kind of time.

Fortunately, Steve had thought to purchase rudimentary camping equipment. Staying in Morefield Campground
would save him almost seventy dollars a day compared to
staying at the lodge. So, the next order of business was to
set up camp. He could start his investigation of the park
in the morning.

*   *   *

Alexander returned the receiver of the pay phone to its cradle, exhaling in a soft "whew." That had been an informative phone call.

According to the staff researcher at the *Clarion*, the blue pickup with the New York plates had just been purchased by one Steve Wilkinson. Mr. Wilkinson was a student at New York State in Albany, or at least he had been. About a week ago he had dropped all of his classes and, apparently, headed straight out here. That was about the time the issue with Alexander's story had hit the stands.

The rest got even more interesting. About seven months ago, the twenty-year-old Wilkinson had fallen into a coma as a result of some experiment at the university. He had missed the next semester while convalescing and was only just now returning to school—only to drop everything at the emergence of Alexander's article.

None of that was the reason for Alexander's alarm, however. No, that was something even more interesting. According to police records, young Mr. Wilkinson had been involved in a minor altercation with three football players in a locker room at the college about two weeks ago. One of them suffered some broken ribs and a concussion. Another had gotten a shattered elbow out of the deal. Wilkinson, himself, had come out of it without so much as a black eye. *Not* the type of person one wanted to have decide that life would be simpler if you weren't around.

Alexander had just made it back to his rental car when Wilkinson came out of the Knife Edge Cafe. He watched as the young student climbed into his truck and pulled out of the parking lot. Alexander waited until Wilkinson was almost out onto the road before pulling out after him. Wouldn't do to go tipping his hand this early, after all.

It quickly became apparent that Alexander's quarry was heading for the campground below Morefield Village. That made sense—Wilkinson didn't have much in the way of a budget. It was a lot cheaper to camp than to pay the room rates at the lodge.

Alexander turned around and pulled back into the parking lot. There was no other way out of the camping area. Wilkinson would have to pass this point to go anywhere else in the park.

The campground was very nice, Steve supposed. Small, pre-prepared pads lined the narrow roads that twisted through the campground. Right now, though, he was more concerned with how to set up this stupid tent.

The only tents he had pitched before had been in Quarin. There, he had simply been one of many setting up Theron's nightly camp. Here, not only was he alone, but he had to decipher these cryptic instructions.

After several embarrassing attempts, he finally got the four-man tent erected. He walked around and inspected the canvas bag that was going to be his home for the next few days. It certainly looked more comfortable than the legion's tents had been.

Ah, well—it would keep the rain off him. Right now, that was all that mattered. Steve glanced up at the sky. He would have another hour or two of daylight to go over the park brochures some more before turning in.

The next morning found Dick Alexander waiting for Wilkinson to emerge from the campground. His stomach growled softly. Hopefully, Wilkinson would get breakfast at the Knife Edge before going anywhere else. That way he could grab a bite to eat, too.

Less than an hour after dawn the blue pickup pulled into sight. Alexander smiled as Wilkinson parked in front of the cafe. God was on his side for a change. Alexander got out and followed Wilkinson into the cafe for breakfast.

There was no doubt that the kid was in a hurry. He wolfed down his breakfast in less than fifteen minutes and was on his way back out the door. Alexander grabbed his coffee and hurried to follow.

Fortunately it was fairly easy to follow someone through the park. Especially when they weren't familiar with the park and you were.

Not to mention that Alexander had a good idea of where Wilkinson was headed. It was no surprise when the kid turned off at Cedar Tree Tower. That was the only site that had been specifically mentioned in the article. Further confirmation that Wilkinson was here *because* of that article.

Alexander drove past the turnoff, around the next curve. There he made a U-turn, no small feat on these narrow park roads, and headed back. There had been no sign that Wilkinson was watching for a tail. It should be safe to just pull in behind him.

When he pulled up to the ruins, there was no sign of the kid except for his truck. Again, no surprise. Wilkinson was probably back in the brush looking for some sign of whatever *he* was hunting.

Alexander carefully made his way back to the edge of the mesa. He didn't want to risk revealing himself to Wilkinson, who would no doubt be a little jumpy. Soon, he caught sight of Wilkinson, scanning the far mesa through a pair of binoculars.

A nearby pile of rock gave Alexander the cover he needed to watch from. Wilkinson could head back at any moment. It might not be very healthy if Alexander were standing right behind him when that happened. It was a long way to the bottom of Soda Canyon. . . .

There was nothing to be seen on the opposite mesa except more of the scraggly vegetation that topped this one. Steve made another sweep with the binoculars. Nothing.

Of course, what had he expected? Belevairn wasn't exactly going to have left a billboard behind stating that he'd been here. It was beginning to look as though an extended hike along Park Mesa would be in order. It was unused by the park—no roads or facilities—so getting caught shouldn't be too much of a risk.

Just as he was about to turn away, something caught his attention. He lifted the binoculars to his eyes for a closer look. A thin wisp of smoke was just beginning to rise over the juniper. Forest fire? Steve watched for a moment.

The fire wasn't spreading. That one thin wisp continued to rise above the trees—campfire. *Someone* was over on the other mesa. Someone who wasn't too concerned with drawing attention to themselves, which meant they were either stupid or they were authorized to be there.

Steve took out his map of the park. That fire should be just about . . . there. A little north of Cedar Tree Tower and almost on the near edge of the mesa. He drew a circle around the estimated location. Much better than having to search the entire mesa top.

Alexander ducked behind the rockpile when Wilkinson finally turned back from the edge of the mesa. It was obvious that he had seen something—he had even marked it on his map.

Once Wilkinson was out of sight, Alexander walked over and took a look across the canyon. The only thing visible was a lot of brush. Nothing to get excited about. He glanced up the mesa to where he knew the newly discovered kiva was being excavated. It was certainly not visible from here.

However, a small puff of smoke *was* visible there. Someone must have started a cookfire or something. That must have been what caught Wilkinson's attention. Alexander turned back from the edge of the mesa. If he didn't hurry, he would lose the kid.

Steve studied the map of the park on the picnic table in front of him. The campfire he had seen today was about six miles along the top of Park Mesa from where the park road crossed it. Unencumbered, he could make it there in about an hour, maybe less. In this terrain, he had best figure two hours and, at night, probably three.

So three hours out and three hours back was six hours. That still left him four hours of darkness to check out the area. Better figure on leaving at least an hour after sunset and hope to get back at least an hour before. That left two hours. Hopefully that would be more than enough time.

Steve folded the map and placed it into his pack. He had best get some sleep and then get a good dinner under his belt. It was going to be a long night. He gathered up his pack and carried it into the tent.

About eight-thirty that night Wilkinson's truck came back out of the campground. Alexander started his car. If the kid was going to head out to that site, Alexander was going to be there to see what he did.

Wilkinson was not headed out to the site, however—at least not yet. Instead he pulled into the cafe parking lot and went inside. Dinnertime. Alexander killed his engine and got out. Hopefully Wilkinson would eat a little slower this time.

Steve finished his drink and glanced out the window. The sun had set a few minutes ago. By the time he made it to the lookout tower on the north end of Park Mesa, it would be just about time for him to head out.

Steve paid his check and left, feeling a little anxious. If the park rangers caught him at this, he could lose twenty years in a federal prison somewhere. That wouldn't do his quest much good—but then, neither would not going at all.

Alexander followed Wilkinson's truck more closely now that it was dark. He was, indeed, headed back into the park. When they reached the turnoff to the lookout tower at Park Point, however, Wilkinson turned off the main park road.

Damn! If Alexander tried to follow him up there, Wilkinson would *know* something was up. After all, who would go to the lookout in the middle of the night? For that matter, why was Wilkinson going up there?

Alexander drove on past and pulled off to the side of the road. He carefully guided the car behind a stand of juniper trees. In the dark that should be enough concealment. He walked back to where he could watch the lookout road. Should he head up that way on foot? No, it would be too easy to miss him in the dark—or run into him.

He hadn't waited long, maybe ten minutes, when he saw a furtive figure, carrying a rifle, cross the road and disappear into the juniper not ten feet away from him. Good lord, was Wilkinson going to *walk* all the way to that new site? It had to be miles from here!

That was obviously what he intended to do. Alexander moaned mentally as he took off after the youth. He hadn't counted on this . . .

Not quite three hours later, they arrived at the new site. The excavation crew had long since departed. Presumably they would return shortly before dawn to resume the dig. A tarpaulin laid on the ground protected the kiva beneath.

Alexander collapsed to the ground as he watched Wilkinson inspect the ground around the site. The kid was good—he kept his flashlight shielded from the far side of the canyon so that its light only illuminated the ground he was searching and didn't give him away to any nocturnal observers.

Alexander unlaced his shoes and gently massaged his sore feet. He hadn't had to travel that far over rough terrain at night since Nam. He tried to keep his ragged breathing as quiet as possible. He hadn't killed himself to follow Wilkinson this far only to give himself away now.

Wilkinson continued to search the ground around the site. Alexander wondered what he was looking for. Whatever it was, he finally found it. Wilkinson stopped for a moment, studying one patch of ground. After a moment the youth's head dropped, as if in resignation.

"Damn," Alexander heard him say. Then Wilkinson began studying the ground again, walking as if he were tracking something. Alexander watched him closely. What had he found?

"Damn," Steve said. He hadn't realized it, but some part of him had been hoping this was all a wild-goose chase. The cloven hoofprints in the ground dashed that final, desperate hope. Some scorched vegetation lay in the bottom of one track—it was the *goremka*, all right.

But now what? These tracks were old, had possibly even been rained on once. Two weeks, perhaps? This was not a place frequented by Belevairn. But why had he come here at all?

Power, Belevairn's voice answered in his mind.

What power? Steve asked. This was the first time that his private demon had spoken since leaving New York. Steve had almost begun to hope he was gone—but such was apparently not the case.

There is almost no Power in your world, Belevairn replied. *The* goremka *will only be able to enter at places where the Power is strengthened. This was once a holy site— it has Power. My counterpart probably arrived during the full moon, which would provide additional power for his entrance.*

Steve glanced up at the sky. The barest sliver of a moon hung there. What Belevairn said made sense. If that was the case, though, then this was just a wild-goose chase. Steve had no way of knowing where Belevairn would show up next or what he was doing. He needed some answers, or this was the end of his quest.

There may be a way to get some of those answers, Belevairn said.

Steve blinked in surprise. Was Belevairn actually trying to be helpful?

How? he asked.

The Rite of Past Visions, Belevairn said. *But you will have to give me control long enough to perform it.*

When Hell freezes over, Steve replied, laughing sharply.

Limited control, Belevairn countered. *Just enough to perform the ritual—no more. You can keep control of your legs. If I don't surrender the body, you don't let me leave.*

Why, Steve asked suspiciously, *are you suddenly becoming so cooperative?* He felt Belevairn become more guarded.

I have my reasons, the sorcerer replied. Steve didn't like the sound of that.

And those are?

As I said, they are my *reasons.*

Steve wasn't certain that he liked Belevairn's proposal. That bit about him keeping control of the legs—was that even possible? Or was it just a ploy to gain Steve's trust long enough to take over?

Still, if he didn't accept Belevairn's offer, he might never find the *real* Belevairn. Steve took a deep breath. As much as he didn't like the idea, it was still the best game in town.

Now? Steve asked hesitantly.

No, Belevairn replied. *There is not enough Power here. We shall have to wait for the new moon.* Steve was actually relieved to hear that. If Belevairn were just trying for control, there would have been no reason to refuse to do it now, even if the ritual would not work.

We should also bring a sacrifice, Belevairn added.

I don't *think so*, Steve replied.

Just an animal—a rabbit, say, Belevairn continued.

No!

Belevairn somehow managed to convey a sigh mentally. After a short pause he began to recite. . . .

> *The Power is strengthened*
> *at the Full and New Moons,*
> *Sunrise and Sunset,*
> *Midnight and Noon,*
> *Springtime and Summer,*
> *Winter and Fall,*
> *But where Blood is spilled*
> *is the strongest of all.*

No sacrifice, Steve reasserted.

Then I withdraw the offer, Belevairn stated flatly. *I shall not allow you to endanger me by returning here for a rite that will probably not work.*

The Power is that weak? Steve asked.

It is, Belevairn replied.

That left Steve back where he had started. Did he give in to Belevairn's demand or surrender his quest? He sighed— there was really no choice.

A rabbit? Steve asked.

That should suffice, Belevairn replied.

A . . . live rabbit?

Belevairn's contemptuous laugh made Steve flush. Angrily, he turned and headed back north, toward the park road.

Once Alexander was certain that Wilkinson was not going to return, he left his hiding place to inspect the site for himself. He began his search where Wilkinson had apparently found whatever it was he had been looking for.

The reporter's small penlight didn't provide anything near the amount of light that Wilkinson's flashlight had, but it was more than enough to show him the prints in the sandy soil. The tracks were much like a horse's hoofprints, with one important difference. Each track was cleft in the middle—like a goat's hoof would be.

Alexander sat back, letting the penlight go dark, trying to ignore the goosebumps that rose at the back of his neck and down his arms. The kook theory had just lost a *lot* of strength. Wilkinson had come here *knowing* what he was looking for, had *known* when he had found it and did not seem particularly happy to have done so.

Now the question to answer was, what did a college student from Albany have to do with some demonic horseman in Colorado? Alexander rose to his sore feet—he wouldn't find the answers here. Only Wilkinson and the demon he was hunting knew what was going on. Alexander winced as he began the long walk back to his car.

Chapter
-------- **Four** -------------

BELEVAIRN STOOD ATOP the ancient Aztec temple, waiting. The feathered robe he wore was far from his normal attire, but it served his purpose today. Today was the day of the new moon and soon it would be noon, bringing the ambient Power of the temple to its peak. Behind him, three master *kaivir* also waited in feathered robes.

Finding this temple on his first trip to Earth had been a remarkable stroke of luck. He could still remember emerging from the Gray Plain atop a vine-covered hill and feeling the dark Power that throbbed beneath him. He had been able to immediately summon the *kaivir*, almost depleting what had remained of that Power.

Now the vine-covered hill had been excavated to reveal the ancient temple in all of its glory, and the Nicaraguan jungle had been pushed back almost five hundred feet around it. The restored temple made a perfect base of operations in addition to being a source of the Power that was so rare in this world.

And that Power was increasing. Every full and new moon, fourteen people had been sacrificed at noon atop this temple. Double that number had been slain on the spring equinox and again on the summer solstice. Fresh blood now stained the ancient altar as sacrifices to the Sun were once again offered.

He looked down to the camp at the base of the pyramid where twenty-five canvas-backed, camouflaged trucks waited. This would be the last exchange. The rest of their plan could proceed as soon as the ambient Power of this site was restored.

Today, double the normal number of sacrifices would be made to provide the Power for this ritual. He had calculated that merely an additional six would provide the necessary power, but Belevairn wished to leave nothing to chance. Any excess would only serve to raise the permanent level of the Power here.

The light of the sun finally fell onto the altar—it was time. . . .

Maria Gonzales was frightened, despite the drugs the ancient priests had given her. Almost a month ago she had been taken prisoner by the strange soldiers in Guatemala. She had watched as her parents and older brothers were killed in the attack on her village.

Maria had been brought here, along with the other survivors from her village, to this new village built around the ancient temple. Here she had been made to work for the soldiers as their cook and maid—and their whore.

Her face and body were always bruised and cut. She didn't even cry anymore when they beat her, or when they forced her down and raped her. Crying made it worse. Crying made them beat her longer—more viciously. She cried only late at night, when the soldiers were asleep and there was no one to hear her—when it was safe.

She had thought about escape once, when they first brought her here. But then they had all been shown the demons that lived in the jungle. Horrible things, like large monkeys. The soldiers had taken one of the boys from her village and thrown him to them. His screams as they tore him apart still haunted Maria's dreams. It could have as easily been her. . . .

So she had resigned herself to her life here, such as it was. She did anything she was asked, and hated herself for all of it. Her mama would be so ashamed of her—if she were still alive.

This morning had been different, though. This morning she was not taken to cook the soldier's meals. Instead, she had been taken to the foot of the ancient temple. There, a man in a serpent mask and a feathered robe had made her drink bitter water.

Her mind seemed to fade away after that. The pain from the cuts and bruises that the soldiers had inflicted on her also faded. There were others with her, all sitting at the foot of the ancient temple.

They were allowed as much of the bitter water as they wanted. As the sun rose in the sky and the day grew hot, she willingly drank more when it was offered to her. With each drink, she became more tired, less able to think or remember.

Something bad was going to happen. Somehow she knew that something very bad was going to happen. But the fear would not stir her from the stupor the drugs had placed her in.

Then, when the sun was high in the sky, the soldiers came and lifted her by the arms. She tried to resist, or wanted to, but her drugged body would not do what she wanted. They dragged her up the stairs of the pyramid to the temple at its top.

Another man in a feathered robe waited there, wearing a golden mask. It shone like the sun itself. Two other men in feathered robes took her from the soldiers and cut away her clothes. They lifted her between them and laid her across the altar.

She looked up at the golden mask. He lifted a knife over her and she knew—knew she was going to die. The ancient ones were going to take her life, as her mother had always told her they would if she were bad.

She tried to scream, but only a whimper escaped from her lips. She tried to struggle, but all she could do was roll her head away.

Mother of God, she thought. *Do not let them kill me, please*. Finally, tears ran from her eyes as the knife swiftly descended.

No, please! she screamed silently. *Virgin, I am only fourteen! Please!*

It only took Belevairn a few seconds to carve the woman's heart from her bosom and throw it into the burning brazier. He hurried to complete all twenty-eight sacrifices before the sun left the altar. With each, the amount of Power available to him climbed until, at last, he wielded something approximating what he was accustomed to in his own land. When the last human heart had been consigned to the fire, Belevairn turned from the altar.

His mind took firm hold of the Power and shaped it into a lance of energy. Driven by his will, the Power leapt through the barrier to the Gray Plain, leaving a trail of Power behind as it sought Belevairn's homeworld.

Well before its strength had been expended, the probe reached its destination. Belevairn could not afford to gloat over his accomplishment, however. He must maintain this feeble link with his homeland until it could be strengthened.

Then he felt it—felt the link strengthen and stabilize as every *kaiva* in Morvanor, masters and apprentices alike, poured their Power into it. Belevairn began to expand the link and below, at the edge of the cleared ground north of the Aztec pyramid, a portal appeared.

At first the image within the portal was unfocused and blurred. However, as the portal grew, the image cleared until not the Nicaraguan jungle, but a tunnel to the Burning Hills, lay at the northern end of the camp.

The *kaivir*, knowing that their master had stabilized the gateway, ordered the trucks forward. Twenty-five truckloads of ammunition and supplies passed between worlds. Shortly after the last truck cleared the tunnel, twenty-five trucks returned from Delgroth. The exchange was a success.

Belevairn allowed the portal to slowly collapse once the last truck had left the tunnel. As the portal vanished he sat, yielding to the fatigue that followed the release of the Power.

The first thing that struck Lieutenant Garth about Earth as he stepped from the truck was the heat. It was easily as hot as the hottest day in the Burning Hills, but with a cloying mugginess that could never occur in that arid region. Breathing the thick air was difficult, at best. Garth was perspiring heavily before he could make it to the back of the truck to debark his men.

From the knowledge that had been placed in Garth's mind by the *kaivir*, he knew that this was one of the hottest regions on the world. Still, he had not been expecting anything like this. Nor had he been expecting the almost solid wall of vegetation that surrounded the camp. It was more dense than even the thickest Olvan forest.

He called his men into formation at the foot of the . . . pyramid—the alien word came reluctantly to his mind. The other four lieutenants did likewise—two hundred and fifty men in all. Garth had not commanded this small a group of men since he'd been commissioned in the Mistress's army. Still, the fifty men under him could defeat ten times that number of the Morvan cavalry—possibly without losing a man.

Garth and his men had trained in the Burning Hills with the new weapons for almost a year. Now they were to face actual combat against similar forces for a month here on Earth. Five such groups had been trained before theirs—another had begun training as soon as they left.

Garth's men had been picked from among the best of Lord Jared's forces. All had been sergeants and officers—demoted to the rank and file of these new forces. Garth had been a captain before being selected for this duty. Still, the honor of being selected far outweighed any stigma that could conceivably be attached to the demotion. Garth had risen quickly, first to sergeant and then to lieutenant.

Each of the *Kaimordir* would eventually command one unit of the new Special Forces, including Lord Belevairn. With these forces, the Mistress hoped to sweep over the Northern Kingdoms and the Empire without effective resistance. Garth could believe it, although he had had his doubts before training with the new weapons.

Still, the Olvir could pose a threat. Even with the new weapons, Garth did not see how the Morvir could hope to ferret the forest-dwellers out of their trees. An Olvan arrow could kill a man just as dead as a bullet. He knew—he had been trapped in an Olvan ambush in Umbria several years ago. Had not Lord Jared personally rescued him, Garth would not have survived the encounter. What good would a gun do against an enemy one could not see to shoot?

A man wearing the insignia of a Special Forces captain walked to the head of their formation. Garth and the other four lieutenants saluted, empty handed in the new fashion. The captain returned the salute.

"At ease," he said in the language Garth knew as English. Garth and the others relaxed from attention.

"I am Captain Korva," he continued. "I am the senior captain here and, as such, am your commanding officer." He paused before continuing.

"I know that all of you think you know everything there is to know about fighting with these new weapons you've been trained to use. The truth is, you don't know shit."

Garth tensed at the insult and could feel the similar response of his men behind him.

"We've all thought that when we arrived here," Korva continued. "However, you are going to learn more in one month of combat here than in your entire year of training back in Morvanor.

"The opponents you will be fighting have fought with these weapons all of their lives," Korva added. "They know them inside out and they know all the tactics that go with them. You don't have that advantage." Korva paused again. Garth was beginning to be annoyed at the senior captain's melodrama.

"The advantage that you *do* have is that you are Morvir," Korva continued. "The fiercest warriors ever bred—on either world. The Morvir are spoken of in whispers here. Those who have fought us, and lived, remember us well. Those who have hired us want no one else. If you raw troops sully that reputation, you *will* answer to the rest of us.

"To help prevent that, each lieutenant will be assigned a senior sergeant from the experienced troops. You are in command of your platoon, but you would be well advised to listen to this man. He just might keep you alive.

"Now, each sergeant will take his squad over to the central Quonset hut behind you and get quarters assigned for his men. I want each of you green lieutenants to report to the briefing room in the Quonset hut north of the temple, *with* the gold your platoons have each brought from Delgroth. We've got a lot to do before sunset.

"Atten-tion!" Korva barked and Garth resumed position. He could hear the cascade of feet behind him as his men quickly formed to attention as well.

"Dismissed!" Garth saluted before turning to dispatch his sergeants. It was going to be a long month . . .

Garth wiped the sweat from his brow as he peered through the thick foliage at the narrow dirt road that wound its way through the Costa Rican jungle. His first assignment had been described by Korva as a "milk run," whatever that meant. Ambush and destroy a military truck convoy and then return to the pickup point for transport back to Nicaragua.

Only two of his squads had been hired for this job—twenty men. The convoy was supposed to be carrying twice that many Costa Rican troops. That and a few hundred pounds of cocaine. The Morvir had been hired by a rival drug cartel to destroy the shipment.

Earth was a complex world. The divisions of power were far from obvious. The various small kingdoms, or rather countries, had their own divisions. Some men held power only within those borders, but others held power across the world, to varying degrees. It all seemed to be driven by wealth rather than by force of arms.

The greatest single power on this world seemed to be America. That seemed odd, however, because this shipment of brain-rot was on its way there. What Garth had heard of America reminded him of the Nymran Empire of his own world. Secure in their power, the members of the populace were becoming decadent—pursuing their own diversions rather than defending their position. Only their vast size kept them from being toppled from power, and that could only last for a time.

The sound of truck engines broke Garth from his reverie. The convoy was approaching. Garth watched from the direction of the sound, waiting for the lead truck to appear.

He did not have to wait long. An olive-drab, canvas-backed truck rounded the curve a few hundred feet from him. Soon, three more trucks followed it. Garth frowned; four trucks—not three. He hoped that the remaining intelligence proved more accurate.

He eagerly watched, tensing as the lead truck approached the section of road where the Morvir had planted explosives. That explosion would be their signal to attack . . .

With a deafening roar, the earth of the road erupted beneath the lead truck, lifting it and hurling it back into the truck behind it as if it were a child's toy. The Morvir opened fire on the remaining vehicles from both sides of the road as the troops guarding the convoy frantically tried to deploy.

It was over in less than a minute. Garth hadn't lost a man in this action. Now he knew what a "milk run" was . . .

"Well?" he asked his senior sergeant as the Morvir began scattering the cocaine across the road.

"Not too bad, sir," the sergeant replied. "You used a little too much explosive—expensive, you know. But other than that, not too bad at all."

"Hm," Garth replied. He hoped that his next assignment would be a little more challenging.

Chapter
-------- Five -------------

STEVE PACED, CAREFUL not to fall into the entrance of the ancient kiva in the moonless night. He could just barely make it out in the light from the stars overhead. He had been waiting for almost half an hour now. Steve briefly turned on his flashlight and glanced at his watch. One-fourteen—two minutes until true midnight. He sighed.

Steve was not looking forward to this. He had spent the last six months fighting to keep Belevairn from gaining control. To simply just hand his body over to the sorcerer's personality . . . he shuddered—the mere thought gave him chills. However, it was the only way to get the information he needed if he ever hoped to find the true Belevairn.

It is time, Belevairn informed him.

Steve sighed and forced himself to relax. It was difficult to fight down the panic as he felt Belevairn come forward and take control. With an effort, he concentrated on keeping his legs immobile . . .

Belevairn blinked in surprise at the feel of the cool night air on his skin. He savored the taste of it as he breathed it in through his mouth. Mistress, he had forgotten the myriad sensations of a living body!

They were little things that Wilkinson took for granted. The light breeze stirring his hair, the feel of the rocky ground beneath his feet, only partly blocked by his shoes. All of these were things that Belevairn had not experienced in centuries. They were wonderfully familiar and wonderfully new at the same time.

Other, more familiar, senses told Belevairn that the Power in this area had reached its peak. With a sigh (a real sigh!) he lit the flashlight and leaned it against a rock before reaching down to take the rabbit from the sack. There was barely enough Power to perform the Rite. The sacrifice would ensure that nothing went wrong.

He drove Wilkinson's hunting knife into the creature's chest. Its feet flailed wildly as the rabbit tried to disembowel him. Belevairn avoided the long claws with practiced ease as he drew the creature's heart from its chest.

He gathered the Power as the small creature's life fled and began the Rite. . . .

Alexander winced when he saw Wilkinson drive the knife into the rabbit's chest. Wilkinson twisted the knife around and pulled a small object out of the rabbit—its heart. What in the *hell* was going on?

With the knife in one hand, the rabbit's heart still impaled on its point, and the lifeless animal in the other hand, Wilkinson spread his arms, tilted his head back and began to chant. Alexander felt the hackles rise on his neck as Wilkinson's voice rose and fell in a strange, almost unearthly rhythm. The kid must have been minoring in sorcery back at Albany. The language was like nothing Alexander had ever heard before.

Finally, the chanting ended. *What now?* Alexander wondered. He stifled a gasp as the first light of dawn broke over the horizon. There was no way it could be dawn already! He glanced at his watch to be certain—had he dozed off?

No, his watch claimed that it was just one-twenty. Dawn should be another five hours or so away. Alexander scrambled further back into the brush. His hiding place had been secure enough in total darkness, but daylight was another matter.

Belevairn watched as the visions began. His counterpart must have arrived at dawn. The *goremka* materialized to the sorcerer's left. His eyebrow raised in puzzlement. There was no rider, tack or harness. What was happening here?

Belevairn glanced toward the ancient kiva. Then back to the *goremka*. Nothing seemed to be happening. Cautiously, he sped up the passage of time in the vision.

After roughly an hour had passed in the vision, Belevairn noticed movement by the kiva. The earth over the entrance began to fall inward. The sorcerer returned the passage of time to normal.

As he watched, a saddle—*his* saddle—was thrust up through the opening. Wilkinson's body laughed. Apparently the real Belevairn had emerged *inside* the kiva. Obviously the *goremka* had been unable to remain inside and had abandoned his rider.

Belevairn himself now emerged from the kiva. His every movement betrayed severe irritation as he gathered up his mount's tack and walked directly toward the *goremka*. The watching sorcerer did not move, contemptuously allowing the image to pass through him on its way to the *goremka*. Once the demon-horse had been resaddled, his counterpart removed a radio from his saddlebags.

Belevairn watched in fascination as his counterpart went through the ritual of determining his location. Apparently he had put Wilkinson's stolen knowledge to good use— had expanded on it, in fact. He was taking sightings to determine his exact position. Why?

In the growing "daylight" he looked over the sorcerer's shoulder at the maps spread out on the saddle. His counterpart was only concerned with his current location, however, and when he finally put the maps away, Belevairn knew no more than before.

Then the image mounted up and rode off. Belevairn watched as the *goremka* stepped off the edge of the mesa. Where was his namesake going?

Belevairn closed his eyes and launched the soul from his body. He quickly caught the apparition as it rode through the air along the little finger canyon toward the main canyon.

Back at the site, Belevairn sneered in contempt. This was what had given his counterpart away—what had exposed

him to that photographer. Only a fool would ride through
the air in broad daylight at a national park where there
would be hundreds of people with cameras. It was a miracle
that he had only been seen by one.

The image made a circuit of its arrival point and returned
to the kiva. Belevairn's astral self returned to his body, and
he rose to his feet. The image settled in, as if preparing
for a long wait, and again Belevairn increased the passage
of time.

Finally, at what appeared to be noon for the image,
Belevairn's counterpart began a Rite of Sending. Belevairn
watched as the message to be sent was consumed in a small
fire. The message itself had been of little interest—just an
order to perform a sacrifice at a specified time. What *was*
of interest was that the missive implied the presence of
some of Daryna's sorcerers, the *kaivir*, on Earth—especially since it had been written in Morvan.

His counterpart was making certain that his base of
operations, wherever it might be, was the strongest point
of Power on Earth. A quick trip to the Gray Plain and back
at the appropriate time, and his counterpart would be where
he wished to go.

With a wave of his hand, Belevairn dismissed the image.
The darkness of the moonless night returned instantly. Finding his counterpart would be difficult, at best. Belevairn's
only recourse was to visit locations of Power and hope that
he was attempting to gain entrance at that time. A long
shot, at best. Hopefully, in the meantime, he would be able
to learn more.

Once he found his counterpart, it would be a simple
matter to kill him with the flares and then reclaim the
golden mask from the corpse. The *goremka* would then
obey him—after all, was he not its master?

He smiled. The real Belevairn had been a fool—almost
as great a fool as Wilkinson had been for performing this
spell and allowing Belevairn to gain the ascendancy in their
internal battle.

Belevairn smiled wickedly and began the trip back to
where Wilkinson had left his vehicle. . . .

*   *   *

Alexander sat in the darkness, shaking, long after Wilkinson had left. Until now he had more than half believed that this was all some elaborate hoax. This was no hoax, however. *No one* could make the sun rise in the middle of the night. No one could turn the clock back and replay an event that had happened over three weeks ago.

Wilkinson had done just that, however. Alexander was certain the sun had not actually risen. If that had been the case, the entire park would be in a uproar about now. No, he and Wilkinson must have been the only ones to see the . . . images that had been conjured by Wilkinson's . . . spell.

Alexander shook his head. He did not believe in the occult and magic and all that related hooey. At least he hadn't before tonight. Now he was beginning to wonder, for the first time, if he had possibly bitten off more than he could chew. Apparently this demon-rider *was* real—and was being pursued by a freshman wizard from New York State. A near-hysterical giggle escaped from his lips.

"Get a grip on yourself, Alexander," he whispered shakily. "You're a pro, you're a vet—you can handle this."

He got to his feet and began to follow Wilkinson back to the park, still not truly convinced that he *could* handle this.

Steve struggled vainly against the ropes that held him. He could smell the moist leaves rotting on the forest floor and the smell of wood burned long ago. He was naked, bound hand and foot to stakes driven into the ground. How had he gotten here? He thrashed madly—he *must* get free!

"Do not bother to struggle, Master Wilkinson," a familiar, rasping voice said. "You are mine now."

Steve looked up into the red, burning eyes of Belevairn. At least, he *thought* it was Belevairn—that was who the voice belonged to. But Belevairn looked . . . different. He wore no gold mask and, instead of the mummified corpse Steve knew him to be, he looked like . . . Steve . . .

Steve saw Belevairn smile as the realization hit him. *Oh, God. Oh, dear God, this couldn't be happening.*

"But it is, Master Wilkinson," Belevairn said, sensing his thoughts. "I defeated you at Quarin and now I have defeated you here, in your own mind. Of course, it was just a matter of time—I have always been your better."

"*No!*" Steve shouted. "Never, damn you! Never!"

"Give it up, Dreamer. You have lost."

Steve screamed then—a primal, wordless cry of rage and terror. He could not, *would* not let Belevairn win *this* way.

The stake holding his right arm pulled free from the ground. Steve screamed again, defiantly, as he also pulled his left arm free. Belevairn fell on him, pinning his arms to the ground bodily. With one last scream of rage, Steve sat up, locking his hands around Belevairn's throat . . .

Then Belevairn, the forest and everything else faded away to darkness and was gone. Steve glanced around shakily—he was in a tent . . . in a sleeping bag. Where was he?

Mesa Verde, he remembered. Memory of the night before returned, as well—he almost *had* lost to Belevairn. This had been more than a mere dream—it had been a battle for his very soul . . .

He opened the tent flap and stepped out into the cold night air. It stung his throat refreshingly—tied him more firmly to his body. He saw a few curious faces peering out of other tents around him—apparently his screams had not been confined to his nightmare.

"Just a nightmare," he said as he felt his face flush. "Sorry."

There were a few sheepish, reassured smiles, and then the faces ducked back into their tents. Steve wandered over to a picnic table and sat down.

Do not ever *try to use magic again,* he thought to himself.

He saw the first, faint glow of dawn to the east, which meant that he'd gotten about two and a half hours' sleep. He didn't feel like sleeping right now, though. Not this soon after nearly losing himself to Belevairn.

So what was the next step? His stay at Mesa Verde was over—he had learned all that he could here.

Belevairn himself had given him the answer. Steve would have to find other, likely places for the real Belevairn to emerge and wait there for him. It wasn't much to go on, but what else could he do?

His next step would be a visit to a major public library. Denver would probably be his best bet. With a yawn, Steve stretched and began breaking camp. It was time to press on . . .

Alexander tried to blink the sleep from his eyes as he sipped his coffee. He had not been able to sleep after what he'd seen last night. The one time he had dozed off, he'd dreamed about watching Wilkinson carve out that rabbit's heart. Only it hadn't been Wilkinson—instead it had been the demon-horseman. Alexander had woken up, screaming, when it had turned and looked at him with those glowing, red eyes.

Alexander shuddered as he took another swallow of coffee. He hadn't had dreams that upsetting in a long time. Not since a few years after Nam, anyway.

Wilkinson's truck pulled onto the short road from the campground to head into the cafe parking lot. With a start, Alexander sat up and stared—Wilkinson's truck was loaded! He had packed up his tent and all his gear and was getting ready to leave.

The kid walked in with a thermos, probably intending to fill it with coffee. Damn! Alexander's luggage was still at the lodge—there was no way he'd be able to get there and make it back here before Wilkinson left.

Alexander swallowed the last of his coffee. There was nothing to do for it—he would have to leave his luggage. He could have someone from the paper come back to pick it up and clear his bill. If Wilkinson thought he was going to shake him this easily, the kid had another thought coming.

Alexander and Wilkinson passed each other as Alexander tried not to hurry too noticeably out of the cafe.

The kid's eyes met his briefly, looking him up and down and then dismissing him as unimportant. The look in his eyes confirmed Alexander's suspicions about one thing. Wilkinson was capable of killing a man, had probably done so before. Alexander was going to have to be very, very careful with this tail . . .

Chapter
-------- **Six** -------------

DICK ALEXANDER GLANCED sidewise over to the small library table where Wilkinson was reading. For five days now the kid had done nothing but devour every book the Denver Public Library possessed on every aspect of the occult and on ancient Amerindian history. Alexander had been able to find no other pattern to Wilkinson's research. To Wilkinson's credit, however, the kid had quickly discarded the kookier books on the occult.

Wilkinson stood up, stretched and began gathering up his materials. Alexander glanced at his watch—closing time. Wilkinson placed pad, pencils and the few photocopies he'd made into his slim attache case—the perfect picture of the American college student.

Alexander left ahead of Wilkinson. He knew where the kid's truck was parked, and it would not do to have Wilkinson spot him. Not after successfully tailing him for this long.

Robert, the photographer, woke up when Alexander unlocked the door to the dark blue Pontiac sedan they'd rented in Denver. He would have to replace it soon—maybe tonight. Alexander wasn't about to take *any* chances with this kid . . .

"Is he done for the day?" Robert asked, rubbing his eyes.

"Yeah," Alexander replied. "He should be out any minute."

"Good," Robert said. Then, after a moment of silence, "I'm starving."

"Fasting is good for the soul," Alexander replied. The

paper had sent Robert out when Alexander had phoned in for assistance. Tailing someone by yourself was not conducive to sleeping and, sooner or later, you would end up falling asleep when you shouldn't. Then you could kiss your story goodbye. Especially when your target was someone as erratic as Wilkinson had proven to be.

Alexander had almost lost Wilkinson when the kid left Mesa Verde the morning after . . . whatever it was he had done. The thought of seeing the sun rise in the middle of the night *still* gave Alexander the shivers.

Wilkinson emerged from the entrance into the underground parking area. Hopefully, the kid would go back to his motel, and he and Robert could have dinner delivered. In spite of his caustic remark, Alexander was more than a little hungry himself.

"Another exciting day at the library," Robert drawled. Alexander sighed, hoping that Robert wouldn't continue on about having had to miss the film festival at Cannes just to tail some college kid.

If it weren't for that, Robert would be pretty easy to work with. The photographer was good at this, but then, as Robert himself had smugly informed him, you didn't get pictures of the celebs without knowing how to shadow a mark. In fact, the photographer had arrived with enough observational gear to equip a small spy ring.

Wilkinson's truck backed out of its parking space and pulled away. Alexander started the Pontiac, making certain to give the kid a little bit of a head start before pulling out after him.

Steve threw the bolt on the door before collapsing into the room's only chair. He had had no idea just how *many* books there were on the occult, nor just how many ancient ruins there were in America. There were mounds and effigies built along the Mississippi Valley, Indian medicine wheels all over the Great Plains, pueblos and kivas in the Southwest and so on.

He had no idea which site might be Belevairn's next arrival point. He had narrowed the list down to half a

dozen or so where supernatural events had been reported and where those reports had sounded at least halfway
reasonable.

Even with all that research, there was no guarantee
that Belevairn would ever arrive at any of the sites he
had selected. There were too many possible sites outside
of North America. Stonehenge, Incan, Mayan and Aztec
temples, Egyptian pyramids—any one of them could be
Belevairn's next arrival point. Most countries wouldn't
have the manpower to cover all of the possibilities. How
was one man going to accomplish it?

"It can't end like this," Steve muttered to himself. "It
just can't."

It can, his mental tenant informed him. *And it probably
will.*

Oh, shut up, Steve replied. *I'm just tired. Things will
look better in the morning.* There was no response from
Belevairn.

With a sigh, he got up and undressed, throwing his
clothes over the back of the chair he had just vacated.
He turned the bed down before turning out the light and
crawling in.

Mortos, he thought before drifting off to sleep, *please
don't let it end like this.*

Alexander snuffed his cigarette out in the ashtray when
the light in Wilkinson's room went out. So ended another
exciting day in the life of Richard Alexander. The kid
was going to make some type of a move soon, though—
Alexander could feel it.

Robert flopped over onto his back and started to snore.
Alexander was glad they didn't try to sleep at the same
time—the photographer's snoring would have kept a deaf
person awake. He lit another cigarette. He was going through
a lot of them lately.

Alexander's gaze wandered across the parking lot to
where the hookers stood beneath the motel sign. Wilkinson
sure had picked a dive to stay in. It was cheap, though.
Only nineteen-fifty a night, which, of course, was probably

why Wilkinson had picked it. The kid's finances had to be running low.

He glanced at his watch—nine-thirty. Time to wake Robert up and get a little sleep himself. Actually, he should send Robert to change cars at the rental agency first. While Wilkinson was asleep would be a good time to take care of that.

The full moonlight shone dazzlingly white off Aerilynn's hair as they walked beside the grassy ridge. Steve was certain that he had never been here before, but the place seemed oddly familiar. Aerilynn took his hand and pulled him to her for a quick kiss before breaking away to walk a little further to a place where the ridge split.

" 'Tis beautiful here, Steven," she said. "Thank you for bringing me."

"My pleasure, milady," Steve replied. He still couldn't shake the familiarity of this place. He turned to look behind him. The ridge extended behind them in a series of curves like a snake. The asphalt sidewalk they walked on circled the obviously artificial mound.

Steve was certain he had never been any place like this, but he still couldn't shake the familiar feeling this place evoked in him. Inexplicably, the landscape began to darken. As it did, Steve could feel some type of dark presence watching him. The hair on the back of his neck began to rise—this was *not* a good place to be.

He turned to tell Aerilynn that they should leave, but she was nowhere to be seen. He ran up the mound to the split in the ridge as the night continued to darken.

"Aerilynn!" he called. There was no answer. He looked about frantically. There was no sign of her—what had happened to her? It was almost completely dark now, and the feeling of some malevolent presence watching him continued to grow.

"Aerilynn!" he yelled again. "Aerilynn!" He turned back to look along the undulating curves of the mound. He could see nothing in the total darkness the once bright moonlight had left behind.

He turned back and looked into a pair of red, glowing eyes behind a golden mask. He screamed as withered hands grabbed him by the throat . . .

Alexander leapt from the light doze he had fallen into in the chair when the scream echoed out of the headphones. *Good God*, he thought. *What the* hell *is going on?* He glanced out the motel window in time to see the light in Wilkinson's room come on.

"Just a dream," he heard Wilkinson say shakily. Apparently the kid was having nightmares. Somehow, Alexander found that reassuring.

Steve sat up in the uncomfortable bed, shivering. Every detail of the dream was still crystal-clear in his mind. Aerilynn, Belevairn, the strange park with the Indian mound—all of it perfectly clear.

He still couldn't shake that strange feeling of familiarity he had experienced. He was certain that he had never been anyplace like that. But still, the feeling persisted—he knew that place. Steve reached over and turned on the light to drive the shadows of the dream away.

"Just a dream," he said softly, reassuring himself.

Aerilynn had been so beautiful in the dream, with the moonlight shining off her silver hair. God, he missed her. He lay back on the pillow as a single tear trickled from his right eye. Angrily, he wiped it away.

Frank had tried to set him up with some of the girls he knew. None of them had ever lasted beyond a few dates. None of them could compare to the Olvan lady who had loved him and who had died in battle against the *galdir*.

He yawned. Now that the initial reaction to the nightmare was ebbing, he was even more tired than before. He turned the light out and crawled back under the covers, praying for a night of dreamless sleep.

The next morning Steve returned to the library one last time. There were still a few books on his list that he hadn't been able to find. He was going to make one last attempt this morning and then, depending on what he found, pick a site to visit.

That would give him six days or so before the next full moon to get wherever he was going. If the first site was a dead end, he would probably still have enough time to make it to a second.

Two of the books he was looking for were in. He took them back to a table and began perusing them. The first he discarded quickly. It was one of the typical crackpot works that were all over the occult section.

The second was much more interesting, with a lot of color plates and insets. Unfortunately, it was mostly about areas outside the United States. He did come across a photo from the States that he recognized, however. One of the large medicine wheels in Wyoming.

Two pages later he came across another picture he recognized. Goosebumps ran down his arms and up the back of his neck . . .

Sprawled across two pages was a grassy, undulating, snake-shaped mound surrounded by an asphalt walkway. The ridge split to form the head of the snake at one end.

He had visited this place in his dream last night. A dream that he still recalled with perfect clarity. Other than the dream, however, this was the first time he had seen this place or any reference to it.

He slowly read the text on the surrounding pages. The site was an ancient Indian mound just outside Peebles, Ohio. Furthermore, it was the site of a supposed supernatural encounter, albeit a minor one.

Steve closed the book after copying the information he needed. *Now* he knew where he was going.

Wilkinson practically jumped up from the table he'd been working at and took off for the elevators. Alexander hesitated for a fraction of a second, torn between following the kid and looking at what Wilkinson had been reading.

Pragmatism won out—Wilkinson was *moving*. If Alexander didn't follow him now, it would all be over. The reporter caught up with him at the elevators. There was no choice—Alexander would have to take the same elevator if he wanted to keep up. Damn! What had Wilkinson found?

The elevator opened and the two of them stepped into it. Wilkinson glanced at Alexander while the latter prayed that the kid wouldn't recognize him behind his ten-day growth of beard. If he did, there was a good chance that only one of them would get off the elevator. Alexander had no illusions about which one that would be.

Fortunately, there was no recognition in Wilkinson's gaze. Just the same head-to-toe assessment and dismissal Alexander had seen at Mesa Verde the one time he and Wilkinson had come face to face. Thank God. After today he would shave off his beard in case this happened again.

The elevator went all the way down to the parking garage without stopping. Wilkinson was first off the elevator, with Alexander briefly lagging behind. It would not do for the kid to notice that he was hurrying too.

Robert hadn't been caught napping this time. He had the car, a dark green Continental, started and ready to go by the time Alexander got to it. Good man.

"What's gotten into him?" Robert asked when Alexander got in.

"Dunno," Alexander replied. "He was looking through some books when he got up and took off like a shot. I'd say he found what he was looking for."

"Hm," was Robert's only reply. They pulled out after Wilkinson. Thank God Alexander had made Robert switch cars last night.

Wilkinson drove straight to his motel room and began packing up the truck. Robert parked across the street.

"Go check us out," Alexander said, handing Robert the room key. He slid over into the driver's seat when Robert got out. The kid wasn't wasting any time. He was on his way to the office by the time Robert came out.

Alexander watched as the two passed each other. Oh, Lord, if he hadn't thought to have Robert check them out, that would have been *him* walking past Wilkinson. There would have been no hope at all that the kid wouldn't have recognized him at that point.

"Man," Robert said as he climbed into the passenger side of the Continental, "I do *not* like the way that kid looks at you."

"Believe me, I know what you mean," Alexander replied. "There he goes."

They pulled out behind Wilkinson after allowing two cars to get between them. The kid took East Hampden Avenue to Highway 25. Not long after getting onto 25 he exited onto Highway 225, eastbound.

"Okay," Alexander said. "He's headed for 70. What's the next major town?"

"Topeka," Robert announced after studying the atlas briefly. "No new freeways."

"After that?"

"Kansas City. Three freeways, but 80 intersects the other two routes." Highway 80 was accessible from Denver more easily via Highway 76.

"So he's probably staying on 70," Alexander noted. "What's next?"

"St. Louis," Robert replied. "Five freeways."

Alexander nodded. That was where they would have to be careful not to lose him. Assuming, of course, that he didn't stop in Topeka or Kansas City.

A day and a half after leaving Denver, Steve pulled into the small country town of Peebles, Ohio. Peebles was a tiny place—one thousand seven hundred and ninety people, according to the city limits sign. Compared to the rural areas he had already driven through on his way up here, Peebles was a remarkably clean and well-kept little town.

Older buildings and homes were mixed with more modern stores and service stations, creating a surprisingly comforting atmosphere. New or old, all of them were immaculate. Peebles was sort of a cross between Mayberry RFD and Smalltown. It almost seemed too perfect to be real.

This was what he was fighting to protect. He hadn't realized that places like this actually existed outside of movies and television. Without a doubt, Peebles at least *looked* like rural America at its best.

A small bed-and-breakfast sat on the left side of the road. It was a delightfully quaint old country house, with even more of a storybook appearance than what he had seen of the rest of the town. It was probably the only place to stay in town, as well.

For a moment Steve considered taking a room there, but quickly decided against it. It was a full four days until the next full moon. If he tried to stay here that long, he would attract attention. Fortunately, Cincinnati was only about two hours away. If he stayed four days in a motel there, no one would notice. Unfortunately, four days in a motel would just about exhaust his remaining funds. Maybe he could find a campground nearby . . .

In Locust Grove, the next small town north of Peebles, he got directions to the mound itself from a friendly woman in a small convenience store. Unfortunately, it was close to closing time—he would probably only get to spend a little over an hour there.

Soon, he was leaving the narrow road and pulling up the drive that led to the park. He stopped at the booth and paid his admission fee. This late in the day, there were very few visitors. Steve pulled into a parking spot and got out of the truck. Taking a deep breath, he headed down the walkway that led to the mound. He didn't notice the dark green Continental that pulled into the parking lot behind him.

Before him lay the site of his dream. Short, mowed grass covered the undulating mound. He walked along the asphalt sidewalk until he came to the split that formed the serpent's head.

Looking back from here, there was no doubt. *This* was where he had had his dream encounter with Belevairn. This was where the sorcerer should arrive next.

There is Power here, Belevairn said in his mind. *It is very weak.*

So this mound is *a source of Power*, Steve noted.

Actually, there are two sources here, Belevairn replied. *A Power of light has been laid over a darker Power.*

Something was imprisoned here long ago.

But is it strong enough for Belevairn to come through? Steve asked.

No. However, that may very well change with the full moon.

Steve nodded. In that case, he would return when the moon was full.

Chapter
-------- Seven -------------

LIEUTENANT GARTH WALKED past the temple on his way to Captain Korva's office. It was approaching noon, and the *kaivir* were atop the pyramid preparing for a sacrifice. Garth spared only a glance for the grisly preparations. The victim was already being led up the stairs to take his place on the altar.

This was the eventual destination of all the prisoners they captured. Garth was glad of the fact that the senior Morvir handled those duties. Killing a man in combat was one thing—leading him like a bull to slaughter to feed the sorcery of the *kaivir* was quite another.

The junior Morvir were too busy being hired out to tend to the camp duties—they were here to be trained. The senior Morvir had already completed their month of combat and were waiting to be transported home—maintaining and guarding the camp was their duty. Garth liked it that way.

Of course, his men would also become the camp guard once the new batch of recruits arrived in a month, Earth time, which would be almost a year back in Morvanor. Once the core group of each Dread Lord's Special Forces unit was trained, all training would be shifted to Morvanor. Training the forces on Earth was simply too time-consuming for the Mistress to tolerate.

Garth entered the headquarters building north of the temple and walked to Captain Korva's office.

"Lieutenant Garth reporting as ordered, sir," he said, saluting.

"At ease, Lieutenant," Korva replied. "Sit down."

Korva looked up once Garth had settled into one of the two chairs facing his desk.

"Good job on that convoy in Costa Rica," Korva began. "Very well done for a first mission."

"Thank you, sir." Garth somehow doubted that the captain had called him in to congratulate him for an inconsequential mission.

"I've got another assignment for you," Korva continued. "One that will test your capabilities quite a bit more."

Garth raised an eyebrow. This sounded interesting . . .

"You will select two squads to take on this mission. Lieutenant Ulan will also be commanding two squads with you."

"Ulan?" Garth asked. Why not just have Garth take all four of his squads instead of sending two lieutenants on this mission? However, Ulan had served with Garth under Lord Jared in Umbria. If Garth had to share command with someone, he couldn't have picked anyone better.

"That is correct," Korva replied. "This mission is extremely sensitive. I will accompany you with three of my own senior squads."

So, Garth would not be sharing command at all—Korva would be in command. Seven squads in all, three of them seasoned troops. This must be an important mission indeed.

"Go select your squads," Korva ordered. "Then report back here to the briefing room with your sergeants. Dismissed."

Garth stood at attention, saluted and left the captain's office. He found that he was looking forward to this mission.

"Our target is a small village in Colombia near Cartagena," Korva informed them. "This village is, for all practical purposes, owned by someone fairly high up in one of the Colombian drug cartels. A very large amount of the cartel's coca production moves through this village.

"Our mission description is quite simple," Korva continued. "We are to destroy Don Raphael's mansion, north of the village, the village itself and the coca-processing house back in the jungle. Furthermore, our orders are that no one is to be left alive and, most definitely, no one is to be allowed to escape.

"I am going to amend those orders," Korva said. "No one is to be allowed to escape—no one. However, you are to take all the captives you can—the *kaivir* need sacrifices and we need camp slaves.

"Garth, you and Ulan will be assigned to raze the village," Korva said. Garth nodded—that was what he had expected. The village would be the place to use green troops. Resistance would probably be much higher at the mansion and even more so at the processing house.

"How you undertake that is between you and Ulan," Korva continued, "as long as you achieve the mission objectives. Two of my squads will attack the processing house and the third will attack Don Raphael's mansion. You will hold your attack on the village until we begin our attack on those sites. Our signal that we have begun will be a starburst flare fired overhead. Are there any questions?"

"Which of us is in command of the attack on the village?" Ulan asked. "Garth or myself?"

Korva leaned forward onto his elbows, resting his chin on his knuckles. Garth suspected that Ulan had just asked the wrong question.

"I doubt that either of you will have much opportunity to communicate once the attack begins," Korva replied. "However, since *you* asked, Ulan, Garth will have battle-field command."

"Yes, sir," Ulan replied.

"Now that we've gotten *that* out of the way," Korva said, "how do you men plan to proceed with the attack on the village?"

"It seems simple enough," Ulan began.

"Oh?" Korva replied quietly.

"Yes, sir," Ulan continued, apparently not noticing the tone of Korva's reply. "We surround the village and tighten the circle, firing all the buildings we come to in order to flush out the occupants. Anyone who flees toward the center of the village we allow to do so. Anyone else, we kill."

Garth frowned. Ulan's plan sounded like the standard tactics used back at Delgroth. It did not utilize the capabilities of the variety of weapons they had at their disposal.

"How many villagers do you expect to capture alive with that strategy, Lieutenant?" Korva asked.

"Perhaps a quarter of the noncombatants," Ulan replied.

"In other words, about twenty people," Korva observed.

"We can do better than that," Garth said. "Assuming that it is worth a little expense to increase the number of captives."

"Depends on how good the increase is," Korva noted, leaning back in his chair and drumming the fingers of his right hand on the table.

"I would estimate double or triple the number that Lieutenant Ulan's plan would yield," Garth replied. "Perhaps more."

Korva smiled and nodded.

"That sounds more like it," he said. "What's your plan, Lieutenant?"

Garth waited in the thick underbrush for the signal. He and Ulan had divided their two squads into three, each lieutenant taking command of three men from each of their two squads. As a result, six seven-man squads waited in the jungle to attack the village.

Each man was carrying a rifle-mounted grenade launcher and five gas grenades in addition to his normal complement. Except, that is, for one man in each squad who was carrying a flamethrower. Additionally, each squad leader was carrying a rocket launcher against the slim possibility that the Morvir might encounter fortified positions within the village.

The signal flare burst high above the village. Taking advantage of the brief illumination, each squad leader used his grenade launcher to destroy the perimeter homes. The attack had begun. Garth slammed a gas grenade into his launcher to replace the incendiary he had just fired.

Garth led his squad's charge from the jungle as the villagers began to rally from their night's slumber. Around him he could hear his men's breathing as it rasped through their gas masks. The first sounds of gunfire reached them from somewhere to the north. The villagers were beginning to resist.

The burning form of a woman staggered from the house in front of Garth, screaming. He fired a single shot, ending her misery. That was one who would not have to face the *kaivir* atop the temple.

The squad had spread out as they advanced into the village, forming an even perimeter. Not so much as a dog was to be allowed to escape. Garth dropped to one knee and fired a gas grenade through the window of another home. A man ran into the street, and Garth cut him down with a short burst. Shortly afterwards a woman staggered out, unarmed.

Garth waited while she recovered from most of the effects of the gas before allowing her to see him. She screamed and ran from him—toward the center of the village. Garth stepped into the gas-filled home. Empty. He stepped back out and motioned to his fireman. A stream of flame shot onto the roof and then through the open door. In seconds the house was burning furiously behind them.

The distant sounds of the heavier battles at the mansion and the coca house reached them. These formed a steady background to the random bursts of nearby gunfire from the village resistance.

Garth ducked instinctively at the sound of one of the rocket launchers firing from across the village. One of the houses almost directly opposite the village from him was consumed in a violent explosion. Ulan. Garth smiled—Ulan had objected that the rocket launchers were unnecessary, even cowardly against nothing but villagers. Apparently he had changed his mind.

Garth stepped around a corner, coming face to face with an armed villager. Garth fired even as he dove to the side. The enemy fell back, dead, as a burning pain raced across Garth's arm. He rolled behind the cover of another house and up onto one knee. He shuddered—that had been *too* close.

He glanced down at his arm. The right bicep had been grazed. It was minor, he could tend to it later.

He rose, back to the wall, before stepping around the corner again. Burning homes garishly illuminated the battle. Garth could see the men of his squad continuing to advance into the village. He jogged between the houses to rejoin them.

He slipped around a corner. One of his men, Kelar, lay in the street. A village man bent over the body, apparently attempting to claim some of Kelar's weapons. The villager straightened and began to turn as Garth fired. His lifeless body fell atop Kelar's inert form.

Garth glanced up and down the street before kneeling to check Kelar. There was no pulse.

"Damn!" he whispered. Now his platoon would be one man short for the rest of the month. He pulled the pin from one of Kelar's grenades and left it by the body before ducking behind the cover of a nearby house. The villagers would get nothing useful from Kelar's corpse.

Garth arrived at the center of the village with no further encounters. A double circle of Morvir surrounded the town center where the noncombatants had been driven. The village's defenders had all been killed. All that were left were the women, the children and the elderly.

"Sergeant Aglar," Garth ordered, "take your squad and search the village. Burn everything to the ground. If it won't burn, use the explosives. Our orders are to leave nothing standing."

"Yes, sir," Aglar replied, saluting before leaving to carry out his orders. Ulan joined Garth as the sergeant left.

"I've radioed for the trucks," he said. "They'll be here any minute."

Garth turned to look at Ulan.

"I've just sent Aglar to search the village," he said. "You should have waited until the search was complete."

"There is no one left alive here," Ulan said. "We went through every building during our advance."

A brief burst of gunfire sounded behind them. Both Garth and Ulan looked back at the sound.

"It seems," Garth said, turning to look at Ulan, "that you are mistaken."

Aglar found no other holdouts, and the trucks arrived safely. Garth supervised the loading of the slaves while Ulan directed the demolition of the village. Korva's men arrived shortly after the trucks arrived. They brought a few captives from Don Raphael's household. One beautiful, young girl with angry dark eyes and long, flowing black hair especially caught Garth's eye.

"Can you finish up here, Lieutenant Garth?" Korva asked.

"Yes, sir," Garth replied, tearing his gaze from the young woman. For some reason he felt sorry for her.

"Good. We'll go on ahead and secure the pickup point. Follow as soon as you are through here."

"Yes, sir," Garth said again.

"You're in command," Korva said, saluting. "You'll be debriefed once we return to camp, but for now, good job, Lieutenant."

"Thank you, sir," Garth said, returning Korva's salute. The captain turned and climbed into the first of the three trucks that would transport the senior squads to the pickup point.

Garth watched as the senior squads drove away. Good job? He had lost one man and two others had been wounded, not including himself. Still, that was better than Ulan's performance. Three dead and three wounded, one severely. And Garth's squads had never had to resort to the rocket launchers. Still, was that a mark of Garth's skill, or had Ulan simply run into fiercer resistance?

"The demolition is complete except for the fountain," Ulan reported.

"Good," Garth said. "Set the explosives. We will detonate them once the trucks move out."

"Where is Korva?"

"*Captain* Korva left to secure the pickup point," Garth replied. "He left me in command. You have your orders, Lieutenant."

"Yes, *sir*," Ulan replied acidly.

*   *   *

Belevairn looked up as Korath entered his office. The *kaiva* bowed before speaking.

"Ramirez has arrived, Dread Lord," Korath said.

"Good," Belevairn replied. "Send him in and tell Captain Korva to join us."

"At once, Dread Lord." Korath turned and left, to be quickly replaced by Ramirez.

Ramirez was a thin weasel of a man with dark features and a pencil-thin moustache. The mouth under his large nose split into a toothy smile as he entered Belevairn's office.

"*Hola*, Don Espantoso," he said, extending his hand. Belevairn took it reluctantly.

"Where is my equipment, Ramirez?" Belevairn asked, sitting back down behind his desk.

"It is on its way, Don Espantoso," Ramirez replied. "It was not easy to arrange transport into Nicaragua. Small arms are one thing, but this . . ." The little man shrugged.

"I . . . see," Belevairn said. Of course, the Nicaraguan government would not allow Ramirez to bring armor into the country. They were already complaining about the number of troops that Belevairn had in camp. Some veiled threats to take action had already been made.

This was a problem that would have to be solved if operations here were going to continue. It might be necessary to engineer a coup of some smaller country to obtain an unrestricted base of operations. Belevairn would hate to leave the temple, though. He would probably never again find such an ideal site. He would have to discuss this problem with the Mistress . . .

"Captain Korva reporting as ordered, Dread Lord," Korva announced as he entered Belevairn's office.

"Sit down, Captain," Belevairn said. "Ramirez says our armor is on its way. Have the crews been trained?"

"Yes, Dread Lord," Korva replied. "I can have them back in camp in a few days."

"Trained?" Ramirez asked.

"Yes, Ramirez," Belevairn replied. "None of our men

have any experience with mechanized armor. Captain Korva has had several crews training in Africa for the last few months."

"Ah, I see."

"That will be all, Captain," Belevairn said. "You are dismissed." Korva rose to his feet, saluted and left.

"Now, Don Espantoso," Ramirez began, once Korva had left, "I believe we can discuss payment . . ."

"You will get your final payment when I take delivery, Ramirez," Belevairn interrupted. "Not before."

"But, my Don . . ."

"That is final," Belevairn said. "I did not get where I am through blind trust. You have eighty percent of the payment. You can wait until delivery for the last twenty."

"Yes, Don Espantoso."

"When will the equipment arrive?"

"In about three days."

"Excellent. You can wait here, or you can return in three days for your payment."

"I will . . . return, Don Espantoso." Ramirez did not relish the thought of spending three days in the Morvan camp. He had seen the bone racks at the base of the pyramid . . .

"As you wish," Belevairn replied. "You may go, Ramirez." After the arms dealer had left, Belevairn leaned back in his chair. He would have to return to Delgroth to consult with the Mistress.

Don Estefan stood on the charred foundation of what used to be his son-in-law's estate. All that was left of the younger Don's home was the foundation and the remains of a few fireplaces. Everything else had been burned to the ground, just like in the village.

The coca-processing house hidden back in the jungle had also been burned. Millions of American dollars lost in a single night. That was only part of the loss, however. The body of Estefan's daughter had been found earlier today. Don Raphael's daughter, Estefan's granddaughter, had not been found among the dead. In fact, most of the women of the village were unaccounted for.

"Who is responsible for this, Juan?" he asked the man next to him.

"The Valdez family, of course," Juan replied.

"Yes, of course," Don Estefan agreed. "But who *did* this?"

"According to Miguel, the Valdez family hired a group of mercenaries called the Morvir to carry out the attack." Miguel was Juan's informant in the Valdez family. His information had always been reliable in the past.

Don Estefan stared over the ruins. He had heard of the Morvir—their name was all over South America.

"These Morvir must have enemies," he said, musing aloud. Juan snorted in amusement.

"Only half the mercenaries in the world," he replied. "The ones they have not fought, they have taken business from. Don Espantoso hires the Morvir out for a quarter of the normal rates."

"*Find* these enemies," Don Estefan said bitterly. "Learn all that you can about the Morvir. They must be made to *pay* for this outrage."

"Yes, my Don."

Chapter
-------- **Eight** -------------

STEVE KILLED THE headlights on the pickup just after turning into the parking lot beside the Louden General Store. The one car that had been behind him drove on past without slowing. Good. He waited until it was out of sight before getting out of the truck.

He removed the shotgun from its case behind the seat. The small store had apparently been abandoned for some time and should make a good place to leave his truck while he paid his evening visit to the mound. Steve glanced at his watch—11:05. He was going to have to hurry to make it into the park by true midnight, less than two hours from now.

Checking to make certain that no one was coming, he crossed the narrow street and hurried down the embankment to the plowed fields below. Travel through the fields was quick with the full moon to give him light. Unfortunately, that moon also denied him any concealment out in the open. He would have to get under the cover of the trees around the park as quickly as possible.

Steve glanced back several times as he jogged across the fields. So far, so good—no one else had even come down the road, let alone sighted him. Less than a hundred yards from the trees, however, his luck ran out. A pair of headlights came down the road. Steve threw himself to the ground as soon as he saw them.

He panted heavily from the run. No sense trying to keep quiet; the road was over five hundred feet away. Steve watched as the car headed down the road back toward Locust Grove without slowing. Good—apparently the occupants of the car had not seen him.

Steve got back on his feet and crossed the remaining distance into the protective cover of the trees. He stopped, still panting from the jog, as he allowed his eyes to adjust to the dimmer light beneath the trees. Now all he had to do was make it to the mound before midnight. Crossing the creek and making it up the fifty-foot bank was going to be a challenge. Still, he had well over an hour in which to get there. He should be able to make it with time to spare.

Steve proceeded slowly through the underbrush. The silvery moonlight lent a dreamlike quality to the patch of woods. Steve shuddered—he had dreamed about a moonlit forest much like this once. That dream had culminated in his arrival in the Burning Hills, summoned by Magus Artemas's misperformed magic.

He finally found the spot he had chosen for his crossing earlier in the day. A fallen tree extended halfway across the creek. Steve gingerly made his way along it. From here he would have to swim to reach the opposite bank.

Fortunately, swimming had been the main program in his physical therapy after the coma. Crossing this creek shouldn't be any problem at all. He gasped as he climbed into the unexpectedly icy water.

Great, he thought, as he held the shotgun over his head with one arm and sidestroked across. *I'm going to get pneumonia on top of everything else.*

The current carried him about twenty feet downstream before he reached the opposite bank. Now, the hard part was going to be following this creek around to the hiking path that led up to the mound. He slung the shotgun over his back and began carefully climbing over the tangled brush that lined the narrow shore of the creek.

It took him the better part of an hour to work his way around to the hiking path. From here he could make it up to the mound and to the hiding spot he had selected in five minutes. Plenty of time.

Alexander drove on past when Wilkinson pulled off beside the abandoned store. He drove down the road

until he was out of sight before killing the lights. Then
he turned around and drove back to where he could just
see the store.

Soon, Wilkinson crossed the road carrying his shotgun
and scrambled down to the fields below. Alexander watched
as the kid jogged across the fields in the moonlight, obviously headed for the cover of the trees.

"We're not going to follow him, are we?" Robert asked.

"No way," Alexander replied. "Not with the firepower
he's packing. Besides, we don't have to—we know where
he's going."

"The park?"

"Bingo."

Alexander started the car once Wilkinson was most of
the way across the fields. No, he wasn't about to follow
Wilkinson on another overland hike. Security at the park
was pretty light—they would just park beside the road a
short distance away and walk up the driveway. He and
Robert could duck into the trees just long enough to keep
from being seen. It would make for a much easier trip than
the one Wilkinson was taking.

Steve sat on the steps that led down to the observation
lookout over the creek. This location gave him a good view
of the head of the serpent while also providing cover. He
shivered in the chill of the night air, wishing that his clothes
would hurry up and dry.

The light of the full moon gave an eerie cast to the
surroundings. Steve glanced at his watch—twenty minutes
till true midnight. Soon he would know if this had all been
a wild-goose chase. It was beginning to look like it might
have been. His own resident version of Belevairn claimed
that the Power was hardly any stronger fifteen minutes ago
than when they had first visited here. There was simply not
enough Power for the real Belevairn to arrive.

He squinted toward the head of the serpent. Was it getting darker? He was certainly having more difficulty seeing
the mound. Perhaps it was getting cloudy.

Steve gasped when he glanced skyward. Over half of the lunar disk was gone! It was an eclipse!

Belevairn! Steve called silently.

Yes, Belevairn replied. *The Power has increased by an order of magnitude. It is growing rapidly.*

So, the real Belevairn will *arrive here!* Steve could feel the old familiar rush of impending combat.

If anywhere, Belevairn agreed. *You must kill him the moment he arrives.*

No! Steve objected. *I have to find out* why *he is here.*

Fool! When my counterpart arrives, he will have as much Power at his disposal as anywhere on my own world. You cannot *face him at his full power! You* must *kill him!*

No, Steve replied. *I must know if any of the other Dread Lords know the path to Earth. I have to know what is happening.*

You will get us both killed, Belevairn insisted.

Shut up, Steve thought firmly. *Belevairn may arrive at any moment.*

Steve sighed in relief when Belevairn's presence left his mind. He disliked conversing with the sorcerer, but, as much as he was loathe to admit it, he needed the other's assistance with this. That didn't mean he had to like it, however.

The light was fading quickly. Steve would not be able to see the mound when Belevairn arrived. He cautiously advanced a little further up the hill, taking cover behind some thin brush. In the fading light, that should be sufficient. It wouldn't do to miss his rendezvous after waiting all this time.

Alexander watched the spot where he and Robert had seen Wilkinson go to wait. The kid was good; even from the observation tower near the center of the mound, they couldn't see him in the full moonlight.

Gaining access to the park had been every bit as easy as Alexander had thought. They had simply strolled in and set up their watch on the tower. About an hour later, Wilkinson had appeared, moving stealthily from one of the hiking trails to the creek overlook near the head of the mound. From his appearance, he had obviously swum the creek, making Alexander even more grateful that they had not followed him.

"This eclipse is going to ruin our light," Robert whispered. The photographer had brought some special night equipment and film with him, but from this distance without the moonlight they wouldn't get a damned thing on film.

"Well, I don't think we want to move up any closer," Alexander replied. From Wilkinson's vantage point, he and Robert would be sitting ducks the minute they started climbing down the small tower. As long as they were relatively still, they were as invisible to him as he was to them. Of course, at the rate it was going, it would soon be pitch black. They could probably move then, but Alexander was a bit apprehensive at the thought of bumping into Wilkinson in the dark . . .

"How long are we going to wait?" Robert asked.

"Until he leaves," Alexander replied. "Now be quiet before he hears us."

Robert's exasperated sigh was his only response.

The *goremka* slipped through the barrier to Earth on the first attempt. Belevairn smiled at the pleasant surprise. It usually took him almost a day, if not longer, to find an entrance.

He emerged atop a grassy mound to discover another pleasant surprise. The Power here was extreme—as powerful as anything he had ever wielded on his own world. This was an unexpected boon. He would be able to transport himself immediately to Nicaragua.

But first, he wanted to see where it was that he had emerged. What was the source of such incredible Power on a world so devoid of any of it? He arrogantly summoned a light before turning to inspect his surroundings. With this much Power at his disposal it did not matter if anyone saw him.

* * *

The darkness had grown to the point that Steve could not see the mound from his current position. He was considering advancing to a better vantage point when a gleam of light opened atop the mound like a rip in the air. A mounted figure stepped from it onto the grass of the mound. The portal winked shut behind it.

Paydirt! Steve thought.

An unexpected, brilliant light suddenly illuminated the area, and Steve hastily ducked further behind the brush. He smiled—Belevairn was being arrogant. The sorcerer had Power to burn, and knew it. He was invincible—or so he thought.

To Steve's surprise, Belevairn dismounted and began inspecting the mound. Of course—the sorcerer would be curious about the level of Power here. Good; that got him off the *goremka*.

Steve took a deep breath—he would have to get this right the first time. He tensed, waiting for Belevairn's attention to become fully focused on what he was doing.

The *goremka* looked away, back down the mound toward the observation tower. Now! Steve launched himself up the short hill toward the walkway. At the first smack of his foot on the asphalt walkway, both Belevairn and the demon-steed looked up with a start.

Without hesitation, Steve raised the shotgun to his shoulder and fired. Belevairn flew backwards as the lead shot impacted him. The buckshot wouldn't hurt Belevairn, but it would keep him off balance long enough for Steve to close the distance. Steve leapt to the top of the short mound and aimed the shotgun at the prone sorcerer.

"The next one's a magnesium flare, Belevairn," Steve said in Morvan. "If either you or the *goremka* make a single move, you'll be ashes."

"W-Wilkinson?" Belevairn asked incredulously. "It . . . it cannot be! How . . . ?"

"Rumors of my death have been greatly exaggerated," Steve replied, smiling. "I want to know why you're here. Now."

The sorcerer slowly shifted to a sitting position. Steve tracked his every movement with the shotgun.

Kill him, you fool, Steve's Belevairn hissed in his mind. *Now, while you still can.*

Shut up!

"Why should I tell you?" the real Belevairn asked, resuming his normal, arrogant tone now that the initial shock of encountering Steve alive had passed.

"If you don't . . ." Steve began.

"You shall destroy me?" Belevairn interrupted. "That is exactly what will happen if I *do* tell you. As long as you need me, I remain alive—so to speak."

Steve frowned. Belevairn was right. No matter what happened, Steve could not let the sorcerer leave here alive.

Kill him now!

"Now," Belevairn continued, "if you were to swear that you will allow me to leave unharmed if I tell you what you want to know, perhaps we could negotiate."

"*You* would trust my word?" Steve asked.

"Yes, were it sworn in Mortos's name and on the honor of your liege. These concepts are ridiculous to me, but I *know* that they are binding to you."

Belevairn was right—if Steve swore such oaths, he would be bound to honor them. Now he had a dilemma on his hands. Should he agree to this to get the information he needed? Killing Belevairn might not stop the Mistress's plans for Earth, whatever those might be.

No! Steve's tenant insisted. *Kill him now before he tricks you and kills both of us. He* cannot *let you live!*

That was certainly true. The dark goddess would have Belevairn's hide if the sorcerer left here with Steve alive.

"No deal," Steve said, squeezing the trigger.

Belevairn rolled away as Steve fired, and the burning flare buried itself in the mound. Simultaneously, the *goremka* leapt at him, its fangs diving for his throat.

Steve threw up his arms, shoving the shotgun crosswise into the monster's mouth like a bit. The force of the impact knocked him onto his back as he desperately struggled to keep the demon's maw forced back.

The muscles of his arms strained against the shotgun, struggling to force the horselike muzzle away. Mortos, it couldn't end like this!

The demon jerked back, snapping its jaws shut and shearing through rifle stock and barrel as though they were balsa wood. Steve rolled away as the fangs dove toward him. He came up into a crouch and leapt from atop the mound, feeling the *goremka's* fangs brush his back as he jumped.

Steve's shoulder struck the asphalt walkway hard. He tucked his head as he began to roll down the hill toward the trees. The *goremka* must be right on top of him.

Steve managed to stop his roll and come to his knees halfway down the hill. The *goremka* was hurtling down toward him from above. Steve heard his voice shouting words he did not recognize as his hands wove an intricate pattern through the air. The demon-horse struck the hastily erected ward with an impact like a physical blow.

Together we might *survive this,* Belevairn said in his mind. *Do not fight me.*

Belevairn increased the flow of Power to the ward. Steve screamed as it burned through his body, fighting to remain conscious.

Belevairn watched from atop the mound as the *goremka* reared, striking the ward with its fiery hooves. Where had Wilkinson learned to fashion a ward? There was nothing in the memories he had stolen from the youth about sorcerous training.

He would have to assist his steed in defeating that ward—Wilkinson must not be allowed to live. He reached for the Power he would need to shatter Wilkinson's ward, only to discover that the Power here was ebbing.

Belevairn glanced skyward. A sliver of moon had returned to the sky—the eclipse was ending. At the rate the Power was fading, he would barely have enough to send himself to Nicaragua if he began the ritual now.

There was no choice. If he was forced to remain here, he would risk discovery by others. This place showed all the signs of being a tourist attraction. He would have to deal with Wilkinson at a later time, curse the luck!

Each blow of the demon's hooves against the ward sent waves of agony through Steve's entire being. Sweat ran down into his eyes from the strain of the Power that Belevairn poured through him. How much longer could he maintain this?

Another blow landed against the ward, and darkness gathered at the edge of his vision. He pushed the darkness back by sheer force of will—he dare not black out now!

The next, expected blow did not come. Steve blinked and looked up from his prone position in time to see the *goremka* vanish over the top of the mound. With a sigh of relief, he felt the release of the Power. It was over.

Suddenly, Steve rose on his hands as realization hit him. The real Belevairn must be leaving! He scrambled up the slope, ignoring his protesting muscles and joints, in time to see Belevairn mount his steed.

Forgetting his pains, Steve bolted for Belevairn, leaping onto the *goremka*'s back in a maneuver he had not used since returning to Earth. Before he could try to pull the sorcerer from the saddle, Belevairn twisted, driving his elbow into Steve's side with the superhuman strength that all of the Dread Lords possessed.

Steve tumbled from the back of the demon-horse, clutching at something that supported him only briefly before snapping and letting him fall to the ground. He watched helplessly as mount and rider vanished into nothingness.

Steve rose slowly to his feet, staring at the place where Belevairn had vanished. *Now* it was over. Now there was nothing to do but return home and wait with the rest of humanity to see what the Mistress had in store for Earth.

His gaze fell to his feet. Lying on the ground in the returning moonlight were a pair of saddlebags. He dropped to his knees, opening one of the saddlebags. Maps! Maps and papers. He hadn't lost yet!

Steve rose to his feet, alerted by the sounds of someone approaching. The battle had apparently attracted some attention. He quickly gathered up the saddlebags and the remains of his shotgun before heading back into the forest trails.

"Did you get all that?" Alexander asked.

"Yeah! I think so," Robert replied. "Man, we've got to get back so I can develop this film!"

"Robert," Alexander said, pointing back down the walkway, "we have a more immediate problem."

"Huh?" Robert said, looking to where Alexander was pointing. A group of men with flashlights were approaching.

"Oh, shit!" Robert said. "We can't let them get the film!"

"Get it out of the camera, man!" Alexander said. "Throw it into the woods."

Robert quickly removed the film, placing it in the plastic film case before tossing it into the trees. Hopefully, no one had noticed. That film was priceless.

"You on the platform," someone shouted from below. "Come down with your hands in the air."

Alexander and Robert complied, holding their press cards over their heads as they gingerly walked down the stairs. Something about having half a dozen revolvers pointed at you made one move carefully.

"I'm Richard Alexander," he said once they had reached the bottom of the stairs. "My partner and I are on a story for the *Clarion*. Official press business."

"That's nice, Mister Alexander," the sheriff replied. "You're under arrest."

Belevairn emerged atop the Aztec temple in Nicaragua. Curse Wilkinson and all his kin! Who would have thought that he could survive the Ritual of Transfer? And how had he learned of Belevairn's presence on Earth? For that matter, how had the *rega* managed to track him down? Not even Belevairn could predict the location of his arrival.

He guided his mount down to its stall at the base of the

temple. The *kaivir* came to assist him as he dismounted. Only when he reached for them did he discover that his saddlebags were missing. For a moment he merely stared, as if his disbelief could make the stolen saddlebags reappear.

Then he did curse Wilkinson, long and loudly. There had been two stoneweight of gold in those saddlebags—over one hundred thousand dollars, American. For an instant he considered going back for his saddlebags, but only for an instant.

It would be more efficient to return to Delgroth. For every hour that passed here, roughly ten passed back there. Also, the Mistress would want to know of this . . . development.

"Tell Captain Korva that I have been unavoidably detained," he told the *kaivir*. "And that I shall go over the mission schedules with him upon my return from Delgroth."

"Yes, Dread Lord," they replied.

"From this day forward," Belevairn added, "I want a sacrifice performed atop this temple every day at noon, in addition to our normal schedule." To hell with the attention it might draw—these random appearances had just become far too costly. Belevairn wanted to make certain he did not accidentally run into Wilkinson again.

"Y-yes, Dread Lord," they replied, shaken. Belevairn remounted and began the journey back to Delgroth, hoping that Daryna would not be too displeased.

Chapter
-------- Nine ------------

IT WAS FOUR in the morning when Steve got back to the motel room he had rented in Cincinnati. He was exhausted—every single muscle in his body ached. He couldn't be certain if that was from the battle with the *goremka* or from the searing flow of the Power through his untrained body.

He knew what the pain in his chest that came with every breath was from, though. If Belevairn hadn't broken some of Steve's ribs, he had at least cracked them. Tackling a Dread Lord unarmed had not exactly been the brightest move he had ever made. Of course, he hadn't had much choice in the matter.

To add insult to injury, he was still wet from his second trip across that damned creek. If he didn't wind up with pneumonia, it would be a miracle. Fortunately, he had packed a change of clothes in the truck, so he wasn't completely sodden. Still, he shivered in the predawn air.

He winced as he lifted Belevairn's saddlebags from the truck. What did Belevairn have in them, anyway—lead bricks? He would have to check them as soon as he got into his room.

Actually, a hot shower and a night's, or actually a day's, sleep sounded better. The saddlebags would keep until tomorrow. He needed to take care of himself right now.

It was just after noon by the time Alexander and Robert were released by the Adams County Sheriff. Alexander was pissed. By now, Wilkinson was *long* gone. The paper wasn't extremely happy with him, either. That was all right—Alexander was certain they would become a lot happier once they retrieved and developed that film.

Still, it was going to be hell trying to catch up with Wilkinson. That kid moved fast when things broke—Alexander had to give him that. He was probably two or three states away by now.

"What now?" Robert asked. "Can we go get my film?"

"Are you crazy?" Alexander said. "Do you think the owner of that park is going to let us anywhere *near* there? I've already asked someone from the *Clarion* to retrieve the film. They'll develop it and send us the prints."

"Hey, those are *my* shots!" Robert objected. "I don't want someone else developing the prints that I spent a night in jail to get!"

Alexander smiled. Robert certainly was beginning to seem a little more enthusiastic about this assignment.

"Don't worry," Alexander reassured him. "I'll make sure you get the credit for them, and there will be other shots. Trust me."

"Yeah . . . right." Robert did not sound convinced.

"As far as your earlier question," Alexander continued, "we have to try to pick up Wilkinson's trail."

"Back to the motel," Robert said.

"Right."

Alexander blinked in surprise as they pulled into the motel parking lot. Wilkinson's truck was parked a few doors away from the room he had rented. Could he still be here? Surely he hadn't abandoned the truck.

"Looks like picking up the trail won't be too hard," Robert noted.

"God likes me," Alexander mumbled.

"It makes sense, you know. Wilkinson had an even worse night than we did. He probably hasn't woken up yet."

"God *really* likes me," Alexander replied.

"I doubt that," Robert said, smiling.

Steve groaned and rolled over, which was a mistake. Fire flared along the ribs where Belevairn had struck him. The coughing fit that followed didn't help any. At least there still wasn't any blood—he didn't have to worry about a punctured lung.

Once the coughing fit had passed, Steve sat up. Another mistake. A throbbing pain erupted in his head, and the room spun about him. Great—so he had a concussion as well as some cracked ribs.

"Oh, God," he moaned, falling back onto the pillow. The worst part was that Belevairn had gotten away clean.

No, he thought, remembering the saddlebags, *not clean.* Steve sat up carefully. He managed to get out of the bed and make it to a chair without falling. His empty stomach threatened to heave—another symptom of the concussion. He should get to a hospital. . . .

No, that wouldn't do. He didn't want to draw any attention to himself this close to Great Serpent Mound. Not after last night. The concussion would fade and the ribs would heal just as fast if he took a few days to rest.

He lifted the heavy saddlebags from the floor and laid them on the bed, wincing at the strain this placed on his injured side. The ruined shotgun lay on the floor next to them. Steve picked up the three main pieces of it, laying them on the bed as well.

He shook his head. At least he had been smart enough not to leave it at the mound. That would have identified him immediately as last night's intruder. Other than that, he might as well toss the remains. He would dump it in a dumpster somewhere outside Ohio.

Steve unfastened the clasp on the saddlebags. He pulled out a stack of navigational charts—the same ones he had seen Belevairn refer to in the vision at Mesa Verde. He set them aside for now.

Other navigational items emerged from the saddlebags. A sextant, a radio, a flashlight—Steve smiled when he pulled out a folding shovel. Belevairn was apparently determined not to suffer a repeat of his entombment at Mesa Verde.

Steve gasped when he saw what lay in the bottom of the saddlebags. He slowly removed one of the small bars of gold. On it was stamped, in English, "One Troy Pound."

"Oh, my God," Steve said softly. There were twenty-eight bars in the saddlebags. He laughed, then cried out at the pain it caused in his side. He couldn't help chuckling, though. Belevairn himself had just financed Steve's quest.

Now, Steve had to find out where that quest would take him. He began to look through the navigational charts. They were of little help. There were charts for the entire world—Belevairn had no way of knowing where he would emerge.

Finally, he found something of interest. One chart had a location clearly marked, with a latitude and longitude written beside it. The coordinates matched the marked location—Belevairn must refer to this area often. Steve sat back.

"Nicaragua," he whispered.

Belevairn waited outside the gilded doors to the throne room. He displayed an air of calm to the guard who stood beside those doors, despite the agitation he truly felt. Daryna would *not* be pleased by this unexpected development.

The guard who had gone to inform the Mistress of his presence returned, holding the door for him.

"The Mistress will see you, Dread Lord," he announced.

Without a word, Belevairn walked into the throne room. Green eyes stared down at him from the shadows enveloping the throne.

"Greetings, Belevairn," the Mistress's silken voice said. "I did not expect you back so soon. It has scarce been three days since you departed."

"I bear grave news, Mistress," Belevairn replied, kneeling on the marble steps to the throne.

"Proceed."

"The Dreamer lives, Mistress."

"*Wilkinson?*" she asked incredulously. "Alive? Impossible."

"I could hardly believe it myself, Mistress," Belevairn said. "He ambushed me when I arrived on Earth. Had I not escaped, he would have destroyed me."

Daryna rose to her feet—Belevairn could *feel* her anger. He cringed, abasing himself more fully on the marble steps.

"And you let him escape?" she whispered angrily. "Have you gone mad? You *know* the prophecies!"

"I-I had no choice, Mistress!" Belevairn pleaded. "If I had remained to battle him, I would have been discovered by the American authorities. I *could* have destroyed him, had he not raised a ward to protect himself."

"A ward?"

"Yes, Mistress. I do not know how he did this. I am certain he was not trained in sorcery during his stay in this world."

"The Ritual of Transfer," Daryna mused aloud.

"Mistress?"

"The Ritual of Transfer, Belevairn," she replied. "By its very nature, none have survived it ere now. Even as you stole his memories, he was given yours."

"Then . . ."

"Aye. Master Wilkinson is not only a *kaiva*, but a Master. Your equal, in fact."

"Yes, Mistress." Wilkinson his equal? Preposterous!

"Hear me, Belevairn. The Dreamer *must* die. His death is of greater import than any other aspect of your mission." She paused. "When next you return, it had best be with his head."

"Y-yes, Mistress."

"You may go." She dismissed him with an idle wave of her hand.

"M-Mistress? There is more . . ." The green eyes narrowed, transfixing him.

"More, Belevairn?" she asked coolly.

"Y-yes, Mistress."

"Continue."

"During my escape, Wilkinson . . . stole my saddlebags."

"The gold?"

"Yes, Mistress." Belevairn replied. He heard her sigh wearily.

"No matter," she finally said. "Gold is an insignificant

price to pay for my final victory. Take what you need from the treasury."

"Yes, Mistress." Belevairn rose and, after bowing once again, turned to leave.

Daryna rested her chin on her palm as she watched Belevairn leave. So—Steven yet lived and, even now, sought to thwart her. A pity that she must delegate his death to Belevairn. It would have been so much more satisfying to destroy him herself. . . .

When Steve woke again the next morning, the pain in his head had all but vanished. However, it had been replaced by a hollowness in his stomach that would not be denied. He wasn't surprised. After going through Belevairn's saddle-bags, he had gone back to bed without eating. He doubted that anything would have stayed down yesterday, anyway.

He needed to head on—get out of Cincinnati. First, though, he would have to unload some of that gold so he could pay his motel bill and get some operating capital.

"He's packing up," Robert announced. Alexander glanced out the window. Sure enough, Wilkinson was loading up the truck.

"Go check us out," Alexander said.

"Right." Robert left the room and strolled casually over to the office. They could check out before Wilkinson and be ready to move when he left.

To Alexander's dismay, Wilkinson did not go check out. Instead, he simply climbed into his pickup and drove off. The son of a bitch was jumping his bill!

"Shit!" Alexander ran out and jumped into their latest rental car, a beige Chevrolet sedan. He couldn't wait for Robert.

Fortunately, Wilkinson stopped a few streets away at a pancake house. Alexander kept on driving and circled back to the motel where Robert was waiting for him. The photographer quickly climbed in on the passenger side.

"Did you lose him?" Robert asked.

"No, he went to eat," Alexander replied. "Scared the shit out of me."

"I'll bet. Let's go."

From the restaurant, Wilkinson drove into downtown Cincinnati, stopping at several gas stations. Finally, he stopped at the Cincinnati Gold & Silver Exchange and went inside.

"What do you suppose he's doing in there?" Robert asked.

"Probably hocking some jewelry, or something," Alexander replied.

After about half an hour Wilkinson came back out and headed off. They followed him to another gold exchange where he spent another twenty minutes.

"He must have a lot of jewelry," Robert observed when Wilkinson stopped at the third exchange.

"Follow him in," Alexander replied. "Get a price on this." Alexander handed him the gold ring he wore on his right hand.

"*Don't* sell it," he admonished. "Just get a price on it and see what Wilkinson is up to."

"Right."

Alexander waited as Robert followed Wilkinson into the gold exchange. What in the hell was the kid up to? Soon, Robert came back out and climbed back into the sedan.

"Well?" Alexander asked. "What did you see?"

"He's selling gold bars," Robert replied. "Big fucking gold bars."

"How big?"

"One pound. I could read the stamp as I walked past the table he was at."

Alexander whistled. Wilkinson should have about ten thousand dollars, or more, if he had unloaded three of those things. Where had he gotten them?

"There he goes," Robert interrupted.

Alexander pulled out behind the blue pickup as Wilkinson left the exchange. After stopping back at the motel to check out, Wilkinson left town headed south on 75.

"Here we go again," Robert quipped. This time, though, it sounded excited instead of bored. Alexander smiled.

"Yep," he replied. "Here we go again."

A little under three hours driving from Cincinnati brought Steve to Louisville, Kentucky. It was still well before noon, but Steve had a lot to do now that he was out of Ohio. Besides, he was still worn down from the night he had found Belevairn.

He checked into a Holiday Inn. It would be nice to stay on the decent side of town for a change. He couldn't rest yet, though. It was time to go shopping. He'd had an idea that just might work against the *goremka*.

"Sporting goods," Alexander noted. "He's replacing his shotgun." Alexander was still wondering why Wilkinson had stopped at a Catholic church before coming here. What was he up to now?

"Looks like he's replacing more than his shotgun," Robert said, interrupting Alexander's musings.

Wilkinson emerged from the sporting goods store with the anticipated shotgun and three other large boxes as well as a few paper sacks.

"Christmas came early this year," Alexander noted as Wilkinson loaded the stuff into his truck.

"What do you suppose he's got?" Robert wondered.

"I don't know," Alexander replied. "But, if the other night was any indication, he *ought* to buy a tank."

Hauling all of his purchases up the stairs to the room had aggravated Steve's cracked ribs. He opened a brand-new bottle of aspirin and swallowed a few of them before setting to work.

He cleaned and loaded his new shotgun and cleaned his new .44 revolver. He couldn't load it yet—he hadn't made the bullets.

The bars of silver he had set to melting on the hot plate were starting to sag by the time he finished cleaning the guns. He filled a cup with some of the holy water he'd

gotten from the church and started setting up the reloader.
If silver bullets, quenched in holy water, couldn't hurt the
goremka, then nothing on this planet could.

About an hour later, Steve had managed to manufacture
about a dozen silver bullets. His pace was picking up,
though. He ought to be able to manage another two or
three dozen tonight.

After I eat, that is, he thought when his stomach growled.
At least now he could afford something a little better than
fast food. A steak sounded pretty good. . . .

"He's leaving," Alexander said.

"What?" Robert sounded anguished.

"He'll be back," Alexander assured him. "He left all his
junk in the room. You tail him while I go and take a look
around his room."

"Be careful."

"Always am. You stick with him."

"I'll do my best."

Alexander walked over to the kid's room. There was no
one about, so he took the picks out of his pocket. In a few
seconds he had the door open and was inside.

Christmas *had* come early for Wilkinson. In addition to
the shotgun, he had bought himself a brand new .44 Colt
revolver and a reloader. A melting pan, with a few bars of
metal in it, sat on a hot plate—a definite violation of hotel
rules. Why was Wilkinson making his own bullets?

An examination of one of the bars lying next to the
melting pan answered that question. It was pure silver—
the kid was making silver bullets. Alexander snapped a
few pictures with his little 35mm camera. Robert would
have done a better job, but this would suffice.

A quart jug of water sat on the table by the bullet molds.
This must have been what he saw Wilkinson carrying out of
that church he spent two hours in this morning. Alexander
chuckled. Silver bullets quenched in holy water. The kid
was resourceful, all right.

A brief search turned up a pair of saddlebags. These
must have come from the battle at the mound. Interesting—

somehow, Alexander doubted that some type of demon or monster would have saddlebags on its mount.

Especially saddlebags full of gold. Twenty-four bars of gold—all marked as one troy pound. So that was where Wilkinson had gotten the gold bars he sold this morning. He had gotten them from his enemy's saddlebags.

There were maps too. Navigational charts from all over the world. One place was clearly marked, though, with a latitude and longitude marked in pen beside it. Some place in Nicaragua.

Even if ghost horsemen carried saddlebags, Alexander doubted that they would carry modern navigational maps in them. Or radios and flashlights, for that matter. It was about time to ask Wilkinson some questions, face to face.

The next night, Steve was sitting in a cafe in Memphis, sipping a cup of coffee. Unloading these gold bars was slowing him down. He had dropped off four more before leaving Louisville and another four in Nashville before coming on into Memphis.

He had just unloaded another four bars here and was going to leave for Little Rock as soon as he finished his meal. He would spend the night in Little Rock, then unload another four bars of gold there. As long as the IRS didn't get on his tail, he'd be fine.

Almost on cue, someone stepped up to his table, attaché in hand. Steve glanced up—the man was of medium height and build with brown hair and eyes. He was clean shaven and was wearing a brown sport jacket with darker brown trousers.

"Do you mind if I join you, Mister Wilkinson?" the person asked. Steve tensed. Who the hell would recognize him in Memphis?

"Who are you?" Steve asked, sitting up. The guy didn't look like a government employee, but Steve wasn't certain. The answer proved to be even worse.

"I'm Richard Alexander with the *Clarion*, Mister Wilkinson," he replied. "I'd like to ask you a few questions, if I may."

Steve blinked. This was the reporter who had covered the story of Belevairn's appearance at Mesa Verde. How the hell had he gotten onto Steve? Alexander sat without waiting for permission.

"What could you possibly want to ask me?" Steve said, attempting to feign ignorance. What had he done to deserve *this*?

Alexander smiled humorlessly. He opened his attaché case in such a way that Steve could easily see the contents.

"Look, Steve—may I call you Steve? Good. Let's cut the bullshit. You're not good at it, and I've interviewed the best." Alexander removed a large manila envelope from his attaché.

"I beg your pardon," Steve replied coldly, "but I don't think there's anything you need to know from me. Good night." Steve started to get up from his chair. He had to lose this guy—fast.

"What about this?" Alexander asked, laying an eight-by-ten glossy photograph on the table.

Steve glanced down at the photograph. It was a close-up of himself, lying on his back while the *goremka* tried to rip his throat out. Steve sat down, staring at the photograph. How long had this guy been following him?

"Well?" Alexander asked. "What do you have to say to that?"

Kill him, Belevairn urged inside his mind. *He knows too much!*

"At least I didn't look as scared as I felt," Steve muttered, ignoring the sorcerer. Damn. This guy had him cold.

Alexander chuckled.

"I can imagine. If something that looked like a cross between Black Beauty and *Jaws* tried to have me for lunch, I'd need a new suit."

"I still don't think I'm going to tell you anything," Steve replied. "All you have are a few pictures, and no one believes the rag you work for anyway."

"I'd reconsider that if I were you, Steve," Alexander said. "I've got a good imagination. I could weave a hell

of a story around these pictures. Of course, I'd make sure
your folks got a complimentary copy."

"You son of a bitch," Steve said, almost under his breath.

"Now, before you start deciding how convenient it would
be for me to disappear, let me tell you that my photographer
is watching this meeting."

"I don't work that way, Mister Alexander," Steve
replied.

I do, Belevairn interjected. *Find his partner and kill them
both, you fool!*

"The people I'm following do, however," Steve continued. "They won't be real happy with anyone I talk to.
Neither will they be overly concerned with the consequences
of their actions."

"Well, that's my lookout, then, isn't it?"

Steve looked back down at the photograph. There had to
be *some* way out of this. For the life of him, though, Steve
couldn't figure out what it was.

Then stall, Belevairn suggested. For once, the sorcerer
had a good idea.

"All right, Mister Alexander. You've got your inter-
view."

What! Have you lost your mind, Wilkinson?

"Great—we'll get a room where we can talk more privately, and . . ."

"No," Steve interrupted.

"No?"

"No," Steve repeated. "I don't have time to sit around
here answering your questions. I'm headed from here to
Little Rock and then on to Dallas. You can ask your questions en route and your photographer friend can follow us.
It's that or nothing."

Excellent, Belevairn said. *We can kill them out on the
highway.*

Shut up!

Alexander thought for a moment. It was obvious that he
wasn't certain whether or not he should trust Steve. The
reporter in him finally won out.

"Okay. Let me inform my partner."

"You do that," Steve replied. He watched as Alexander walked out to a beige Chevy two-door sedan. It was going to be a *long* trip to Little Rock.

Chapter
-------- Ten -------------

"THAT'S SOME STORY," Alexander said. Steve had talked to the reporter for the entire trip from Memphis to Little Rock and then, this morning, from Little Rock on into Dallas. What surprised him was how good it felt to finally tell someone. Especially when it was someone who didn't automatically think he was some sort of nutcase.

He had told the reporter everything—from the dream experiment that had started all of it, to his arrival in the new world, to his own eventual acceptance of it and, finally, of his eventual return to Earth—everything.

"And then you saw my article about this sorcerer?" Alexander asked.

"Yeah," Steve replied. "A friend of mine and I walked into a convenience store and there was Belevairn's picture plastered all over the front cover. I couldn't believe it."

"And so you started trying to track him down?"

"That's right."

"Why?"

Steve glanced over at Alexander, incredulously.

"What do you mean, 'why'?" he asked. "What choice did I have?"

"You could have just sat back and not worried about it. Why throw your whole life away to chase off after this guy?"

Steve shook his head.

"That's not an option. It's my fault that Belevairn is here—my memories that brought him to Earth. I *have* to stop him—it's a matter of honor."

"If you say so. What are your plans now?"

"I'm afraid I can't tell you that."

"Steve, I haven't followed you all the way from Mesa Verde for half a story."

"I'm afraid that's all you get, Mister Alexander. If I tell you what I'm planning and Belevairn reads whatever you print, then I've tipped my hand."

Alexander thought for a moment.

"Look, Steve," he said, "I'm not going to print half a story. What I mean by that is, I'm planning on seeing this through to the end—right up to your final confrontation with this Belevairn person."

Steve looked over at Alexander again. As far as he could tell, the reporter was dead serious.

"You're crazy," he said.

"I've been called that before," Alexander replied, smiling. "Look, Steve—I've covered dozens of these stories and they've always turned out to be crackpots or hoaxes. Not yours, though—you've got the real thing on an epic scale. I'm not letting go of this one."

"That's out of the question," Steve replied, shaking his head. "You'll get in the way and slow me down. I don't need to be looking out for you when I get in a jam."

"Hey, I can take care of myself, kid. I've been doing it for a long time now."

"You don't know what you're dealing with here, Richard. You're not coming along and that's final."

Alexander sighed. Good—maybe Steve had finally gotten it through his thick skull. Then the reporter reached up and shut off his cassette recorder.

"I didn't want to have to tell you this," Alexander said, "but . . . I know where you're going."

"What? How?"

"In Louisville, where you made your silver bullets. I . . . took the liberty of looking around your room. I found those maps you've got."

"That's breaking and entering!"

"Fine," Alexander replied, shrugging. "Call the cops and turn me in." Of course, Alexander knew that Steve couldn't do that.

"You know just how far to push, don't you?" Steve finally said.

"I've been doing this a long time, Steve. Like I said, I know where you're going. You can either have me along and know where I am, or I can just keep following you."

Steve remained silent for a time, gathering his thoughts. It would be better to have Alexander where he could watch him rather than just tailing along.

That way we can kill him and leave him in the jungle, Belevairn added.

"Can you use a pistol?" Steve asked, ignoring Belevairn.

"Uh . . . yeah," Alexander replied nervously. He hadn't carried a gun since Nam. "Steve, I'd really rather not . . ."

"If you're coming along, you're going to carry a pistol. If the *goremka* goes after you, I want you to be able to defend yourself."

"Silver bullets?"

"Right. If you want to come along, that's the condition."

"Whatever you say, *Kemo Sabe.*"

"That's it," Steve said to Alexander as they left the last gold exchange. "Let's go pick up the Jeep and turn in your rental car." They had lost several days here in Dallas outfitting for the trip. Steve was anxious to finally get started.

"Right," Alexander replied. The reporter was starting to chafe at the delays himself. Not to mention that if Robert said how bored he was with all this just one more time . . .

They pulled into the customizing shop where Steve had left his new Jeep Cherokee for the last week. He walked over and inspected the vehicle. The original paint job had been sanded off and replaced with a heavy, flat olive drab. The rear side windows had been replaced with steel, and a jerry can was mounted on the rear.

Steve walked around to the front, where a winch had been mounted and metal cages placed over the headlights. This baby ought not to have any trouble getting through the jungle. Steve didn't bother to look underneath—he had already inspected the hard black rubber pad that had been placed over the gas tank two days ago.

"She's a beauty," Alexander observed. "I still wish we'd gotten the Range Rover, though," he added, smirking.

"I offered to get it if you were willing to shell out the extra thirty thousand," Steve replied,

"Hey, you're the one with all the gold," Alexander retorted.

Steve smiled. He had dumped a considerable amount of his recently acquired capital on this Jeep and the modifications to it. After that and the new pistols for Richard and Robert, along with tents, jungle clothing and other essentials, Steve only had forty thousand out of the hundred thousand he'd gotten for Belevairn's gold. Outfitting a jungle expedition, even for just three people, wasn't cheap.

"Will you two cut it out?" Robert interrupted. "Here comes Billy." Billy Joe was the owner of the customizing shop—a tall, heavyset blond man with a thick moustache and a quick smile. At least, it was quick when someone handed him several thousand dollars' worth of work.

"She's all ready, Mister Wilkinson," he said. "Includin' that one special modification you requested."

"Great," Steve replied. "What's the balance?" Steve had stopped by every day to check on the Jeep's progress and to make payments as Billy Joe got work completed on the Jeep.

"Right here," Billy Joe replied, handing him an invoice. The final bill came to a little over four thousand dollars. Steve handed over the cash.

"It's been a pleasure doing business with you, Mister Wilkinson," Billy Joe said, handing Steve the keys. "Have a nice trip to Mexico."

"Thank you," Steve replied.

"Hey, Billy," one of the mechanics said, sticking his head into Billy Joe's office, "there's some guy in a suit wants to talk to you."

"Be right out," Billy Joe replied. Probably some downtown lawyer or North Dallas type wanting a paint job.

"Howdy," Billy Joe said, walking out and shaking the guy's hand. He revised his estimate in a hurry—cop.

"Special Investigator Andersen," the cop said, displaying his identification. "Drug Enforcement Agency."

"Huh?" Billy Joe replied. What the hell did the DEA want with him?

"I'd like to ask you some questions about the gentleman who just left with the Jeep. . . ."

Steve packed the shotgun, the .30-30 and the three Colt revolvers along with ammunition for all of them into the secret compartment Billy Joe had built into the back of the Jeep. His sword and a lockbox containing the remaining cash also went into the compartment. After the panel and the carpet had been replaced, all of the camping and photography equipment was packed in on top of it. That should escape anything except an exhaustive search of the Jeep or gunpowder-sniffing dogs.

"Next stop, Nicaragua," Alexander said as they climbed into the Jeep.

"Hopefully," Steve replied. "Let's get going."

"You're the driver," Alexander said. "Whenever you're ready. You ready, Robert?"

"No, but I suspect we'll be leaving anyway. I still think it would be easier to fly there."

"What?" Alexander said. "And miss all the scenery?"

Steve started the Jeep and pulled out into traffic, smiling as Robert and Alexander traded jibes.

Belevairn sat back and allowed the image in the pool of quicksilver to vanish. So, Master Wilkinson had acquired two companions and was putting his stolen gold to good use. He was apparently still in America, but that would be changing soon.

The questions now were, who were Wilkinson's companions and how would they be travelling? Probably by ship, if Wilkinson planned to use his new vehicle in Nicaragua. That amount of air freight was simply too expensive for the amount of money he had stolen from Belevairn.

As for his companions, they must be hired guides. If so, then Wilkinson could not have told them the true nature of his mission. That meant they would likely abandon him once the exact nature of the expedition revealed itself.

Carrying out the Mistress's orders should be simple, once Wilkinson arrived in Nicaragua. A single squad of Morvir should be more than enough to guarantee the Dreamer's death, whether or not his companions remained with him.

Manuel Garcia walked into the director's office. The DEA office in Nuevo Laredo was very small—and nonexistent, at least as far as was publicly known. Their operations were run out of a small brokerage trading in American securities. They had very few customers . . .

"Good morning, Manuel," the director said. "Got an assignment for you."

"Yes, sir," Garcia replied.

"We've got a possible new runner," the director elaborated. "Steve Wilkinson."

"What's his history?"

"Very little. To date the only police record on him is a brawl in his college gym. He dropped out right after that. We didn't get on him until he showed up in Ohio selling one-pound gold bars in Cincinnati."

"Sounds more like a job for the IRS," Garcia observed.

"It gets more interesting. There was some type of gun battle at a park outside Cincinnati. We're not certain, but the timing is coincidental. Wilkinson may have been involved."

"That's a little more indicative, but it still . . ."

The director held up a hand. "Let me finish. Wilkinson travelled from there to Dallas, dropping gold bars at exchanges all along the way. In Dallas he bought a Jeep and had it modified for jungle use. He also had a secret compartment built into the back. According to the mechanic who did the modifications, Wilkinson told him he was going to Mexico to explore some Aztec ruins. That fits with the fact that he got a passport from the Dallas passport office."

"Okay," Garcia agreed. "That's starting to sound interesting. But it seems a little too obvious."

The director nodded. "We think the kid's actually a red herring. We're supposed to spend a lot of time worrying about him while something else goes down—at least that's the theory."

"That would be my guess, too."

"I want you to follow Wilkinson," the director continued. "Pay as much attention to what happens *around* him as to what he actually does."

"Right."

"Here's his dossier," the director said, handing Manuel a surprisingly thin folder. "And dossiers on the two men who are travelling with him. A reporter and a photographer."

"What?" Why on Earth would a new runner be travelling with reporters? The dossiers on Wilkinson's two companions were thicker than the kid's file.

"Yes, we don't know how they tie in."

"The reporter was in Viet Nam," Manuel noticed as he flipped through Richard Alexander's file. There was nothing notable in Wilkinson's file.

"That's right," the director said. "And the photographer is an expert in electronic surveillance. He's been sued a couple of times for invasion of privacy. That's the most notable thing about either of them."

"Where do I pick them up?"

"When they cross the border. Wilkinson should arrive late this afternoon, or early tomorrow morning—assuming he comes through here. DEA offices in all of the border towns have been notified. Be careful—all three of them are armed."

"Yes, sir," Garcia replied, rising to leave. This assignment sounded like it had potential.

Crossing the Mexican border into Nuevo Laredo had almost been anticlimactic. They had simply been required to stop and talk to the border guards for about twenty minutes. The stop might have been shorter if they hadn't been using Alexander's press affiliation as a cover.

Actually, it probably would have been longer, come to

think of it. If Steve had come through the border with this type of equipment and no credentials at all, the federales might have had a lot *more* questions for him. As it was, they hadn't even searched the Jeep, beyond a cursory inspection.

It was beginning to seem as though running afoul of Alexander had actually been a blessing in disguise. Besides, Steve was beginning to enjoy the company of his new associates. They made the long trips pass more quickly.

"Where to now?" Alexander asked.

"Monterrey," Steve replied. "Then over to Saltillo and down to Mexico City."

"Seems a little out of the way," Robert noted.

"I want to stay on the major roads," Steve explained. "This baby is still being broken in, and I don't want to push her until we have to."

"Makes sense to me," Alexander agreed, as they left Nuevo Laredo behind.

Steve glanced at his watch anxiously. This was not going as quickly as he had hoped.

"Are you going to check your watch every five minutes all the way there?" Alexander asked.

"I had planned on being in Monterrey an hour ago," Steve complained. "If this keeps up, we won't be able to make it to Mexico City tonight."

"Mexico City!" Alexander said. "How fast are you planning on driving, kid?"

"I was only figuring on sixty," Steve began. Alexander laughed, interrupting him.

"This is Mexico, Steve," he explained. "Figure an average of forty-five, and you'll be doing good to make that."

"But . . ."

"Oh, there will be stretches where you can hit sixty for a little while, I'm sure," Alexander continued. "Just don't plan on it—they won't last for very long."

"Oh," Steve replied. That was going to throw his timetable behind.

"I hate to interrupt your lesson on international driving,

Dick," Robert said, "but I think we have a tail."

"What!" Steve said, letting his foot off the gas as he looked in the mirror.

"Keep driving!" Alexander commanded. "Don't let him know we've spotted him, kid!"

Steve obeyed, resuming his previous speed and looking away from the mirror. Who would be following them? Of course, that's what he'd thought before Alexander had turned up . . .

"Are you sure?" Alexander asked without turning around.

"Fairly sure," Robert replied. "Dark green Chrysler four-door. It's been with us since Nuevo Laredo."

"If it's a Chrysler, then it's American," Steve noted.

"Not necessarily," Alexander replied. "After all, they build them down here now. Have you been able to make the plates?"

"Yeah," Robert said. "They're Mexican."

"What do we do?" Steve asked.

"As long as he's just following us, we ignore him," Alexander replied. "We'll see if he's still with us in Saltillo."

It was pushing ten o'clock when Wilkinson made it to San Luis Potosi. Garcia followed them to a small inn and watched long enough to make certain they were checking in.

Garcia didn't know whether or not Wilkinson was a runner, but he certainly wasn't a tourist. He had just driven five hundred miles into Mexico without making a single stop until tonight. Once they started unpacking the Jeep, Garcia left. He would report in to the embassy and then return to resume surveillance.

Belevairn passed his hand over the bowl of mercury—he had seen enough. Wilkinson was driving to Nicaragua. Unfortunately, Mexico was outside his sphere of operations. Once Wilkinson entered Guatemala, however, Belevairn could probably take action. It would certainly be easy to arrange something once Wilkinson entered either Honduras or El Salvador.

*   *   *

We are being watched, Belevairn said inside Steve's mind. Steve rolled over and grumbled. He was going to have to set down some rules with Belevairn on nocturnal conversations.

This is important, Belevairn insisted.

I know we're being watched, Steve told him. *Robert spotted the tail this morning.*

I am not referring to the person who is following us, Belevairn replied. *That is of little concern. My counterpart is watching us.*

"What?" Steve said aloud, sitting up. In the next bed, Alexander snorted and rolled over. All sense of Steve's fatigue had vanished. Belevairn was watching them?

Please avoid waking your companions, the sorcerer said.

Sorry, Steve replied. *How do you know Belevairn is watching us?*

I felt the Power he used to call our image. In this Power-hungry world even the simplest working causes a notice-able drain. I woke you as soon as it passed.

So he's not watching us now? Steve surmised.

I do not believe so.

Steve lay back on the bed. That was great—if Belevairn had enough Power to use the Rite of Far Visions on a regular basis, they didn't have a chance of reaching him. It also reduced the odds that whoever was following them was working for the sorcerer, however.

Is there some way of blocking this? Steve asked.

Technically, yes—practically, no, Belevairn replied.

Explain.

With sufficient Power at my disposal, I could fashion an amulet that would temporarily protect us from my counter-part's attention. There is no practical way to raise such Power in this world.

Temporarily? Steve asked.

A week at best before the amulet was consumed by the Power, Belevairn explained. *It would last about a month back in my homeworld, but here the gold would be con-sumed more quickly.*

So we have no way of preventing this, Steve concluded.

I will endeavor to keep you apprised of any time that I believe we are being watched, Belevairn assured him. *For now, that is all I can do.*

Why are you being so cooperative? Steve asked.

As I said before, Belevairn replied, *I have my reasons.*

That's what I'm afraid of, Steve thought. There was no reply.

Chapter
-------- Eleven ------------

"WERE YOU ABLE to penetrate the camp?" Don Estefan asked.

" 'Fraid not, Don Estefan," Sergeant Williams replied. The mercenary leaned back in his chair and propped his feet up on Estefan's desk.

"Their perimeter is too . . . well defended," he continued. "Unless you want to hire enough men for an outright attack, we're not going to able to get inside to find your granddaughter."

"Could you possibly bribe your way in?"

Williams laughed. Juan began to step forward from his position beside the Don's desk, but Estefan ordered him back with a slight nod of the head.

"Maybe," Williams replied, once his laughter had stopped. "Sorry 'bout that, Don, but it occurred to me that we'd prob'ly need a truckload of bananas for the bribe."

"Bananas?"

"Yes sir," Williams replied, taking his feet from the desk and sitting up. "Don Estefan, my boys an' I got something out in the truck you *need* to see."

"Very well . . ." Estefan said. "Juan?"

They followed Williams outside to where his men were waiting and around to the back of Williams's canvas-backed truck.

"Open 'er up, boys," he said. Two of Williams's men zipped open the canvas flap sealing the back of the truck and flipped the two halves aside.

"*Madre de Dios!*" Juan said, stepping back and crossing himself. Estefan took an involuntary step backwards as well.

The creature that shrieked and leapt at them, before the chain attached to the collar around its neck stopped it, resembled a baboon. It was over four feet tall, however— almost five feet. Estefan had never seen such a creature.

"These . . . things guard the Morvir camp?" he asked.

"That's right, Don Estefan," Williams replied. "We ran into a couple dozen of them. There must be at least a hundred of them around the perimeter."

"And you cannot get past *monkeys?*" Juan asked derisively.

"These damned things ain't monkeys, bud!" Williams replied. "Watch this." The mercenary stepped beside the truck, out of the ape's sight. He drew the pistol from his holster and removed the clip, then worked the chamber before placing an empty clip back in the pistol.

"Unloaded," he said, showing the pistol to Juan and Estefan. Then he tossed the pistol into the back of the truck.

The ape immediately stopped shrieking and looked down at the pistol. Estefan thought that it looked surprised. Then, with what could only be described as a gleeful screech, the monster pounced on the pistol. It brought the weapon up, aimed at Williams and pulled the trigger.

When the weapon did not fire, the creature fell silent. A somewhat puzzled expression crossed its face, and it tried to fire a few more times. Apparently it was not smart enough to work the chamber. Then, with a screech of anger, it threw the pistol at Williams.

"No, asshole," Williams said, turning to Juan, "we *can't* get past these monkeys. At least not without makin' enough noise to wake the whole damned Morvir camp. And I do *not* feel like takin' on over a thousand men with just me and my boys."

"What are we dealing with here?" Estefan asked. "Who *are* these Morvir?"

"Well, Don," Williams replied, "I've seen their leader. After that and now runnin' into these things, I'm beginnin' ta think they're from Hell."

"What do you suggest?" Estefan asked.

"Simple," Williams replied. "We can't sneak into camp, so I drive into the camp."

"I beg your pardon, *señor?*"

"Don Estefan, you ain't gonna bust your granddaughter outta there," Williams explained. "But you probably could ransom her outta there. Let me go in, alone and unarmed, with ten thousand American dollars to get their attention."

"*No posible!*" Estefan shouted. "These *monstruos* must pay for what they have done to my family!"

"Don Estefan," Williams said, "you can take your revenge *after* you get the girl outta there. That ransom ain't gonna do them any good if you kill them all a week or two later. But if your revenge is more important, then I'll see about roundin' up the men to do the job . . ."

"No," Estefan said, calming. "No, you are right, *señor.* Maria is more important—my revenge can wait. Juan will . . . give you the money you have requested."

"Thank you, Don Estefan."

"And I want to keep this . . . monkey. Transfer it to one of the cells in the basement."

"You pig!" Maria shouted. Garth dodged the boot she hurled at him. He stepped in, blocked her attempt to claw out his eyes, and backhanded her. The force of the blow spun her half around before she fell onto the bed.

"I ask very little of you, Maria," Garth said, looking down at her. "I know that you are still grieving your family. Other officers would not be as . . . understanding as I have been. I *do* demand that you refrain from attacking me or insulting me. I also demand that you wear my collar when you leave my quarters, but only so that the men will not think that you are available and make use of you. You would not like that."

"I am not your slave!" she screamed. "I want to go home!"

"You have no home," Garth reminded her. "It was burned to the ground. Your life is here, now—with me."

"Bastard!"

Garth backhanded her again. She squealed and cringed away from him.

"I have to go on a mission," he told her sternly. "While I am gone you *will* wear the collar whenever you leave here. Otherwise you will be raped—is that clear?"

Maria nodded, fear in her eyes. Garth did not like that.

"Maria," he said softly. "I do not wish to hurt or frighten you." Garth knelt by the bed and stroked her hair.

"I cannot allow you to continue to defy me like this, however. You are safe with me—but if you continue to be difficult I will release you, and you will be given to someone not nearly as patient with you as I have been. Or to the *kaivir*."

Garth picked the boot up from the floor and stood, handing it to her.

"I have to go. Clean up this mess. We will talk more when I return."

Garth turned and walked from his quarters. As an officer, he enjoyed certain privileges. Private quarters was one of them—Maria was another. Korva had given Garth his pick of the females after the raid on Don Raphael's village for his success in capturing so many of the villagers alive.

Garth had chosen the young woman with the long, dark hair and the soulful eyes. He could not explain his feelings about this woman. Any other prize he would have simply taken, but he did not want that. He wanted Maria to give herself to him at least willingly, if not eagerly.

Garth hoped that she got out into the camp, with the collar. It might do her good to see how the other women were treated. Then she would realize how patient he was being with her . . .

"We've hired out your entire platoon for this mission, Lieutenant," Korva told Garth. "You are to help destroy an American installation in Somalia."

"Then what do we do *after* breakfast?" Sergeant Dalin asked. The other sergeants chuckled.

"Sergeant Dalin!" Garth ordered. "Unless you have something serious to add to this briefing, hold your tongue."

"Yes, sir!" Dalin replied.

"This is no joking matter," Korva continued. "You will be facing primarily American troops. Until now you have been facing obsolete hardware in the hands of undisciplined peasants. On this mission you will be facing the best technology this world has to offer—in the hands of *disciplined* peasants. You will be outnumbered by over seven to one, and they have an entrenched position."

"This does not sound reassuring," Garth observed.

"You will not be acting entirely alone," Korva continued. "Your platoon will be reinforcing a unit of five hundred Somalian rebels. Also, two of our tank crews will be there operating tanks furnished by our employers."

"What exactly will we be facing?"

"A reinforced infantry company," Korva replied. "One platoon of M-1 tanks, a couple of noncombat support helicopters."

"They have five top-of-the-line tanks and we have two obsolete pieces of shit?" Garth asked.

"Precisely. Your platoon will have to make certain those M-1's *never* get rolling. If they do, it's all over."

"So, top priority is to neutralize the tank platoon."

"Wrong," Korva said. "Top priority is to knock out their communications. Otherwise, you are going to have American helicopter support to deal with, and those tanks will be the least of your worries. Neutralizing the tank platoon is the *other* top priority."

"How many other top priorities do I have to deal with?"

"Just one," Korva replied. "Destroy those helicopters, or someone will get one of them in the air and call for air support. After that, it will be up to the Somalians and the tanks to take out the base."

"Are there any other objectives?" Garth asked.

"That's it," Korva replied. "This is a tough mission. Once you're in the field, it's your decision when, if necessary, to abort the mission. If it gets out of hand, get your platoon out of there."

"Yes, sir."

"Lieutenant Garth?"

"Yes, Captain?"

"The Morvir have *never* aborted a mission. I would be highly disappointed if your platoon set such a precedent."

"Understood, sir."

Mike Williams climbed onto the motorcycle. He didn't want to take the truck in—the Morvir would probably confiscate it. The bastards wouldn't have any use for a bike, though. They'd let him ride it back out—assuming they let him live. He kicked the ignition, waved to his boys and took off down the dirt trail that would eventually lead him to the enemy camp.

Damned Morvir bastards. He hoped the Don decided to go on with the attack after he got his granddaughter out. The other mercs that Williams knew were willing to cut their normal rates in half to get a shot at these bastards. Not Williams—he was workin' for free. Plus expenses, of course.

No, that wasn't right. He was workin' for Jack. After what those bastards did to his brother a few months back, Williams wouldn't be able to sleep until he'd seen the whole bunch of them sent *back* to Hell.

Mike leaned into a turn, sending a spray of dirt into the jungle. He couldn't afford to let any of that show now. He would have to smile and be as pleasant to these scumbags as if he'd gone to school with all of them. Later, he could correct the impression he was going to give them today.

After about half an hour's ride he approached the perimeter of the Morvir camp. Hopefully he was right and the monkey-men wouldn't attack someone approaching openly on the road. Damned things had wounded two of Williams's men before they'd been able to get out. Took to the trees just like the monkeys they resembled, but a hell of a lot quieter.

Apparently he was right. The apes were nowhere to be seen, and he could see the camp ahead. He slowed the bike and approached at near idle.

"*Alto!*" an unseen sentry shouted. Williams spun to a stop as ordered.

"Howdy," he called into the jungle. "I know y'all speak English. I need ta see your commander."

Korva looked up when his aide came into the room.

"What is it, Orlas?"

"Someone is here to see you, sir," Orlas replied. "A mercenary with ten thousand dollars."

"Ten thousand dollars? Does he want to hire us?"

"No, sir. He says the money is just to get our attention."

"Well, if someone wants to pay ten thousand dollars just to see me, I suppose we can oblige him—before we kill him. Has he been searched?"

"Thoroughly, sir. He won't give up the money except to you."

"Very well. Send him in."

The man who walked in was obviously American and obviously a mercenary. He was also an undisciplined slob. He had not shaved for at least a few days, or washed either. He walked up and held his hand out over Korva's desk.

"Williams," he said as Korva stood and took his hand. "Mike Williams."

"Captain Korva," Korva replied. "What can I do for you, Mister Williams?"

"Well, you can start by taking me to the commander."

"I *am* the commander here."

"Uh, no, I don't think so," Williams insisted. "I've seen him before. Thin guy, gold mask, black cape."

"Lord . . . Don Espantoso is not here," Korva replied. "I am the commander of the forces here."

"I need to speak to someone with the authority to ransom one of your captives."

Korva raised an eyebrow. How would anyone know whether or not a particular person was being held here?

"Indeed?" he said. "I have that authority, Mister Williams. Who are you working for?"

"A Colombian gentleman named Don Estefan," Williams replied. "I guess I can give this to you, then. The girl's picture is in the bag with the money."

Korva accepted the bag from his guest, opening it and

taking out the picture that lay on top of the money. He set the bag of money on the floor beside him as he inspected the picture. Korva frowned. This was going to be a problem . . .

"She is not here, Mister Williams," Korva lied.

"Bullshit. I know you took her, and a couple dozen other women, captive from your last raid in Colombia. My boss is willing to pay a considerable sum for her safe return."

"If he sent ten thousand American dollars as an appetizer, I don't doubt that," Korva agreed. "And I did not say that we did not take her—just that she is not here."

"That could be a problem," Williams noted.

"It may be . . . possible for me to arrange her return. If so, what is your employer prepared to offer?"

"One hundred thousand American dollars," Williams replied.

"That is not worth the effort. We would have to pay that much just to get her back—not to mention replacing her. Our price is one million dollars, American."

"I don't think my boss will agree to that," Williams said.

"Then get him to make a counteroffer. This is all assuming that I *can* get her back, of course."

"Of course. When will you know?"

"Come back in a week with your counteroffer. We will have an answer for you then." A week's delay would give Korva the time he needed to speak with both Lord Belevairn *and* Lieutenant Garth.

"Great. See you then."

"I shall be looking forward to it, Mister Williams," Korva lied.

Orlas stepped in as Williams left. "Kill him?" he asked.

"No, let him leave," Korva replied. Orlas left, closing the door. Korva leaned back in his chair.

This *was* a problem. His orders had been that no one was to survive that attack. If he ransomed the girl, the Valdez family would know that those orders had been violated. If he did *not* ransom the girl, this Don Estefan would almost certainly attempt to rescue her. Furthermore, the woman in question had been given to Lieutenant Garth as a reward for his success on that raid. Korva would be damned before he took one of his officer's prizes for the sake of some Colombian poison merchant.

Still, if Estefan was willing to pay even half of what Korva had demanded, it might be worth talking to Garth to see if he would voluntarily give her up. After all, it was only a woman . . .

"*Señor* Williams is on the phone, my Don," Juan said.

"Thank you, Juan." Estefan lifted the receiver from the phone on his desk.

"Do they have her?" he asked.

"Oh, they got her, all right," Williams replied. "Tried to tell me some bullshit story about her not bein' there but they could get her back. She's there, all right."

"Will they ransom her?"

"They want a million, Don Estefan."

Estefan was silent for a moment. A million U.S. dollars would put a sizeable squeeze on his operating capital.

"Do you think I should accept, Williams?"

"No, they're expecting a counteroffer. You could prob'ly get her for two-fifty."

"Then offer that to them. If they will not accept, you can negotiate up to five hundred."

"You got it," Williams replied. "They want me back there in a week."

"A week! *Maldición!* Why so long?"

"Beats me, but they're callin' the shots for now."

"*Sí,*" Estefan agreed. "Now that you have seen the camp, what would you need to take it?"

"Don, that place is crawlin' with the Morvir—at least a thousand of 'em. And they got some kind of fuckin' pyramid in the center of it. God only knows what they got in there. I'd want five hundred *damned* good men *with* armor and maybe some air support before I hit that place."

"Can you arrange such an operation?" Estefan asked. He waited while Williams considered his answer.

"No, Don—but I can put you in touch with the people who can."

"Do so, Mister Williams. After we get Maria out of there, I want to squash these Morvir filth."

"You got it, boss."

Estefan hung up the telephone and turned to look out the window. This Don Espantoso would regret the day he had attacked the Estefan family.

Chapter
-------- Twelve -------------

IT TOOK THEM almost two hours just to make it through Mexico City. Steve remembered hearing somewhere that Mexico City was the largest city in the world. From the pollution, he believed it. He had almost smelled the city before he had seen it.

The traffic had been an absolute nightmare, as well. They were almost an hour past the city, and it still hadn't completely let up. There was no way they were going to make Oaxaca by tonight.

"Is Pancho Villa still back there?" Alexander asked.

"Uh . . . yeah," Robert replied. "He's a ways back, though."

So what? Steve thought. He hadn't told his two companions that Belevairn was watching them. After all, how would he explain knowing? Of course, government intervention could be a real problem to them—especially outside the United States. Steve had no desire to see the inside of a Mexican prison firsthand.

Even so, Belevairn was still a more pressing concern. Steve had to find some way to prevent the sorcerer from knowing his every move. The immediate concern, though, was where they were going to stop for the night. It would be past midnight before they made it to Oaxaca.

"Okay, navigator," Steve said, "we need to find a place to stop for tonight. We're not going to make it to Oaxaca."

"Obviously not," Alexander agreed, digging out the map. He spent a couple of minutes examining it.

"We ought to be able to make Huajuapan de León by

109

nine o'clock," he said. "Population fourteen thousand. They ought to have a place to stay."

"Sounds good," Steve said.

"Hey!" Alexander exclaimed. "There's Juxtlahuaca."

"Is that a better place to stop?" Steve asked.

"Hardly," Alexander laughed. "Tiny place—they don't even give the population here. I just know someone from the *Clarion* who did a story on a church near there."

"What kind of story?"

"The usual," Alexander replied. "One of those places where people are always seeing the Virgin Mary and such. There've supposedly been a few miraculous healings there and so forth."

"Any legitimacy to it?" Steve asked.

"Why—*all* of the *Clarion*'s stories are legitimate," Alexander replied innocently.

Steve snorted. He only knew of one story the *Clarion* had done that was legitimate, and he was smack dab in the middle of that one.

"I repeat—any legitimacy to it?"

"Hard to say, really," Alexander replied. "Chuck didn't see anything himself, but everyone there swears to have seen something or know someone who has. Why?"

"How far is it?"

"You're not seriously thinking about stopping there, are you?"

"That depends on how far out of the way it is," Steve replied. If nothing else, he doubted that Belevairn would be able to spy on them if they sought sanctuary there for the night.

"Looks like it's about an hour off the main road from Huajuapan de León," Alexander said. "That would have us arriving around ten o'clock."

"Let's see if we can't cut our travel time a little," Steve replied, pulling out to pass.

It was nine-thirty by the time they found Saint Michael's. It was surprisingly small—Steve had expected a large cathedral instead of the small, adobe building that was the church. Several other buildings sat behind it, forming a small compound.

This is ridiculous, Belevairn said. *There is no Power here. We should continue on.*

It won't hurt to check it out, Steve replied. *Now be quiet.* Belevairn had become more and more agitated the closer they had gotten to the church.

People still packed the yard of the compound. Many had settled down in a makeshift village of homemade tents; some just slept under the stars. Several others were gathered around a small shrine set off in a field north of the complex.

"That's the site of the original appearance," Alexander said, indicating the shrine.

"Good," Steve replied. "I'll be right back."

"Whatever you say," Alexander replied. "Do you mind if Robert takes some pictures?"

"No," Steve replied, walking off. He worked his way through the small throng around the shrine. He crossed himself as he knelt before it and bowed his head.

Well, is there Power here? Steve asked. Curiously, there was no response.

Belevairn?

The force of the unexpected assault was overwhelming. Steve collapsed to the ground as Belevairn's presence flooded his mind. The sorcerer was trying to seize control!

Steve's arms and legs jerked in response to conflicting orders. Belevairn would try to make the body stand and run while Steve struggled desperately just to keep control. Through it all, Steve noted that Belevairn was in a state of near panic. For some reason, the sorcerer was terrified of this place.

Steve didn't notice that the other petitioners had cleared away from around him. His concentration was completely focused on his battle with Belevairn. A battle he was rapidly losing.

Steve's feet suddenly found purchase beneath him, and his body stood. Any second now Belevairn would have complete control. The sorcerer was like a cornered animal, trying desperately to escape.

"Mortos, help me!" Steve cried. He did not notice that he had spoken in Nymran.

As quickly as it had arrived, Belevairn's presence departed. Steve collapsed to his knees, shaking, as complete control of the body was once again placed in his hands.

"Ask and it shall be given," a voice said above him. It spoke in Nymran.

Steve looked up. In the air above the shrine, mounted on a gaunt, pale horse, was . . . an angel. This was not the standard depiction of the half-clad, chubby female with wings. This man was armed for battle, wearing heavy armor fashioned of some glowing white metal with large, powerful wings spread behind him.

Steve swallowed nervously. He had seen the gaunt features of this being before—on a statue in the chapel at Quarin.

"M-Mortos?" he asked, hesitantly. The angel shook its head slowly.

"You have known me as Mortos," the angel replied. "Here, in this world, I am known as the Angel of Death—Apollyon."

"Huh?"

"Did you not know that God was the same there as here?" Apollyon asked. "There is but one God, Dreamer. He wears many faces in many different lands and he has many lesser servants such as myself, but he is still one God."

"Forgive me," Steve said. "I never thought about it."

"No, you have not," Apollyon agreed. "You do not consider such matters to the extent that you should, Dreamer. This is why you have turned from God and started down the path of Darkness."

"What?" Steve said. "That's not true! I have thrown aside everything that matters to me to pursue Belevairn!"

"Do you accuse me of lying?"

"N-no," Steve said. "Forgive me. What . . . how have I . . . done this?"

"You have practiced foul sorcery, Dreamer!" Apollyon accused. "You have dealt with the Powers of Darkness and made blood sacrifice to them. If you continue to commit these blasphemies, not only your quest, but your immortal soul will be imperiled by them."

"Oh, my God," Steve whispered. He hadn't considered how allowing Belevairn to practice his arts would affect him. He had thought of Belevairn as a separate person—not as himself.

"How . . . how can I atone for these acts?" he asked. The angel pointed back toward the church. "The answer to that question lies within God's Church, Dreamer," Apollyon answered. "The answers to all of your questions and needs lie within. Seek them out."

"But, Lord Mortos . . ." Steve began.

"Here I am neither Lord nor Mortos."

"Apollyon," Steve corrected, "Belevairn has the means to watch me and to use the Power against me. How can I fight that?"

"The way the knights of Christendom have always fought such things," Apollyon explained. "With your faith—if you can find it."

"What of the memories of Belevairn that threaten to control me?" Steve asked.

"I have already given you the answer to that, if you will see it," Apollyon replied. "Seek and you shall find, Dreamer. May the Almighty have mercy on your soul."

With no flashy exit, Apollyon was gone. One moment he was sitting there astride his mount and the next he was simply no longer there. Steve sat back on his heels and exhaled sharply, allowing his head to fall. A divine chewing-out was not exactly what he had been looking for when he sought this place out.

It was what he had gotten, however. Now it was up to Steve to put Mortos's words into effect. His legs trembled as he rose to his feet—the battle with Belevairn had drained him.

Turning back toward the chapel, Steve found that every pilgrim in the tent city had gathered behind him. Dozens of faces looked back at him with unconcealed awe, some even with adoration, in their eyes.

They wouldn't be so happy if they knew what he'd said, Steve thought. The entire conversation had transpired in Nymran—a language no one here spoke.

He took a step toward the church, and the spell was broken. The people surged toward him, babbling at him in Spanish, touching him. Mothers shoved babies at him while making incomprehensible pleas. Steve now understood how Belevairn had felt. He wanted to bolt—to flee, but there was no way to win free of the press.

Then a priest appeared at Steve's right as if from nowhere. He held up a hand and faced the crowd.

"*Por favor!*" he shouted, and the throng fell silent and backed away a step. He spoke to them some more and the crowd reluctantly parted for them to pass.

"Come with me, *señor*," he said to Steve in flawless English. "I am Father Rodriguez. We will grant you sanctuary for the night. In the morning, there will be much to discuss."

"Thank you, Father," Steve replied. Alexander approached them once Steve had cleared the press of the crowd.

"Boy, that was some show, Steve," he said. "Robert got it all on film."

"Yeah!" Robert agreed. "Man, I never would've believed it if I hadn't seen it!"

"Do you know these men, *señor*?" the priest asked. Steve briefly wondered what the priest would do if he said no. Only briefly.

"Yes, Father," he said. "These are my . . . companions."

"Then they shall be granted sanctuary as well," the priest said.

Agent Garcia mopped his brow after Wilkinson had retreated into the church with the priest. If he had not just seen what had happened with his own eyes, he would not have believed it. He wasn't certain he believed it as it was.

Whatever was going on, Wilkinson was *not* just another

new drug runner. Either he had just spoken with an angel from Heaven, or someone had managed to pull off one hell of a scam.

Come to think of it—Wilkinson *was* travelling with two reporters affiliated with one of those sensationalist magazines. The whole purpose of this could be nothing more than one of those hyped-up stories those people liked to print.

No, that didn't make sense. They wouldn't pay someone a hundred thousand dollars for something like that. Even if they did, they wouldn't pay with gold ingots.

Whatever had happened, Garcia was going to have to find a way to put this in his report without being retired to a nice, quiet funny farm somewhere. He didn't even notice that he crossed himself at the thought.

Steve stifled a yawn as he waited for Father Rodriguez to finish writing down the details of last night's "miracle." He had slept poorly last night and was woken at dawn to attend morning mass. Then he was fed a breakfast of something that resembled oatmeal but had more flavor.

After breakfast, Father Rodriguez had ushered him into a side room to record the events of last night.

"And what did the angel say to you, Steven?" Father Rodriguez asked.

"Huh?"

"What did he say? You talked with him for some time— in a tongue that none here understood."

"Oh. That is . . ." Steve didn't know quite where to begin. He couldn't just repeat the conversation without giving a lot of background.

"Yes?"

"Well, he sort of chewed me out," Steve finally said.

"Well," the priest said, smiling, "that certainly explains your reluctance. We do need to know what was said, though."

"That's going to take a lot of explaining," Steve said. "Including some things that are not . . . pleasant. Before we go any further, Father—will you take my confession?"

Father Rodriguez walked out the chapel office several hours later in a much more somber mood than he had entered it. Young Steven had confessed some very disturbing things to him. Things that he would have had difficulty believing, had it not been for the dreams that had foretold the young knight's arrival.

He knelt a little longer before the altar than normal as he passed through the sanctuary. The abbot would not be pleased by the news he was delivering. It had been many, many years since they had been required to perform an exorcism.

He rose to find Steven's reporter friend, Richard, waiting to speak with him.

"What's going on in there, Father?" he asked. "You two have been in there for almost three hours."

"I cannot answer your question, *señor* Alexander," Father Rodriguez replied. "My lips are sealed by the vows of the confessional. If young Steven wishes to tell you, that is his decision."

"Oh. Can I see him?"

"Neither you, nor anyone else, will be allowed to see him for the next several days."

"What? Why not?"

"Again, I cannot say, *señor*," Father Rodriguez said. "If you will please excuse me, I must speak with the abbot."

Steve was led from the small office into the sanctuary. Two priests walked in front of him and two more walked behind him. Perhaps telling Father Rodriguez about Belevairn had been a mistake.

Alexander and Robert were waiting in the sanctuary as Steve came out. Some alarm was evident in the way they looked on.

"Is everything okay, kid?" Alexander asked. Steve smiled, displaying a confidence he did not truly feel.

"Yeah, it's okay," he replied. "I'll explain it all when I see you later."

"If you say so," Alexander replied. He and Robert continued to watch on as Steve was led from the sanctuary. Steve hoped they didn't try anything stupid like a rescue. From what Father Rodriguez had told Steve, it wouldn't be him they would be rescuing in a few hours—it would be Belevairn.

They led him to the monastery behind the church. Down a flight of stairs, they came upon a hallway lined with small rooms. The two monks in front of him opened the door to one and stepped aside. Steve passed between them into the small cell. These must be the cloisters.

A small window, high on one wall, let in the noonday sun. A cot sat on one wall, and on the other a wash basin sat on a small table. The wall opposite the wash basin housed a small altar with a crucifix mounted on the wall above it.

The door shut behind him, and Steve heard a bar being laid into place across it. He turned around to see Father Rodriguez's face in the small window.

"I shall return soon, Steven," he said. "Then the abbot and I shall begin the exorcism."

"Oh, boy," Steve replied unenthusiastically.

"Do not fear," the priest reassured him. "All will be well. Have faith—the archangel Apollyon would not have commended you to us if there were no hope." He sealed the window and was gone.

Steve sat on the hard cot. This was *not* going to be the most pleasant experience he'd ever had. But then, it probably wasn't going to be the worst, either.

I guarantee it will be, Belevairn hissed from inside his mind.

"You have to allow him to come forth, Steven," Father Rodriguez said. "If you do not, we cannot drive him from you."

"Don't tell me!" Steve said, pacing back and forth across the small room. "He's the one that's not showing! He's found some corner to hide in and won't come out."

"Do likewise," Father Rodriguez said.

"Huh?"

"If you withdraw, then this other *must* come forward."

Steve looked from Father Rodriguez to the abbot and back. Both looked back at him expectantly.

"But . . . I don't know how . . ." Steve said.

"Have you ever been hypnotized?" Father Rodriguez asked.

"No."

"Would you cooperate if I attempted to do so?"

Steve blinked in surprise.

"Do they . . . teach priests that?"

Father Rodriguez laughed. "No, they do not," he said. "I have a master's degree in psychology from the University of Texas at Austin. I am also a certified hypnotherapist."

"Oh," Steve replied. "Sure . . . I suppose so."

"Good," Father Rodriguez said. "Now, just sit down on the cot and try to relax."

Steve did so. The hard cot was not exactly conducive to relaxation, but he would give it a try. Anything to get rid of Belevairn.

"Now," Father Rodriguez said, "I want you to take a slow, deep breath. In through your nose, filling your lungs completely." His voice slowly softened, becoming a resonant monotone. Steve did as he was told, filling his lungs with air.

"Then exhale slowly, out through your mouth," Rodriguez continued. "Try to force all of the air out of your lungs." Steve did so, exhaling as far as he could.

"Again—in through your nose."

Steve closed his mouth, slowly filling his lungs.

"Then out through your mouth."

Again, Steve slowly forced the air out of his lungs, feeling some of the tension ease from his shoulders. He was going to have to remember this trick . . .

"Now I want you to imagine yourself someplace relaxing," Father Rodriguez said. "A meadow or perhaps your own room at home, anywhere that is quiet and relaxing." The priest's monologue paused for a moment.

"Are you there yet?" he asked.

"Yes," Steve replied.

"Where is it?"

"A field near my home," Steve answered.

"Very good," Father Rodriguez said softly. "Now, imagine yourself lying in the grass with the warm sun shining down on you."

Steve did so. It wasn't difficult—he had spent many summer afternoons doing just that.

"Continue to focus on your breathing," Father Rodriguez urged him softly. "In through your nose . . . and out through your mouth."

Steve's breathing slowly fell into the monotonous rhythm of Father Rodriguez's voice. He could almost feel the grass on the back of his neck and his hands.

"The birds are singing softly," Father Rodriguez continued, "and you feel at peace. A cloud passes over the sun, shading your eyes—but it is still pleasantly warm. You feel yourself getting drowsy."

That was no lie. Steve could probably go to sleep right now. That probably wouldn't be conducive to what Father Rodriguez was trying to do, though.

"I am going to count backwards from ten," Father Rodriguez said. "When I reach one, you will no longer be here, but safely in your meadow instead. You will have left your body completely behind. Ten . . . nine . . . eight . . ."

Belevairn's eyes snapped open. He was in a small cell with two men. One was sitting on the bed by his feet and the other was standing near the barred door. With a snarl of rage he sat upright and tried to backhand the one sitting next to him.

The priest jumped away from him, and Belevairn followed him to a standing position. Damn these ignorant fools! How had they managed to force him to the surface?

Rodriguez grabbed Belevairn's right arm, trying to pin it behind Belevairn's back. But the body obeyed the mind, and Belevairn's mind was powerful. He simply willed the arm to straighten, and it did so. Rodriguez was unable to let go before Belevairn had lifted him from the floor and hurled him across the room.

The abbot and Rodriguez then each grabbed an arm, trying to force him back to the cot. Belevairn would have succeeded in breaking free of the priests had not two more monks entered to assist them. Manacles appeared from somewhere, and Belevairn soon found himself chained to the cot. He struggled briefly before deciding that it was pointless.

"Very good, priest," he said to Rodriguez. "But now that you have me, what do you intend to do with me? I am not some demon that you can wave your crucifixes at and drive back into the abyss."

"I know very well what you are, sorcerer," Rodriguez replied. "I intend to drive you out. I intend to reduce you to what you truly are—a collection of memories with no will or personality of your own."

"I will see you in Hell first, priest."

"We shall see, sorcerer," Rodriguez replied. "We shall see."

Chapter
-------- Thirteen -------------

BELEVAIRN FROWNED AT the bowl of quicksilver. For two days now, he had been unable to summon Wilkinson's image in the pool of mercury. The Dreamer was not dead—Belevairn knew that much at least. So the pertinent questions were, how was Wilkinson blocking him and what was Belevairn going to do about it?

The Power of the temple began to fade as the sun passed its zenith. Belevairn released the Power. This was not a good sign. If Wilkinson had succeeded in finding some way to block the Rite of Far Visions, Belevairn was at a severe disadvantage. It was imperative that he find some way of holding Wilkinson at bay—some way to gain an advantage over the *rega*. Wilkinson must have some weakness that Belevairn could take advantage of . . .

Belevairn paused in mid-stride on the way back to his desk. Of course! He had been such a fool not to think of this before. Belevairn quickly crossed the room and sat down at his desk, pulling out his navigational charts.

Yes, this solution *would* work! He would have to inform the *kaivir* to prepare seven sacrifices for tomorrow near sunset. Belevairn sat back in his chair and smiled. If this worked as well as he thought it might, he would actually be able to take Wilkinson back to the Mistress alive.

Wilkinson's body longed for sleep. One of the disadvantages of having a living body, Belevairn mused. Along with sensation and vitality came fatigue and hunger.

The two priests once again began the ritual that was

intended to drive Belevairn from Wilkinson's body. This had continued all night and into the next day. What would they do once they decided that he could not be driven out? Kill him, perhaps?

Belevairn blinked. To his fatigue-glazed eyes, each of the two priests was surrounded by a faint nimbus of golden light. He blinked again—the illusion did not fade. Belevairn reached out with other senses, and his eyes widened in surprise.

The priests were wielding the Power. Here, on an almost Power-less world, these two men were wielding almost as much Power together as any single *kaiva* in Morvanor. They shaped it between them and then directed it at him.

"Belevairn," the one called Rodriguez said, "I command you in the name of God the Father, God the Son and God the Holy Ghost to quit the body of Steven Wilkinson and return to the nothingness from which you were created."

Belevairn could feel the Power strike him—saw darkness gather about the edge of his vision as he began to lose consciousness. No! He fought back the darkness, clung desperately to his hold on Wilkinson's mind. He would not let these ignorant, peasant priests overcome *him*—master of the *kaivir*.

This made his situation more desperate. He had not noticed the assaults of Power before—presumably, they had increased in potency with the dawn. However, it was possible, likely in fact, that the priests would eventually succeed in destroying him if he did not escape.

Once the force of the Power had washed over him and ebbed, Belevairn cast his mind outward. There was only one hope of escape. Fortunately, the exorcism was not being conducted in the church itself, or even this slim chance would not exist.

Belevairn hoped that his counterpart was currently on Earth. He did not want to face too many more of these assaults. He almost sighed in relief when his mind touched that of the *goremka*.

Belevairn felt the demon's confusion as he wrapped his will around the *goremka*'s mind and commanded it to come to him. It hesitated—it had thought its master safely nearby. Belevairn concentrated, forcing his will to overcome the demon's hesitation. The demon reluctantly submitted. Now Belevairn could only hope that his counterpart would not have need of his mount for the next few moments. It would not do for him to find it missing . . .

Belevairn opened his eyes, careful to maintain his link with the *goremka*. Father Rodriguez glared back at him, waiting to see if the sorcerer had fled. Belevairn smiled.

"Your faith is strong, priest," he said. "Against a chained man, that is."

"You will not goad me into releasing you, sorcerer," Rodriguez said.

"I would not even attempt it," Belevairn replied, smiling. "However, I cannot help but wonder how your faith would fare, face to face against a true demon—unbound and craving your flesh."

All the residual Power from the priests' ritual was abruptly consumed as the *goremka* used it to reenter the physical world. Rodriguez and the abbot recoiled as what must appear to them to be Satan's own steed reared to crush them with its cloven hooves.

Rodriguez recovered quickly, placing himself between the abbot and the *goremka*. He shouted something in Latin, not even flinching as the *goremka*'s hooves descended on him. Fool.

Belevairn's arrogance was replaced with astonishment as the *goremka*'s hooves struck an unseen barrier. Rodriguez glared at the demon as it reared and struck again, with the same ineffectual results.

"Begone, demon!" he commanded, taking up the same crucifix staff they had been waving in Belevairn's face all night. "Depart from here and return to the abyss whence you came! Begone!" He struck the rearing beast in the chest with the crucifix.

The *goremka* dissolved into mist and was gone as quickly as it had appeared. Belevairn could feel it nearby, on the Gray Plain, awaiting his commands. Angrily he dismissed it, allowing it to return to its true master. Now Belevairn could only hope that his counterpart had not noticed his mount's brief absence.

"Does that answer your question, sorcerer?" Rodriguez asked, setting the crucifix aside. Belevairn simply glared at him.

Alexander suffered from an odd mixture of boredom and concern. He was bored because there was absolutely nothing to do. He was concerned because Steve had been missing all day. He hadn't lost a story yet, and he didn't want to start now.

Of course, there was more to his concern than just a story, but Alexander would not have admitted that to anyone—including himself. His gaze wandered over toward the monastery where Steve was being held. If the priests didn't bring the kid out of there by tomorrow morning, Alexander was going to go in there after him. After all, what were they going to do, excommunicate him?

The Jeep pulled back into the compound. Robert must have gotten back from his search for a place to get his film developed. Alexander hoped it had been successful—he wanted to see those shots.

"Any luck?" Alexander asked.

"Yeah, but I had to drive all the way into Oaxaca for it," Robert replied.

"How'd they come out?"

"Not too good," Robert said. "Here, take a look at these. All you can see of the angel is a blurry glow that looks like it *could* be someone mounted on a horse."

Robert was right. Alexander had hoped that the photographs of the angel would be as clear as their photographs of the demon-horse. Even so, they would still be useful for the book.

"Okay," he said, "let's get an article for the *Clarion* wrapped around these pictures. It'll make them happier if they get a little something for their money this early."

Agent Garcia switched the headphones to the microphone trained on the monastery. He had no desire to listen as the two reporters worked on their story. The tapes could be listened to later to see if anything illegal were discussed.

Now, the exorcism—*that* was interesting. Garcia smiled at the thought of what the agency would make of that. In a few days, they would probably take him off this assignment. That would be just fine with him. It was obvious that Wilkinson had nothing to do with drug trafficking. He might be crazy, but he wasn't a runner.

Belevairn screamed as the Power burned through him, his back arching up away from the mattress of the cot. All day long the two priests had bombarded him—not allowing him to rest. At noon they had almost overcome him. Now it was nearing sunset, and their Power was cresting again.

Belevairn was not certain that he could withstand another onslaught at the peak of their Power. If he could just find Wilkinson, then he could elude them. But the young man he shared his body with was nowhere to be found. Somehow the priests had managed to conceal Steven's ego in a place where even Belevairn could not reach it.

The wave of Power passed and Belevairn settled back onto the cot, his breath shuddering out in a ragged sigh.

"Damn you," he said. "Damn you to your own Hell, priest." He spoke only to Rodriguez, as the abbot did not speak English. "You shall *not* drive me out."

"I think we shall," Rodriguez replied. "You are weakening, sorcerer. Your hold on Steven's mind is slipping."

"Damn you."

Belevairn waited atop the temple as the *kaivir* prepared for the first sacrifice. He barely heard the feeble cries of the first victim—his attention was completely focused on the image of the red brick house reflected in the bowl of quicksilver.

As he watched, an old sports car of some type pulled up to the house. The owner had painted it some horrid shade of flat purple—apparently some time ago. The passenger door opened and a young woman climbed out of the car. It was time—Belevairn quickly mounted his steed, gathered up the Power that the *kaivir*'s sacrifices had produced and slipped from reality onto the Gray Plain.

Tammy Wilkinson waved to her date as he pulled away. What a jerk. She'd spent more time blocking his hands than watching the movie. On nights like this she was actually grateful for her parents' ten o'clock curfew.

She was getting tired of the football guys. As a cheer-leader, she was always being taken out by them and they always had just one thing on their minds. Of course, no one else ever asked her out.

She was walking toward the front porch when a bright light split the air in front of her. Through the glowing rift, a black horse with a black rider emerged. The eyes of the horse glowed red in the night and the yard light glinted off the golden mask the rider wore.

Tammy screamed before her mind truly registered any of this. She turned to run, kicking off her high-heeled shoes. The horseman pulled up beside her. She screamed and dove to the right as he reached out to grasp her.

She rolled to her feet and turned back toward the house in time to see her father run out the front door with his shotgun. The horse had cut back and was again bearing down on her. Tammy threw herself down on the ground, still screaming, as her dad fired.

The blast knocked the rider from his horse, and he landed next to Tammy. She stood to run toward the house, only to find herself face to face with the horse. However, it wasn't a horse. It threatened her with bared fangs. She started to scream again when a blow from behind knocked her unconscious.

Jerry Wilkinson could do nothing but watch in disbelief as the horse carrying his daughter rode up into the air. He had already fired two slugs into the thing with absolutely no effect. Several neighbors were also watching, but he didn't notice them. He couldn't tear his eyes away from the sky.

He sat down on the front steps, still holding the shotgun as he watched horse, rider and his daughter vanish into a bright light that appeared in the sky. When the light vanished, everything was gone, as if they had never been.

He was still sitting there, staring, a few moments later when the police arrived.

Belevairn emerged atop the Aztec temple shortly after sunset. Tamara Wilkinson was still unconscious across the back of the *goremka*. The *kaivir* lifted her down from his mount.

"Imprison her within the temple itself and tend to her injuries," Belevairn commanded them. "Be certain that those who guard her know that she is not to be harmed. If any man touches her, he shall answer to me personally."

"Yes, Dread Lord," the *kaivir* replied.

Now the only problem was how to find Wilkinson and inform him that his sister was now in Belevairn's possession. Belevairn had been unable to locate him before leaving to abduct Tamara. Where on Earth could he be?

Steve blinked and slowly opened his eyes. Every muscle in his body ached, and his throat was raw and sore. Where was he?

He tried to sit up, but found that his wrists and ankles were chained. He'd been captured! His eyes snapped open and he looked into the concerned gaze of Father Rodriguez.

He sighed in relief and sank back onto the cot. No, not captured.

"I take it, Belevairn gave you a bit of trouble," Steve said, wiggling one wrist.

"A bit," Father Rodriguez replied, smiling. "Can you find him?"

Steve closed his eyes and searched for Belevairn's presence. There was no trace of the sorcerer. He *did* find memories of Belevairn's life, if it could be called that, but there was no sign of the sorcerer's presence in his mind.

"I . . . don't think so," Steve replied. "I can remember things that he knew, but I can't find *him*. Oh my God."

"What?" Father Rodriguez asked. "What is it?"

"Did . . . did I actually summon the *goremka* here?"

"If that is the demon-horse we fought, yes you did."

"Was . . . anyone hurt?"

"No, we drove it off successfully."

"Belevairn's gone," Steve said, hardly daring to believe it. "Thank God, the son of a bitch is finally gone."

"Sleep now," Father Rodriguez said as he gently removed the manacles. "We will talk more in the morning."

Steve settled into the cot. He was asleep before the priests had left the room.

The first sensation that Tammy felt on regaining consciousness was the pain in her head. It began at the back of her head as a sharp stabbing pain and radiated around the sides and over the top, wrapping her entire head in throbbing agony.

The second thing she noticed was the heat. It was an oppressively humid, stifling weight that made each breath an effort. Where was she?

She sat up slowly—the dizziness she felt would not allow her to move quickly. She was in a stone room, lit by a single, bare bulb overhead. The stone walls were covered in what looked like ancient South American carvings. Her bed was a stone block covered by a thin, lumpy mattress. To her dismay there was no door.

Memory returned quickly—the nightmare horse and the equally horrible horseman. She was still wearing the jeans and blouse she had worn on her date, now pasted to her body with perspiration. She remembered her father rushing to her rescue. Had he been hurt? She feared that he must have been—he never would have let someone take her, otherwise.

A section of wall opposite the stone bench began to swing inward. Tammy backed away until she was wedged into the corner of the room furthest from the formerly concealed door. As soon as it was open far enough, the man who had kidnapped her stepped into the room.

He was even more hideous than she remembered. His gaunt form was clad all in black, and his face was covered by a hideous, snarling gold mask. The eyes behind that mask glowed red in the shadowed eyeholes. Tammy shuddered and looked away.

A guard had stepped into the room behind him. He was big—real big. He was dressed in camouflage fatigues and was wearing a pistol. The guard was dark-complected and clean-shaven—and not bad-looking. Apparently he thought the same of her, judging by the slow twice-over he was giving her. Jerk.

"Hello, Tam," her kidnapper said in a dry, rasping voice. "I trust you are well?"

Tammy didn't answer at first, surprised by the unexpected use of Steve's nickname for her.

"My head hurts," she finally said, angrily. The guard snorted in amusement. Double jerk.

"It will for a few days," her kidnapper replied. "I have been assured that the injury is not severe, however."

"Who are you?" she demanded. "Why have you kidnapped me?"

"Let us say that I am . . . acquainted with your brother," he said.

"Steve?"

"Obviously, since that is the only brother you have. You are here to make certain that he does not interfere with my operations here."

"Steve?" she repeated. What threat could Steve possibly be to this . . . thing?

"Yes. With you here, your brother will not dare attack me."

"Steve? Attack *you*?" Her kidnapper nodded in response.

"Mister," she said, "you're crazy. And you've got the wrong person. I love my brother, but Rambo he's not."

"Enough," her captor said. "Come here." Tammy cowered further back into the corner. He said something to the guard in a language that she didn't recognize. The guard walked over and plucked her off the stone bed as simply as if she were a doll. He set her on her feet next to the . . . thing in the gold mask.

"Come along," her kidnapper said, grabbing her by the arm. His grip on her arm was painful.

"You're hurting me!"

"If you do not cooperate, I will not hesitate to break it," he replied. "Now come along."

She obeyed as he led her out of the room and outside through a stone archway. Tammy blinked in surprise as they stepped into the sunlight. They were on a landing halfway up the stone steps of a South American pyramid.

In the distance, the jungle surrounded a busy camp at the base of the pyramid. There were hundreds of people here, most wearing the same uniform as her guard. Her heart sank as she realized there would be no escape from this place. She would never make it out of the camp and, even if she did, the jungle would make certain that she didn't get out alive.

"Stand still," her captor ordered. Someone, wearing black robes instead of the fatigues the soldiers wore, took several pictures of her standing between the guard and the man in the gold mask.

"That should be enough to convince Master Wilkinson that I have his sister," he said. "Take her back to her cell and see that she is fed and given fresh clothing."

The guard took her by the arm and led her back inside the temple. He shoved her back into the room she had woken up in, and the door slowly swung shut behind her. Tammy sat on the stone ledge that served as her bed and began to weep.

Chapter
-------- Fourteen -------------

ALEXANDER LOOKED UP as Steve walked into the sanctuary for First Mass. The kid looked like death warmed over—pale and hollow-eyed. He met Alexander's gaze and smiled, briefly, before crossing himself and taking a seat across the aisle. Alexander got up and went over to sit next to him.

"You all right, kid?" he whispered.

"Fine," Wilkinson replied. "Or at least I will be once I've had breakfast."

"Oatmeal again," Alexander said. "Yum, yum."

"We'll be leaving soon," Steve assured him. "Father Rodriguez wants to talk to me about something after breakfast and then we should be able to get back on the road."

"No offense, kid," Alexander said, "but you don't look like you're in any shape to get back on anything but a bed."

"You may have a point there," Steve agreed.

The remainder of the service passed in silence. Once it was over they went into the dining room for breakfast. Alexander was right—it was oatmeal again. Apparently, that was served for breakfast every morning. It didn't matter; as hungry as he was, cardboard would have tasted better than the best steak he'd ever had.

Steve ate in silence. He honestly did not have the energy for conversation. The last two days had taken a severe toll on him. Still, it was worth it to finally be rid of his unwanted guest. He hadn't realized just how much Belevairn's unwelcome presence had pervaded his entire existence.

If only getting rid of the real Belevairn would be so easy.

Then Steve could go back to his own life and forget all of this. Yeah—if only.

After breakfast he found Father Rodriguez waiting for him in the sanctuary. He crossed himself before sitting down beside the priest.

"How are you feeling?" Rodriguez asked.

"Exhausted," Steve replied. "Exhausted and relieved."

"Understandable," Rodriguez said, nodding. "You should probably spend the rest of the day at rest. I was surprised to see you at First Mass this morning."

"I wanted to attend."

"Commendable," Rodriguez said, "but you should not overly tire yourself. There is still much to be done."

"Oh?" Steve asked.

Rodriguez glanced around the sanctuary, as if making certain no one could overhear them. "I did not want to bring this up before you were exorcised," the priest continued, lowering his voice. "We were foretold of your arrival here. More specifically, the abbot and I were sent dreams that spoke of your arrival."

"Dreams?" Steve asked. His arrival at Saint Michael's had been prophesied?

"Yes," Rodriguez replied. "These dreams were quite specific—although they did not prepare us for the exorcism. However, it was made clear that we were to help you in whatever way possible."

"And I thank you for all of your help, Father," Steve replied.

"You have not yet received *all* of our help," Father Rodriguez said.

"What . . . do you mean?"

"The dreams led us to believe that you would bring a sword with you. Did you?"

"Yes—I did," Steve replied. "It is . . . in the Jeep."

"Good," Rodriguez said, nodding. "We will need that. It must be consecrated. Also, you are to be invested and ordained."

"Ordained?" Steve only knew one meaning behind that term. "As a priest?"

"Not . . . exactly," Father Rodriguez replied. He glanced around nervously and dropped his voice to an even quieter whisper.

"You must tell no one of this," he said. "The dreams and visions were clear on this. You are to be ordained into an Order that was banned by the Church seven centuries ago. Officially, you will be a Franciscan, which is our Order."

"Officially?" This didn't sound good. What would happen if Steve agreed to this and someone found out about his true Order? From the way Father Rodriguez was behaving, excommunication would probably just be the *first* step.

"What would I be . . . unofficially?" Steve asked.

Father Rodriguez paused before answering. "A Knight Templar."

Steve knelt before the altar as the abbot placed his hands atop Steve's head. The ordination had been performed early this morning before the congregation. The investiture was being performed privately with only a small group of priests attending.

After a few moments of Latin, the abbot removed his hands and indicated that Steve was to rise. Steve did so, and the attending priests stepped forward to vest him. Over the white robe Steve had worn to the service, a white mantle, trimmed in red with an equal-armed red cross centered on the front and back, was placed.

Then Father Rodriguez lifted Steve's sword, which had been consecrated the previous night, from the altar and approached him.

"Receive this sword," he began, "as a sign of the authority given you to defend the Word of God and to protect his Holy Sacraments. Do not forget the trust committed to you as a priest of the Church of God and a Knight of the Temple."

The remembered words of another priest in another world echoed through Steve's mind. *Never shame it.* Steve lifted the sword from Father Rodriguez's hands and bowed his forehead to touch it as he'd been instructed. He then placed it in the scabbard at his waist.

"I shall not forget," he said.

"Are you certain you would not rather spend the night here?" Father Rodriguez asked. "You are still weak from your ordeals."

"I'm certain, Father," Steve replied.

"Brother," Rodriguez corrected him.

"Brother," Steve replied a little sheepishly. He still didn't feel like a priest—although he certainly felt like a knight and would for the rest of his life. But then, Erelvar had given him that a long time ago.

"Every hour I delay is that much longer that Belevairn has to work against me," he continued. "I'll stop for the night in Oaxaca. I promise."

"I understand," Rodriguez said. "You must be about your quest, Don Quixote."

"Well, I won't be tilting at any windmills tonight, for certain," Steve replied, smiling. "I know my limits, Fa . . . Brother."

"I would like the abbey to have this," Steve concluded, handing Father Rodriguez one of Belevairn's saddlebags. Rodriguez's eyebrows raised when he looked within.

"There must be . . ." he began.

"Ten thousand dollars, American," Steve said. "I'm sure the abbot can find a good use for it."

"Without a doubt."

"Goodbye, Brother," Steve said, shaking the priest's hand. "Thank you for all your help."

"Good journey, Templar," Father Rodriguez replied. "God be with you."

"And also with you," Steve answered. He walked over to where Richard and Alexander were waiting in the Jeep and climbed into the driver's seat.

"We should make it to Oaxaca right around sunset," Richard said. "It's about three hours from here."

"Then let's hit the road," Steve replied, pulling onto the narrow dirt road from the abbey.

"So," Alexander said, "what all did they do to you in there?"

"I can't tell you that," Steve replied. "Let's just say that they performed a service that should protect me from Belevairn's magic."

"They needed your sword for that?" Alexander sounded skeptical.

"They consecrated my sword," Steve said, avoiding the full answer. "Hopefully, it will work against the *goremka* at this point."

"Hopefully?"

"It's a matter of faith," Steve replied. For a moment, Alexander said nothing.

"They certainly didn't seem to have any trouble accepting your story," Alexander observed. "I find that a little hard to believe."

"They knew I was coming a week ago," Steve said.

"What!?" Alexander said. "How? You didn't even know you were going to stop here until we were two hours from the place."

"They were told, in dreams and visions, that a knight would arrive who needed their aid," Steve explained. "They had everything prepared ahead of time—except for the exorcism."

"Yeah, you're going to have to tell me about that," Alexander said. "You sure look like they took it out of you. The extra day's rest did you a lot of good, though. A short drive into town and a proper bed, or at least something closer to it, should have you back on your feet."

"I bounce back pretty well," Steve said.

"So I've noticed. You were back up and moving two days after fighting that horse thing."

"Every day here is ten back in Delgroth," Steve replied. "Every hour counts."

The sound of the heavy stone door opening woke Tammy to her third morning of imprisonment. Room service was calling.

The same young Spanish girl who had taken care of Tammy's needs for the last two days entered. She set Tammy's breakfast on the small table that had been added

to the cell's meager furnishings. Tammy sat up on the bed
and watched as the girl laid out fresh clothing for her.

The girl couldn't be much older than Tammy—maybe a
year or two at the most, if any. Her face was pretty, except
for the fading bruise on her left cheek. The baggy dress,
a clone of the one she was laying out for Tammy, still
showed a fairly nice figure—almost as full as Tammy's.
Her dark eyes held a subdued, haunted look—a broken
look. What had these monsters done to her?

The sound of a commotion of some type reached them
from outside. The guard glanced inside the cell and back
out toward the temple exit. Apparently, he decided that
whatever was happening needed his attention because the
heavy door began to swing closed.

Tammy got up from the bed and stripped off her sweat-
soaked dress, taking the rag from the wash basin the girl
had brought in. The girl stared at her, and Tammy smiled
back as she began to rinse the night's perspiration from her
body. About now she'd kill for a bottle of shampoo.

She bent over and rinsed her hair in the wash bowl. It
wasn't much, but it was the best she could do. Still bending,
she groped for the towel, and the girl placed it in her hand.
Tammy towelled her hair and began to dry off. The Spanish
girl took the towel and dried Tammy's back for her.

Tammy smiled and her impromptu chambermaid smiled
back, sheepishly, as she helped Tammy get the new dress
slipped on. Once dressed, Tammy sat down to her breakfast—a plate of eggs, some type of sausage and soft tortillas. They certainly weren't trying to starve her. If she
ate all of the food they gave her at each meal, she'd be
a blimp within a week. The Spanish girl sat on the edge
of the bed and watched.

She, on the other hand, Tammy thought, *doesn't look
like she's had a decent meal in a month*. With a smile,
Tammy picked up the wash bowl and dumped the water
on the floor. In this heat, it wouldn't take it long to dry.
Using the towel from her bath, she dried the bowl out and
scooped about half her breakfast into it before handing it
to the girl.

The girl certainly ate as though she hadn't had a decent meal in a month. She was completely finished with her meal before Tammy was even halfway through. She silently watched Tammy eat for a few moments.

"*Señorita*?" she said, questioningly.

"I'm sorry," Tammy said, smiling and shaking her head. "I don't speak Spanish."

"*Sí*, I know," the girl replied. Tammy straightened from her breakfast.

"You speak English!" she said.

"*Sí*, a little."

"How come you've never said anything before?"

"The guard . . ." was all the girl said.

"Oh. What's your name?"

"Rosita."

"I'm Tammy." Rosita smiled her brief, timid smile again and fell silent.

"*Señorita*?" she asked again after a moment.

"Yes?" Tammy replied around a mouthful of sausage and tortilla.

"Why are you here?"

Tammy sat back and slid her plate across the small table to Rosita. She nodded when the girl looked at her questioningly, and Rosita began to finish the last remnants of Tammy's breakfast.

"I'm not really sure," Tammy said. "The guy in the mask says it's to keep my brother from attacking him."

"Don Espantoso fears your brother?" Rosita's eyes widened in surprise.

"That was my reaction."

"Will . . . will your brother come for you?" Rosita asked quietly. Tammy snorted.

"Steve? He might want to—if he knew I was here. Probably would want to, but I would hope he wouldn't try."

"Why not?"

"Well, don't get me wrong—I love my brother. He's a good man, I suppose, but he's no knight in shining armor. If he tried to rescue me, he'd just get himself killed."

"*Sí*, I understand," Rosita said. She looked down a

moment, as if in shame, before continuing. "There is talk in the camp that you are being kept as a prize for one of the officers."

"A . . . prize," Tammy said. That was certainly a horrid notion.

"*Sí*," Again Rosita looked away before continuing. "The soldiers who watch you complain that they are not allowed to . . . take you. You are very beautiful, *señorita*."

That certainly explained Rosita's fear of the guards—and her broken spirit. Tammy had been wrong—monsters was too nice a term to describe these people. Tammy wondered how far her protection extended. How afraid of the gold mask were her watchers?

"Are you a prisoner, too, Rosita?" Tammy asked.

"*Sí*," Rosita replied. "All the women are the soldiers' *putas*. We are nothing but animals, here."

Breeding stock, to be precise, Tammy thought. But that wasn't accurate, either. There was no intent to reproduce— the guards were only interested in getting their jollies. And, if they had been allowed, Tammy would be one of those jollies. She shuddered.

"Has anyone ever tried to escape?" she asked. Rosita's eyes grew wide and she shook her head emphatically.

"No, *señorita*," she replied. "The jungle around the camp is filled with demons. They . . ."

Rosita stopped talking at the sound of the door opening. She rose from the bed and placed her finger against her lips asking for Tammy's silence. Then she quickly gathered up the remnants from the bath and breakfast, as well as the full chamber pot.

By the time the door had opened enough to see into the room, Rosita was standing by it, waiting to leave. She glanced back at Tammy, her eyes filled again with that hopeless look Tammy had first seen. Then she left the room, head bowed dejectedly.

The guard looked back at Tammy, slowly scanning her from head to toe and back again before closing the door. Tammy shuddered. What would happen to her once the guy in the mask figured out he had the wrong girl? She *had* to think of a way out of here before that happened.

They pulled into Tapachula well before sunset. Steve was tempted to push on into Guatemala. It would probably be best to put that off until the morning, though. Just in case they ran into any trouble at the border, it would be better to have the whole day ahead of them than to be scrambling to find a place to stop for the night.

Steve was starting to understand the reason for the slower pace that dominated this part of the world. It was the damned heat. If the Jeep hadn't been air-conditioned, he didn't think he would have been able to make it this far this quickly.

"On to Guatemala?" Alexander asked.

"I don't think so," Steve replied. "I think we should stop here for the night and push on in the morning."

"Sounds great to me," Alexander said. "Why don't we find someplace nice to eat for a change since we've got some time?"

"That sounds *real* good," Robert agreed. "I'm getting tired of sandwiches out of the ice chest."

"I third the motion," Steve replied. A good meal certainly wouldn't hurt anything. Neither would a little extra rest before crossing into Guatemala.

They found a fairly nice little cantina. If it weren't for the fact that Alexander spoke a little Spanish, though, they wouldn't have been able to order.

Steve sat back after the meal. It had been excellent—hopefully they wouldn't regret it later. Alexander lit up a cigarette and leaned forward, with his elbows on the table.

"Something I've been wondering about," he began.

"What's that?" Steve asked.

"All we have is a spot on a map," Alexander continued. "Do you have any idea what we're walking into?"

"Not really," Steve replied.

"Oh," Alexander said. "You mean you have absolutely

no idea what might be there?"

"Nope," Steve replied, smiling. "No idea whatsoever." For a long time Alexander and Robert just stared at him. Finally, Robert turned to Alexander.

"I *could* have gone to the Cannes Film Festival, you know," he said quietly.

"Wish I'd gone with you," Alexander agreed.

Agent Garcia waited until his quarry had settled in for the night before heading in to report. Tapachula had another clandestine DEA office. Since the town was nestled on the Guatemalan border, a lot of drug traffic passed through this general area. Maybe Wilkinson was a runner after all.

Garcia wasn't certain why, but somehow he *knew* that wasn't the case. Runners didn't speak with angels, have exorcisms performed in out-of-the-way churches and then get ordained immediately afterwards. Garcia had it *all* on tape. This was undoubtedly the screwiest case he'd ever worked.

He had phoned ahead, so the office was expecting him, despite the hour. The door was opened for him before he had an opportunity to knock.

"We are closed," the proprietor told him. "May I help you?"

"I have a delivery from the home office," Garcia replied.

"Ah, please, come in." The director stepped aside and allowed Garcia to pass him into the small office. He led Garcia through the investment firm's small front office to a smaller office in the back.

"You have a report?" the director asked.

"Yes, sir," Garcia replied, handing the director a folder from his attaché. Garcia sat back and waited while the director scanned his report. After a few moments the director looked up and met Garcia's gaze.

"Is this some kind of joke, Agent Garcia?" he asked.

"I wish it were, sir," Garcia replied. "I have not been able to formulate any solid theories to explain these events. The only theory that seems to fit is that Wilkinson is perpetrating some type of hoax in conjunction with these reporters."

"Hmm, that's an odd thought," the director said. "However, it doesn't hold water. Especially with recent developments."

"Sir?"

"Wilkinson's sister was kidnapped three days ago."

"I see," Garcia replied.

"The circumstances of the kidnapping sound as bizarre as your report, by the way."

"How so?"

"Witnesses, including half a dozen neighbors, claim that Tamara Wilkinson was abducted by some type of demon on a flying horse."

"Sir, I didn't excerpt it because it did not seem important at the time, but there is mention of a demonic horse on one of the tapes. . . ."

"Stay on this kid Wilkinson," the director said. "I want to find out exactly what in the *hell* is going on."

"Are you speaking literally or figuratively, sir?" Garcia asked, smiling.

Chapter
-------- **Fifteen** -------------

TECHNICALLY, SOMALIA WAS just as hot as Nicaragua, but it certainly did not feel that way. The drier climate was much easier to bear than the stifling humidity of Central America. Garth hoped that his platoon got chosen for more operations in Africa. Of course, the best way to insure that was to do a good job on this assignment.

"Sergeant Dalin," he said, "your squad will enter the compound here. You will then proceed to within range of the command center and destroy it."

"And after that?"

"After that, you get your ass out of there. On your way *out*, not in, I want you to knock out those two helicopters. I don't want anything with a radio left working."

"Shouldn't we attempt to join . . ." Dalin began.

"No!" Garth interrupted. "You get your squad out of there. That compound will be boiling over like an ant's nest once you blow that command center. Sergeant Bryn's squad will be covering your entry point. You will join with him and together proceed to this point where you will join forces with Sergeant Algol's squad and myself for the assault against the gate."

"Yes, sir."

"Sergeant Wyrth, once the command center blows, that's your signal to destroy the tank platoon and get the hell out of there. Sergeant Rashine will be covering your entry point. Join with his squad and proceed to the rendezvous point.

"Our tanks will start rolling as soon as we see the explosions," Garth continued. "Our platoon will perform the

142

initial containment until the Somalians can get into the compound. Then the tanks and, after them, our platoon will retreat and leave the final cleanup to the Somalians. Any questions?"

"Yes," Dalin spoke up. "How come we're not seeing this through to the end?"

"Not our mission," Garth replied. "Our job is just to crack this egg for the Somalians. If we do not retreat immediately, we risk facing an American air response. The Somalians can disperse and blend in with the local populace—we cannot."

"I do not like doing half a job . . ." Dalin grumbled.

"Half a job is *all* we've been hired for, Sergeant," Garth replied sternly. "We do not have the force necessary to stick around and fight. Any *other* questions?" There were none.

"Very well. Go and order your men to get some rest and get some yourselves. Our attack begins at oh-one-hundred hours."

Dalin's squad advanced up to the perimeter fence once the sentries had passed. Garth was a coward—always overplanning every operation and discarding every possible risk, no matter how great the potential reward. Were he not one of Lord Jared's favorites, he would have never made it to lieutenant.

They were through the wire barrier around the installation in seconds. Dalin followed his squad as they jogged, single file, across the perimeter, scattering powdered menthol over their trail. This would keep the sentry's dog from catching their scent—buying them a few more precious moments.

Wyrth should already be in position within range of the tank platoon. Dalin's squad made it past the helicopter pads to the cover of the tents surrounding the center of the base. This was the most dangerous phase of the penetration. One sleepless soldier going to the latrines could raise the alarm.

Dalin's heart pounded with excitement. This mission was what he'd been craving. Matching wits with one of the best military units in the world—beating them on their own ground. It was unthinkable that the real battle would be completed by a rabble of gun-waving, Somalian peasants.

They carefully penetrated the barrier of tents until they were within sight of the command center. Dalin unslung the rocket launcher from his back. Each man had his predesignated target. Dalin's target was, theoretically, the communications center. He took and held a deep breath, sighted and fired. Immediately, the nine men in his squad also fired.

Dalin did not even wait to see the explosions. He had already turned and was running for the perimeter, his squad close behind. Behind them, the command center was engulfed in the fiery explosions of ten missiles.

As they emerged from the tents lining the perimeter, Dalin opened fire, felling one of the two sentries who were closing on their position. His man behind him got the other one. Behind them, they could hear more explosions— Wyrth destroying the tank platoon. An alarm siren wailed from somewhere, and the sounds of shouts and gunfire told him that the camp had been alerted.

Two more rocket launchers fired behind Dalin, and the helicopters far to their right were engulfed in flames. Mission accomplished—a walk in the park. From the sounds of gunfire, Wyrth's squad was not having such an easy time of it.

"We're circling around to rescue Wyrth!" Dalin ordered. "Come on!" The tank platoon was less than a quarter of the way around the perimeter, toward the gate. Dalin could already see the burning husks of the M-1's. Garth be damned—he was *not* going to let Wyrth get butchered.

Garth watched as the American installation burned. The tanks had rolled as soon as the command center had been blown. From his vantage, south of the temporary base, Garth had watched as Wyrth destroyed the tank platoon and then as Dalin destroyed the helicopters.

Everything was proceeding smoothly. The Somalian force should be in the compound by now, and Garth's other four squads should arrive at any moment. Then he could advance the platoon to contain the Americans while the Somalian forces assaulted the base.

Rashine and Wyrth were the first to arrive. Something was wrong here—Garth had expected Dalin and Bryn to return first. They should have started out as soon as they blew the command center. Wyrth would have had to remain in position long enough to destroy the tank platoon.

"Sergeant Wyrth," Garth said, returning the two sergeants' salutes, "any sign of Dalin and Bryn?"

"Yes, sir, they . . . should be right behind us."

Garth's eyes narrowed. Something in Wyrth's manner told him there was something the sergeant was hiding.

"Spill it," he ordered.

Wyrth and Rashine exchanged glances. Whatever they had failed to report, it was clear they knew that Garth was not going to like it.

"Dalin joined my squad in the perimeter," Wyrth reported.

"Why?" Garth's tone was flat.

"We ran into some resistance, sir," Wyrth replied. "The Americans responded quicker than we had anticipated. Dalin heard the firefight and brought his squad in on their flank. Saved our ass, sir."

"I'll be certain to mention that in my report," Garth said.

"Y-yes, sir," Wyrth replied. "Once we left the compound, Dalin circled back to rejoin Bryn." Garth frowned. That would put Dalin and Bryn at least another five minutes from the rendezvous—perhaps ten.

"We cannot wait for them," Garth said. "We will have to contain with just three squads. Fall in for the advance."

"Yes, sir!"

Garth needed to have a long talk with Sergeant Dalin . . .

Dalin squeezed off a burst, cutting down an American who was sighting on the tank he'd attached his squad to. When it had become obvious that they could not make the rendezvous, Dalin had convinced Bryn to enter the compound and provide support for the tanks.

It was a good thing he had, too. Dalin's squad had already kept this tank from getting blown to pieces twice. The tank protected by Bryn's squad was still rolling, as well. Dalin was certain neither one would have been without the support of their squads.

Besides, those tanks were the only way their two squads were getting out of this. As soon as those babies turned to roll out of here, Dalin and Bryn were climbing aboard. The tank commanders had already been notified of the plan. Dalin fired, killing an American who tried to retrieve the fallen antitank weapon.

"Time to roll," the voice of the tank commander crackled in his headphones.

"All aboard!" Dalin shouted. "Let's get out of here!" He leaped onto the slowing tank's tread guard, hooking his arm through an anchoring rung. His squad followed, clambering onto the tank.

"All aboard?" asked the tank commander.

"Affirmative!" Dalin replied. He was missing three men, but they were nowhere to be seen. One of them he had seen fall—the other two would have to be presumed dead. Damn.

"Hang on!" The tank lurched underneath them and began rolling toward the gate, picking up speed. Dalin glanced over to the second tank. He could see some of the men from Bryn's squad clinging to it. It was going to work! They were going to make it out. Dalin smiled—he bet that Garth would have a stroke when he saw them.

Two days later, Garth opened the door to Korva's office with mixed feelings. Dalin's open insubordination during the Somalian mission was an embarrassment to him on several levels. It certainly did not look good for him as a commander to have his men flagrantly disobeying orders.

What made it worse was that, judging from Wyrth's statement and the reports of the tank commanders, Dalin's choices had shored up some weaknesses in Garth's strategy. Garth's strategy would have reduced the casualties his platoon had suffered—at the cost of the two tank crews.

"Lieutenant Garth reporting as ordered, sir!" he said, saluting.

"At ease, Lieutenant," Korva replied. The senior captain leaned back in his chair, studying him.

"Well," he finally said, "now that you've had a day to review the reports, what do you think?"

"Sir?"

"What do you think should be done? He's your sergeant, after all."

"Yes, sir," Garth replied. He swallowed—this was not going to be easy, apparently.

"Captain Korva," he said, "after reviewing the reports I think three actions should be taken."

"Three? Very well, proceed."

"One, I think that Sergeant Dalin should be disciplined for refusal to obey orders."

"Agreed. Go on."

"Two, I think that Sergeant Dalin should be rewarded for his initiative in providing support for the tank crews once he was cut off from the platoon."

"Very good. I agree on that as well. I am curious as to what your third course of action is going to be, however. I, myself, was under the impression that the first two actions you recommended would suffice."

"No, sir. Three, I think that the commanding officer should be disciplined for failing to anticipate the need to support the armored units."

"Meaning yourself."

"Yes, sir."

"I see," Korva replied. He leaned forward and rested his forearms on his desk, interlacing the fingers of his hands.

"Lieutenant," he said, "I like a man who steps forward to take his lumps when he fucks up. But I do not like dishing out lumps to a man who does not deserve them."

"Sir?"

"Were you *asked* to support those units?"

"No, sir—but . . ." Garth began. Korva held up a hand, silencing him.

"Lieutenant, you are an *infantry* commander. It was the duty of the tank commanders to *ask* you for support, if they felt they needed it."

"Yes, sir."

"Sergeant Dalin will be busted to private before mess tonight for insubordination and refusal to obey orders," Korva informed him.

"Sir, that seems a bit severe . . ."

"After mess tonight," Korva continued, ignoring him, "Private Dalin will be promoted to sergeant for displaying exceptional valor and initiative during the assault on the American outpost in Somalia. However, he will get to eat one meal with his old squad *before* we give it back to him."

"Yes, sir," Garth replied, smiling. "I understand, sir."

"Good," Korva replied. "Now, I'm afraid I have something of a more . . . personal nature to discuss with you."

Garth glanced down. He had been expecting this. Maria's continued outbursts were starting to reflect back on him. How could he explain his refusal to correct the situation to Korva when he did not understand it himself?

"A few days ago an American mercenary entered the camp with a ransom offer for one of our prisoners," Korva said. Garth looked up, surprise plain on his features.

"That's right," Korva said, misunderstanding Garth's surprise, "Maria. He offered us one hundred thousand American dollars for her release. I told him that we would not release her for less than a million. This man is due back with a counteroffer the day after tomorrow."

"I . . . see," Garth said.

"I also told him that we did not have her," Korva said, "but that we could possibly get her back. Garth, that woman was your prize for that job in Colombia. If you say that you want to keep her, I don't care if he offers us ten million— I'll tell him we could not get her back."

"No, sir," Garth replied quietly. "Accept the ransom offer if you feel it would be advantageous to do so."

"Lieutenant, you get your pick out of the next two batches of females we get in here. Unless, of course, there's an available female in camp already that you want to claim."

"No, sir. Thank you, sir."

Garth opened the door to his quarters cautiously. When nothing flew through the air at him, he stepped inside. Maria was looking out the only window in the small bedroom. She did not even turn around when Garth closed the door. Garth's eye followed her straight, black hair to her narrow waist . . .

"Why do you stay with these pigs, Garth?" she asked.

"They are not pigs," he replied. "They are my fellow warriors. The finest fighting men in two worlds."

Maria spat at the window.

"They are pigs," she insisted. "I had to watch a girl from my village get carried away to be raped yesterday by three of your 'fellow warriors.' "

"That is the lot of captives," Garth replied, shrugging.

"Unless they have the good fortune to be given to an officer as I was," Maria said bitingly. Again, Garth simply shrugged.

"Why have you not raped me, Garth?" she asked. "I saw one of the other officers' women the other day. Spoke with her, even. She could not believe that you had not . . . taken me."

"I . . . do not know," Garth answered. "I have not been so patient with other women who were given to me. I certainly have never let one throw my boots at me."

"Do you love me, Garth?"

"I . . . do not know."

"I think you do," she replied, turning from the window. "Garth, you are not like these pigs—you do not belong with them. Help me escape, come with me—my grandfather will reward you."

"Your grandfather would reward me by skinning me alive," Garth replied. He smiled sadly.

"Besides," he continued, "it is too late for that."

"What?" Maria said, fear growing in her eyes. "What do you mean?"

"You are going to be ransomed by your grandfather," Garth explained. "In a week or two the details will have been worked out and you will go home. I suggest you continue to wear my collar until then, however. It will make it less likely that you will be . . . accosted."

"Home?" Maria said, her voice trembling. Tears hung in her eyes.

"Yes," Garth replied. "I hope this . . . makes you happy." He turned and left his quarters, closing the door behind him.

Belevairn watched as the haul trucks rolled into the camp. Ramirez's three days had stretched into over a week, thanks to the trepidations of the Nicaraguan government. Belevairn himself had been forced to speak with one General Rodriguez to remove the problem. Now the Nicaraguan government had a signed contract with the Morvir.

In exchange for the free passage of military equipment, Nicaragua was entitled to call on any Morvan forces present in the camp for national defense. There were also limits placed on the number of troops and the amount of equipment the Morvir could have in the country. Belevairn was limited to two thousand troops and one armored group, such as he was now receiving.

This arrangement, while it had its drawbacks, solved Belevairn's immediate transport problems. He could now shuttle equipment through Nicaragua to Delgroth without too much difficulty. Only time would tell how much the Nicaraguan government would abuse the new status of the Morvir.

Ramirez's men began unloading the tank from the first haul truck. This Soviet T-55 had been the cheapest, cost-effective tank that Belevairn could find. A T-62 would have been much nicer, but that was far beyond Belevairn's current purchasing power.

Belevairn smiled beneath the gold mask. Not that Lord Erelvar would notice the difference. The T-55 would be more than powerful enough to tear Quarin down around his ears. It might be obsolete on Earth, but it would be a horror in the Northern Kingdoms.

The recalled tank crew began inspecting the T-55 as soon as Ramirez's men had finished unloading it. The empty haul truck pulled away as the truck carrying the armored personnel carrier took its place. The Soviet BTR-60 was also antique, dating back to 1958. The two Soviet ATT ammunition transports were somewhat newer. They had arrived under their own power, carrying supplies for the tank and the APC.

"You are pleased, Don Espantoso?" Ramirez asked.

"I am pleased, Ramirez," Belevairn replied. "I will be more pleased once my men have finished inspecting the equipment."

"*Sí*, of course."

"Here is your payment," Belevairn said as Captain Korva handed the arms dealer a canvas bag. "You may count it while my men finish their inspection."

"*Gracias*, Don Espantoso," Ramirez said, taking the bag. "It is a pleasure to do business with you."

"Likewise. How long would it take for you to locate another armored group exactly like this one?"

Ramirez looked up from counting his final payment. He had obviously not expected Belevairn's request.

"Another, my Don?" he asked. "But your contract with the government says you may possess only one such unit . . ."

"No, it says that I may only have one such unit in the country," Belevairn corrected. "I imagine that by the time you can locate and transport another, this one will no longer be in Nicaragua." The truth was that it would no longer be on the planet, but Belevairn saw fit to omit that detail.

"Ah. A month, perhaps less," Ramirez said, answering Belevairn's original question.

"Excellent. Begin at once."

"As you wish, Don Espantoso!" Ramirez was obviously excited at the possibility of another near million-dollar sale. Of course, it would not be possible this early, had it not been for the unexpected ransom Korva had arranged for that Colombian girl. That alone would cover almost half of the cost of this next purchase.

By the time Ramirez located the equipment, the latest arrivals would have completed their training period. Belevairn planned to send the armor and all of the men except Captain Korva's platoon through on the next exchange. It would not do to have the Nicaraguan government get *too* nervous about the force he had garrisoned here . . .

Chapter
-------- Sixteen -------------

THEY CROSSED THE border into Guatemala with what Alexander assured Steve was very little trouble. Steve, however, did not consider an hour spent searching the Jeep and five hundred dollars to each of the border guards very little trouble. Thank God they hadn't found the secret compartment.

The roads in Guatemala were actually *worse* than they had been in Mexico. Steve actually had to throw the Jeep into four-wheel drive at one point. He doubted that he was even averaging thirty miles per hour, let alone the forty-five that he had used in his estimates.

"Looks like I get to revise my timetable again," he grumbled.

"No shit," Alexander replied. "Hey, Robert, are the *federales* still with us?"

"Hmm?" Robert replied.

"Our tail? Did we lose him at the border?"

Robert glanced back out the rear window. After a moment he turned back.

"No, we didn't," he replied. "Green, four-door Chrysler—Mexican plates."

"Goddamn!" Alexander said. "This guy can't be in his jurisdiction anymore! Want to have a chat with him, Steve?"

"Exactly how do you propose to accomplish that?" Steve asked. "I doubt that he'll pull over if we flag him down, after all."

"Stop in Coatepeque," Alexander suggested. "Let's grab a bite to eat in some cantina. I'll slip out the back, circle around and see if I can get the drop on him."

"Uh, that sounds a bit dangerous," Robert noted. "Are you sure this is a good idea?"

"Kid, if I worried about whether or not approaching someone was a good idea, I'd *never* get any interviews."

"I guess not . . ." Robert agreed.

Agent Garcia watched the cantina from across the street. He had really hoped that the director in Tapachula would shitcan this case. Wilkinson was not a runner—God only knew what he *was*, but he was not a runner.

If it hadn't been for the kidnapping of Wilkinson's sister, that probably would have been exactly what happened. It wasn't the agency's job to investigate either crazy hoaxes or nutcases. Unless they involved drugs.

The suspects had entered the cantina almost twenty minutes ago. He had heard them order, and was continuing to hear just enough conversation to be certain that they were still in there. They were being a lot quieter than normal . . .

His passenger door opened. Garcia was standing outside the car with his weapon drawn before it even registered who was opening the door.

"Hi," the reporter said, ignoring the .38 aimed at his chest. He brandished his press card like a shield.

Estúpido! Garcia thought. Caught with his pants down like a damned rookie! If Alexander had been of a mind to kill him, Garcia would already be dead.

"I'm Richard Alexander with the *Clarion*," the reporter continued. "Care to answer a few questions?"

"Get in the car, Alexander," Garcia ordered.

"And if I don't? Are you going to shoot me down in the street? You and I both know you're a little out of your jurisdiction here, Agent . . . ?"

"Garcia," Garcia replied with a sigh, holstering his gun. "Please get in the car, Mister Alexander."

"Not until I see some credentials, pal."

Garcia slid his official identification across the roof of the car. He was going to get his butt in a sling for this.

Alexander examined the identification carefully.

"I stand corrected," Alexander said. "You're *way* out of your jurisdiction, Agent Garcia. DEA?"

"Do you have to announce it to the entire street, Alexander?"

"I suppose not," Alexander said. "Care to join us for breakfast?"

"I think not," Garcia replied.

"Really? Not even if I make you a deal?"

Garcia frowned suspiciously at Alexander. "What kind of a deal?"

"We'll try to answer some of your questions if you try to answer some of ours? It's got to be better than eating in the car."

"No," Garcia replied. "But if you would be willing to stop at the American Embassy in Guatemala City and make a statement . . . ?"

"That won't get *my* questions answered, now, will it?" Alexander said. "I don't think so. It's over coffee, or it's nothing."

"Very well," Garcia agreed. "But I will be recording the conversation."

"So will I, Agent Garcia," Alexander replied, smiling. "So will I."

Steve looked up as Alexander walked in with someone—presumably the guy who had been following them. That would at least explain the somewhat embarrassed expression Alexander's companion was trying to hide.

"Special Agent Manuel Garcia," the stranger said, "Drug Enforcement Agency."

"The DEA?" Steve exclaimed.

"Let's try to avoid calling too much attention to ourselves, Mister Wilkinson." Agent Garcia glanced around the cantina. Several patrons became intensely interested in their meals.

"Oh . . . yeah," Steve replied, also glancing around the cantina. "Why in the world are you following *me*?"

"Oh, no reason, Mister Wilkinson," Agent Garcia replied

sarcastically. "We get our kicks following honest, law-abiding citizens who sell one-pound gold ingots like Hershey bars, build secret compartments into Jeeps and smuggle weapons across international borders."

"Point taken," Steve replied. Agent Garcia sat down at the table.

"Be careful what you say, Steve," Alexander warned. "He's taping this."

"Are you aware of exactly how many laws you've broken?" Garcia asked. Steve blinked—why had Alexander brought this jerk in here?

"I was not aware that I had broken *any* laws," Steve lied. "All of those guns are legally registered. Ergo, there is nothing of an illegal nature in my 'secret compartment.' And, last I checked, selling gold wasn't illegal either."

"Have you reported that income to the IRS?"

"Uh . . ."

"I thought not. And where did you *get* that gold, Mister Wilkinson? Selling it is not illegal, but I'll bet that you didn't obtain it legally."

"Actually, I believe that it *was* obtained legally."

"Even if you found it lying in a bag, it is not legally yours until it has been surrendered to the authorities."

"Okay, so what?" Steve said, his voice rising. "In case you haven't noticed, buddy, we're not *in* the good old U.S. of A. now, are we?"

"No, we're not, Mister Wilkinson."

"So, unless I am grossly mistaken, you are *way* out of your jurisdiction."

"That is correct."

"Good, so get lost."

"Were you involved in a gun battle at Great Serpent Mound in Ohio, Mister Wilkinson?"

"How . . . ? No, I was not."

"That's interesting, considering that Mister Alexander and Mister Davenport *were* there that night, I believe."

"We were covering a story," Alexander objected.

"On whom?"

"That's confidential . . ."

"Hold it, Dick," Steve interrupted. "Robert, go out to the Jeep and get your pictures from the Mound."

"But . . ."

"Do it," Steve said. "The only way we're going to get supercop here off our backs is to spill it all."

"Steve," Alexander said, "you're going to get yourself in a lot of trouble . . ."

"I doubt it," Steve replied. "I don't expect to survive that long, Dick. And if I do make it back to the States, I'll worry about it then. But I want that damned tape turned off."

"Do you really expect me to *believe* this crap?" Garcia said once Wilkinson had finished his story. For over an hour he had listened while Wilkinson spilled his guts. And, in spite of the fact that he had turned the recorder on the table off, he had it all on tape.

"No," Wilkinson replied, "as a matter of fact I don't. I do expect you to believe that *I* believe it, however. I am not a drug runner, I am not engaged in any illicit activities. I am simply going to go down to Nicaragua and kill this monster."

"And save the world," Garcia added.

"Right."

"You're certifiable," the DEA agent said.

"I don't doubt that," Wilkinson agreed.

Garcia clandestinely switched off his hidden recorder.

"Well, Mister Wilkinson," he said, leaning back in his chair, "off the record, between you, me and the fencepost?"

"Yes?"

"I *do* believe you."

Wilkinson straightened in his chair.

"You do?" he said.

"Yes, I do. But not because of anything you've told me."

"Then . . . what?"

"I was there when that . . . angel appeared to you," Garcia replied. "I've seen some smooth cons in my time, but I've never seen anyone who could pull something like that off. Also, I've heard of the Morvir before."

"What! How?"

"There's a mercenary group in Nicaragua," Garcia explained. "They call themselves the Morvir—do a lot of work for the drug cartels."

"Shit!" Wilkinson hissed. "How many?"

"A lot. They're one of the most feared groups of mercenaries in this part of the world."

"I'll bet. That's *bad* news."

"And there's one other thing . . ."

"What?"

"Three days ago," Garcia began, "according to over half a dozen witnesses, one Tamara Wilkinson was abducted from her home by someone riding a flying horse."

Wilkinson sat back in his chair, face pale. For a moment he said nothing.

"T-Tam?" Wilkinson finally said, his voice shaking. "Oh, my god, not Tam."

"I'm afraid so," Garcia said. "I think you should call home, kid."

Steve returned the phone to its cradle. His shoulder fell against the wall by the phone as he stared through the phone into space.

"Is it true?" Alexander asked.

Garcia had left over an hour ago. It had taken almost that long for Steve to get through to his parents. Belevairn had Tam—that son of a bitch had his sister.

"Steve!" Alexander said, shaking Steve's shoulder. "Is it true?"

"Yes," Steve replied quietly, "it's true."

"What are you going to do?" Alexander asked.

Steve just turned and looked at Alexander. He glanced at Robert and then back to Alexander.

"Do?" he asked, anger slowly replacing shock. "Whatever I *have* to do!"

Tammy opened her eyes as the stone door swung open. Day four. If she ever got back home alive, she would never complain about being grounded again. Not after four days of imprisonment in this empty, stone room.

Rosita left the wash basin and Tammy's breakfast, returning Tammy's gaze with an odd, resigned expression. Tammy
wondered what was wrong as she was sealed in to perform
her morning ritual. She began to wash away the night's
perspiration. With a start she realized that the water in the
basin was perfumed. After washing, she put on the clean
dress that Rosita had brought.

Breakfast was different as well this morning. Instead of
the usual overabundance of sausage, eggs and tortillas,
there was a small bowl of fruit and a couple of tortillas.
Nothing else. She remembered Rosita's odd expression.
Something strange was going on here.

Tammy ate slowly. Although the bowl of fruit was small,
it filled her. She doubted that it would keep her that way
until lunch, however. Tammy sat on her bed and waited for
her captors to come clean away her morning dishes with a
strange feeling of apprehension.

Soon, the door swung open again and Rosita entered to
collect the wash basin and the dishes. She said nothing, but
again her eyes met Tammy's with a hollow, mournful look
that made Tammy's stomach tighten. What was going on?
Rosita left, and Tammy was sealed in to await whatever
plans they had for her.

The morning passed slowly—even more slowly than the
other mornings had. Tammy paced back and forth across
her small cell as the minutes crawled past. Her stomach
began to growl its emptiness and she was certain that lunch
had been skipped. It seemed like an entire day had passed
since breakfast.

She tried to sit in the chair, but was soon up and pacing
again. Lying on her bed was no better. She tossed and
turned and was soon back on her feet. She was up pacing
when the door opened again.

Tammy whirled, her heart racing. Was she going to be
given to one of the officers as Rosita had mentioned? Was
that why they were perfuming her and underfeeding her?

But it was just Rosita, bringing lunch. Lunch was even
more meager than breakfast had been. A bowl of broth

and a cup of water. Rosita set it on the table. Her eyes met Tammy's with the same sorrowful expression before she left.

Tammy sat down at the table with the resignation of someone facing her last meal. Chicken broth. Yummy. Her stomach growled—apparently it thought the broth sounded good. She raised a spoonful of it to her mouth.

The broth *was* good. It was spiced and salty and tasted wonderful. Unfortunately, this would stay with her even less time than the fruit had. What were they doing to her?

She had eaten just over half the bowl of broth when she began to feel strange—numb. She dropped the spoon into the bowl of broth. Her vision went out of focus slightly, and it took an effort to bring her eyes back under control. She felt dizzy.

Drugs, she thought. She pushed the bowl of broth away, sloshing some of it onto the table without noticing. The bastards had drugged her.

She tried to stand but collapsed back into the chair when the room began to tilt and sway around her. A tingly numbness spread across her body. It was not an unpleasant sensation, but the fear that rose in her was anything but pleasant. What were they going to do to her?

She tried to stand again, but instead fell to the floor. What was she going to do? She had to get away before they came for her. The room swam around her—the floor refused to remain still so that she could get to her feet.

She heard the sound of stone grinding against stone and knew that the door to her cell was being opened. They were coming for her. She managed to get to her hands and knees, but the room rocked so wildly that she could get no further.

Hands grabbed her by the upper arms and she was lifted up between two guards. She tried to struggle, but the drugs had robbed her of all her strength. Someone wearing a hawk mask and a dress made of feathers stood in front of her. Tammy tried to scream but all that came out was a weak whimper.

The man in the hawk mask cut away her dress, leaving

her naked. Then a girl came forward to wash her. Tammy forced her eyes to focus on the girl—Rosita. She was crying, silently, as she washed Tammy with more of the perfumed water.

Tammy tried to speak, but her tongue felt too large for her mouth and her words were slurred.

"I'ss a'right," Tammy mumbled to Rosita. "I un . . . un'er . . . stan'. Not . . . your . . . fault . . ."

Rosita pulled another, thinner, dress over Tammy's head. Tammy noticed that it was white as Rosita helped Tammy get her arms through the sleeves. She giggled.

"Here comes'a bride," she sang weakly, still giggling.

Belevairn watched as the guard carried Tamara Wilkinson up the steps to the top of the temple. Seven women waited with him, drugged and prepared for sacrifice. In a few moments it would be noon, and time to begin.

Ever since Wilkinson had stopped at that church, Belevairn had been unable to locate him. That made it difficult to inform Wilkinson that he had Tamara. But Tamara, with Belevairn's help, could make that contact for him.

The *kaivir* manacled Tamara upright between the two pillars that Belevairn had restored atop the pyramid shortly after excavating it. He stepped up to her, grabbed her by the jaw and forced a cup to her lips. She swallowed a sip of the liquid within and he took the cup away.

The noonday sun struck the altar. It was time to begin . . .

Tammy watched, dazed and horrified, as her captor drove a knife into the chest of the woman they had laid across the altar. Her almost empty stomach tightened as she watched him pull the woman's heart from her chest and throw it onto the fire. Tammy's scream emerged as nothing more than a whimper. Another woman was laid across the altar. Tammy closed her eyes and cried.

The cries from the altar stopped. Tammy had sagged between the pillars, only the manacles preventing her from collapsing. She trembled—would they kill her now?

She felt something sticky and warm touch her forehead. Her eyes opened to see the man in the gold mask drawing the flat of his bloody knife across her forehead. She whimpered and tried to turn away, but he caught her by the jaw and forced a cup to her lips.

With horror she realized that the warm, salty liquid in the cup was the blood of the women who had just been killed. She jerked free of his grip and spat the blood from her mouth. He grabbed her again and again forced the cup to her lips. Tammy closed her mouth tightly.

Someone pinched her nose shut, and she involuntarily opened her mouth to breathe. A mouthful of warm, sticky blood flowed past her lips, making her gag. Then her mouth, too, was forced shut.

Starved for air, she had no choice but to swallow. They then released her and she breathed in deep, shuddering sobs. The taste of the blood was strong in her mouth, making her stomach churn. Tears ran down her face.

Gloved hands pressed firmly against the sides of her face, lifting her gaze to meet the red glow behind the eyes of the golden mask. That light seemed to suffuse her with a cold heat, a tingling that started at her forehead and travelled down her back and out into her arms. The red glow of the eyes enveloped her, shutting out the world.

Think of your brother, a voice whispered in her mind. *Think of Steven.*

An image formed in the red light that surrounded her. Far beneath her, a truck drove along a poorly paved road through the jungle. Somehow, she knew that Steve was in that truck.

With that realization she felt herself moving downward, toward the truck. It was dull green, like an Army truck. There were two men in the front seat. She moved closer . . .

Steve shouted and hit the brakes, skidding the truck to a stop.

"Shit!" Alexander shouted. "What is it?"

Steve didn't quite hear him. The feeling of Tam's . . .

presence overwhelmed all of his senses. She was afraid, terrified. He could actually see her face, dimly, streaked with tears.

Steve, he heard her voice faintly in his mind, *help me. Please, help me.*

"Tam?" he whispered. Then he felt another presence, a darker presence behind Tam—Belevairn. Tam's presence was pushed to the back as the sorcerer moved to the forefront. Then it passed as quickly as it had begun and Steve was back in the driver's seat of the Jeep. Alexander was shaking him.

"Steve!" he shouted. "Snap out of it, man!"

"I'm . . . okay," Steve replied. "I'm okay, it's all right."

"What the *hell* happened?"

"We've got to find a phone," was the only answer Steve gave.

Belevairn released the Power and stepped back. Tamara Wilkinson sagged between the pillars, unconscious. Belevairn had been successful, had made contact with Wilkinson. Now it was just a matter of time before Wilkinson made it to a telephone to use the number that Belevairn had carefully implanted in his mind.

"Take her back to her cell," Belevairn ordered. "See that she is bathed. And have her attendant remain in the room with her until she awakens."

"Yes, Dread Lord," the *kaivir* replied.

Belevairn smiled behind the mask. It was almost another week until the new moon—until the next exchange. That would be a great moment for him. The return of a thousand trained troops, the first armored group *and* the Dreamer, alive. Daryna would be very, very pleased with him . . .

Chapter
-------- **Seventeen** -------------

"THIS IS GOING to be your last mission, Lieutenant Garth," Korva informed him. "We have hired your platoon out to a radical subfaction of the PLO. Your job will be to destroy an Israeli armored patrol in the West Bank."

"In Israel?"

"Yes. They specifically requested your platoon," Korva said. "Rewards of that job in Somalia."

"I only have one question," Garth said.

"Yes?"

"How the hell do we get out? Once we have destroyed that patrol, the Israelis are going to tighten the lid on that area down so tight that a fly won't be able to get out of there."

"Good point. Fortunately, the Middle East is the one place on this world where we can pass for natives."

"Except that none of us speak any of the local languages."

"You shouldn't have to stick around that long," Korva replied. "Blend in with the locals long enough to get in touch with our PLO contacts. From that point, they should be able to get you to the transport site."

"I don't like having to depend on someone other than Morvir to get my platoon out of there."

"I understand," Korva agreed. "Unfortunately, it cannot be helped on this mission."

"Very well," Garth said. "However, I will want maps of the area so that I can get my men to that transport site on my own if this subfaction drops the ball."

"Agreed."

"Would it also be possible for my sergeants and I to have language transfers from the local area?"

"Out of the question," Korva replied. "The *kaivir* would probably have to make a dozen sacrifices for each transfer. One such transfer is out of the question, let alone seven."

Garth sighed. He didn't like this mission. The odds were very poor indeed. The mission itself should be relatively simple. Getting out of the area afterwards was almost undoubtedly going to become *his* problem.

"You could refuse the mission," Korva noted. "We have turned down assignments before. We have no goals to accomplish here except to train our men. Is it your opinion that your platoon will be lost?"

"Only if this subfaction fails in assisting us out of the country," Garth replied. "Even then, I would not expect to lose the entire platoon."

"Give me a casualty estimate, Garth," Korva pressed. "How much of your platoon would you expect to lose in that case?"

"Half to three-quarters, sir."

"Do you wish to refuse the mission?"

"That is your decision, sir," Garth replied. "My men and I will go where we are sent."

"Very well," Korva said, smiling. "You leave tonight."

Mike Williams waited with his squad five miles outside the Morvir camp. The exchange was to take place at noon, and it was very close to that now. He had two of his men hidden in the jungle on each side of the road.

If the Morvir tried anything, that precaution would probably have little effect. All they had to do was send out two squads in addition to the squad that was supposed to meet him, and they could have the money without surrendering the girl. If they brought some of those monkey-men with them, those would be on Williams's flank groups before they even realized it.

He heard an engine in the distance. It was going down. Williams lit a cigarette. Now they would find out how smart the Morvir were. If they were smart, they would simply surrender the girl and take the money to avoid antagonizing Don Estefan any further. If they weren't . . . Williams and his men were dead meat.

A canvas-backed truck, much like Williams's, pulled into sight and stopped about a hundred feet away. The Morvir squad filed out of the back, taking position in plain sight. So far, so good.

Two people got out of the truck, a man and a woman. The driver remained behind the wheel. With a deep breath, Williams picked up the gym bag and began walking toward the Morvir. The guy with the girl also began walking toward him. It was definitely Maria. So far, so good.

Williams and the Morvir officer met between the two squads.

"Do you have the money?" the Morvir asked.

"Right here," Williams replied, holding out the gym bag. "Wanna count it?"

"Open the bag, please."

Williams smiled. There was no denying that the Morvir were good. He knelt down and opened the gym bag before standing and stepping back from it. As the Morvir began to kneel to inspect it, the sounds of movement reached them from the jungle.

Williams's four men stepped from the jungle, their hands in the air. Behind them, a full squad of Morvir emerged from each side of the road. Shit!

"Care to explain this?" the Morvir officer said, standing back up.

Williams shrugged.

"Just takin' precautions," he said. "Didn't want an ambush to ruin my day."

"Neither did I," the Morvir replied. "There is yet another squad covering us on each side of the road. Are there any more of your men in the jungle?"

Williams blinked—five squads? He was against a full platoon here with just one fucking squad!

"Nope," he replied, hiding his unease.

"One thing you should know about the Morvir is that we always honor our contracts, Mister Williams," the officer said. "If everything else is in order, you will be allowed to leave here with the woman."

"Glad ta hear it," Williams replied, smiling. *Real* glad to hear it!

The Morvir officer knelt and counted the money—all three hundred thousand of it. After what seemed to be hours later, he zipped the bag shut and rose to his feet.

"Everything seems to be in order," he said, nodding to indicate Maria. "She's all yours, Mister Williams. It has been a pleasure doing business with you."

"Right," Williams replied. "Let's go, Maria. Your grampa's waitin' to see ya."

"You will please wait here while we leave with the money," the Morvir said. "Once we have gone, you will be allowed to depart as well."

"Sure," Williams agreed. "Whatever you say." He watched as the original squad climbed into their truck and left, leaving the two flanking the sides of the road watching. After giving the truck a five-minute lead, the two squads guarding them retreated back into the jungle and vanished. Williams breathed a sigh of relief.

"Let's get the *hell* out of here!" he ordered. His men were all too quick to comply. Now Don Estefan could finish assembling the attack force. It would be nice to take these arrogant bastards down a peg or two . . .

"And you are *certain*," Garth asked, "that Israeli intelligence does not know the location of your . . . headquarters?"

The so-called headquarters consisted of the cellar of a burned-out home a few miles east of Yattah. Garth imagined that next week this splinter group would have found themselves another headquarters. That was the only way a group of this nature could survive here. How they had managed to raise the money to hire Garth's platoon and pay for transport into and out of the West Bank was beyond him.

"They have no idea where we are," Amar assured him. "If they did, we are dead men."

"Why do you want us to return here after the mission?" Garth asked. "Why not just tell us where the helicopter is going to be and what time to meet it? There is less risk of us leading the Israelis back to you that way."

"We will not know where or when, until tonight," Amar replied. "You come back to find out. Maybe stay here until it arrives."

"Amar," Garth said, "the Israelis are going to be searching this area with a sieve after we hit that patrol. Your headquarters will be discovered within a few hours of our assault."

"We will know by time you return," Amar said. "We abandon this place then."

Garth leaned back in the chair and studied Amar. He did not like this—did not like it at all. If the smallest thing went wrong, Garth's platoon could be stranded in the West Bank. Still, it was too late to blow the mission now.

"All right, then," he continued. "How reliable is your information on this patrol?"

Garth waited near the exit of the small defile they had chosen as the site to ambush the Israeli patrol as it headed into Yattah. The sun was just setting—they were late, if Amar's information was to be trusted.

The faint sound of diesel engines reached him. Garth listened carefully, but it was impossible to tell how many vehicles were approaching. This was going to much more difficult than that convoy in Costa Rica. According to Amar's information, they would be facing three armored personnel carriers, fully loaded with Israeli troops. Garth would be outnumbered by about fifty percent to begin with. If the Israelis deserved the reputation they had, Garth's platoon had best kill at least half of them in the initial assault.

Garth saw the headlights of the first APC as it entered the shallow defile. Two of his squads were foxholed in at the top of that defile on either side. Their job was to disable the APC's. Garth with Dalin's squad and Wyrth's squad waited at the exit to the defile. Bryn's squad was foxholed back at the entrance.

Amar's information had been correct. Three APC's entered the defile. Any moment now . . .

Six rocket launchers fired almost in unison. Even before the impact, Garth could see men leaping from the APC's. Garth would have thought it impossible for anyone but Morvir to react that quickly.

The explosion was the signal for Garth's men to charge. As they ran up the road, the two lead squads were firing on the remains of the convoy, trying to pin down the Israeli soldiers. The Israelis were returning fire. Garth watched one Morvir fall into the defile. Damn! He had hoped the two squads atop the defile could avoid taking any casualties.

The Israelis saw them advancing before the Morvir could distinguish any targets amid the burning wreckage. A man next to Garth went down. Garth dropped to one knee and fired a grenade into the convoy. Several others did the same.

The explosions gave them the cover they needed to close on the convoy. The charge degenerated into individual gun battles amid the burning wrecks—in a few instances the Morvir were forced into hand-to-hand combat. A burning Israeli soldier jumped down on Garth from the middle APC. Garth caught him on the chin with the butt of his AK-47 and sidestepped from beneath the man as he fell. Garth then fired a single round into the prone soldier. Admirable . . .

Another Israeli climbed atop the rear APC and opened fire with the burning vehicle's machine gun. Half a dozen Morvir atop the defile were cut down before someone managed to shoot him down. A grenade launcher insured that no other soldier would try that tactic . . .

A bullet cracked past Garth's ear. He whirled around in time to see one of his men gun down the Israeli who had fired on him. Garth looked around for another opponent— there were none. Other men from his platoon were also searching for the enemy. It was over.

"Tend to the wounded," Garth ordered. "Throw our dead onto the fire and let's get *out* of here!" He would count casualties back at Amar's headquarters. Now, he had to get out of here before this place was crawling with soldiers.

No one challenged the Morvir as they approached the burned-out house. Garth didn't like this—Amar's men should have hailed them by now.

The house was empty. No sentries guarded the entrance to the cellar. Garth opened the trap door, already knowing what he would see.

The cellar was abandoned. Only tracks in the dust showed that anyone had been here since the house was burned.

"Sergeant Dalin," Garth ordered, "take the unwounded members of your squad and post sentries throughout the house."

"Yes, sir."

Garth studied what was left of his platoon. He had suffered nine fatalities during the attack on the patrol, mostly among the squads that had been posted atop the defile.

Eleven more were seriously wounded. Most of the wounded were from the squads that had penetrated the convoy after the initial assault. Eight of the wounded would probably be able to fight. The other three were unconscious or delirious.

"Take these men aside and kill them," Garth said, pointing out the three critically injured. "Strip their gear."

Garth walked over to Sergeant Wyrth. The sergeant had taken a bullet to the thigh. It had missed the bone, but would make it impossible for Wyrth to march with the platoon.

"Sergeant Wyrth?"

Wyrth looked up at Garth, his expression solemn. The sergeant knew what was coming.

"I'm leaving the wounded here with you," he told Wyrth. "The Israelis will probably find you before morning. Your mission is to hold them off as long as you can from here while the rest of the platoon retreats."

"Yes, sir," Wyrth replied. "We won't let you down, sir."

"I know that," Garth said, placing a hand on the man's shoulder. "Die well, Sergeant. Take as many of these bastards back to the Mistress with you as you can."

"We'll give them hell, sir," Wyrth replied, smiling.

Garth turned to his remaining twenty-two men. Almost half of them were lightly wounded. They could all keep pace with the platoon, though.

"The rest of you prepare for march," Garth ordered. "Leave all heavy assault equipment behind with the wounded. I want each man carrying his rifle, and only as many grenades as will fit on his gunbelt. Fill your packs with rations, water and nothing else. These men won't need food or much water. Sergeant Bryn?"

"Yes, sir?"

"When your men are ready, go up and relieve Sergeant Dalin's squad so that they can prepare as well. You men have five minutes in which to be ready."

Garth left the cellar, pulling out his field satellite phone. He had a call to make . . .

Korva looked up from his paperwork when the satellite link rang. There was only one reason for anyone to be calling him on that. He unfolded the compact phone. He had a good idea who it was.

"Korva here," he said in Morvan.

"Lieutenant Garth here, sir," answered the expected voice.

"What is your situation, Lieutenant?"

"We have been betrayed, sir," Garth replied. "There is no transport out."

"The mission?"

"Accomplished. Twelve fatalities, eight wounded."

"Tell me what to do, Lieutenant," Korva said.

"I am leaving the wounded to hold the Israelis while the rest of my platoon retreats east from Yattah. I am going to need helicopter transport for twenty-three men."

"You may have to hold out for a day or two."

"I understand, sir."

"Very good. Proceed as planned. Report back when you find a place to hold out. Good luck, Lieutenant."

"Yes, sir. Thank you, sir. Garth out."

Korva folded the satellite phone shut. Betrayed? Amar and his little band of renegades would pay dearly for this! But first, he had to get those men out of there.

Garth snapped the satellite link closed. Sergeant Bryn's men were emerging to relieve Dalin. Garth glanced at his watch. Two minutes—not bad. That would speed up their departure.

Garth repeated his orders to Sergeant Dalin. He wanted to get out of here in the next few minutes. The attack on the patrol had occurred almost an hour ago. It might be a matter of minutes before this place was found. That was assuming that Amar hadn't already told the Israelis where to look.

Wyrth looked out across the starlit night. Garth had left about an hour ago, and a thin sliver of moon now hung in the sky. Less than a week, and he would have been home again.

He smiled. As it turned out, Wyrth would beat Garth home, and maybe he could take enough of the Israelis with him to cause a stir. Perhaps Daryna would even pluck him from among the dead to become one of the Dread Lords. Not likely, but a man could dream . . .

"Sergeant," Darek whispered. Wyrth looked into the night. A pair of headlights was approaching. A searchlight swept the ruins. Wyrth ducked behind a wall.

"It begins," he said.

It was just a Jeep, probably with half a dozen or so Israeli soldiers on board. Nothing the Morvir couldn't handle.

"Rifles only," he ordered. "Let's keep the next group in the dark about what we've got." He waited as his orders were whispered among the troops. The Jeep approached the house, playing its floodlight over the ruins. About a hundred feet away it stopped, and four soldiers got out to approach on foot. The driver stayed in the Jeep. Wyrth sighted on him.

He fired a single shot through the windshield. At his signal, his men also opened fire on the approaching troops. In a few seconds the entire patrol had been killed.

"Darek, get that Jeep out of sight," Wyrth ordered.

"Yes, sir." Darek ran out to the Jeep, dumped the driver onto the ground and pulled the Jeep around behind the house, killing the lights.

Wyrth toyed with the idea of leaving in the Jeep, but eight wounded men would not get far in this country. Besides, Lieutenant Garth was counting on them to convince the Israelis that his squad, and the dead that had been left behind, were all there was to find.

"Look alive, men!" he ordered. "They'll be all over us in a few minutes!"

The Israelis did not disappoint them. Less than fifteen minutes later, Wyrth spied figures stealthily approaching the house.

"Prepare to fire," Wyrth whispered. His order was relayed among the men. Wyrth sighted on one figure. The Israelis were probably using night scopes.

He let his target gain about another twenty feet before he opened fire. This time, the enemy was able to return fire. Wyrth heard a cry as one of his men was hit.

Wyrth fired his grenade launcher into an area where the return fire seemed especially heavy. He was rewarded with the flying bodies of four Israelis. The enemy withdrew.

"Listen for air support!" Wyrth ordered, no longer concerned if the enemy heard him. He was speaking mostly in Morvan anyway. "We might be able to nail a helicopter!"

Each man waited, straining to hear the sound of jet engines or helicopter rotors. Time passed—ten, twenty minutes. It wasn't a helicopter or a jet that Wyrth heard next, though. It was a diesel engine. The sound of tracks on gravel followed it.

"Armor!" Wyrth shouted. "Darek, give me the night glasses."

Wyrth scanned in the direction of the sound, desperately searching for the vehicle producing it. If the Israelis had brought in a tank, they could be in big trouble. He spotted the tank as it topped a nearby rise. It stopped atop the rise.

"Goddamn!" Wyrth shouted. "They've got an M-1! Everyone grab a launcher! We've got to blow that thing, fast!"

Wyrth sighted on the tank, thanking Daryna that the rocket launchers had night scopes. Theoretically, the launchers had enough range to reach the tank. Theoretically.

Darek fired next to him. Wyrth watched as his rocket dropped to detonate far below the tank. Damn! Wyrth squeezed off his own rocket. Before it had crossed half the distance, he knew it was too high. He reached for his last launcher, knowing he would probably not have time to use it.

Darek fired again, along with two other men. Darek's rocket and one other homed in, dead on target. The third detonated somewhere to the left of the M-1 while the first two struck right under the turret. The tank was obscured in the explosion. Wyrth prayed that the rockets had disabled it.

Once the initial blast had cleared, Wyrth could see the M-1, burning atop the rise. He breathed a sigh of relief. He did *not* want to know how close that tank crew had come to firing on their position.

For some time, they saw no further activity. Wyrth smiled—he knew better than that. The Israelis were all out of range, probably waiting for the helicopters.

"I did my best, Lieutenant," Wyrth muttered. "I hope you've made it clear."

Almost twenty minutes passed before Wyrth heard the beat of the helicopter engines. Now they would die, but they had bought Garth another hour by holding their position.

"Launchers ready!" Wyrth ordered. "All men target the lead helicopter! Fire at will after I fire a starburst!" This was probably not going to work, but it was worth a try . . .

He waited, listening carefully. When he thought that the helicopters might be in range, Wyrth fired the starburst flare straight up. Hopefully it would provide enough light for the launchers . . .

Seconds after he fired, six rocket trails launched into the air. Wyrth could see the helicopters now—three flying in staggered formation. One rocket missed . . . and another. The lead helicopter fired a missile—time to die. The other two helicopters fired immediately after the leader.

Wyrth did not take his eyes from the rocket trails. Just before the enemy missiles struck their position, he saw the lead helicopter hit by one of the rockets. Wyrth smiled— not bad for eight wounded men.

It was his last thought.

Major David ben Eliahu watched as the forensics crew dug through the rubble of the terrorist holdout. So far, only eleven bodies had been found, three of those dead before the battle had even begun.

"That's all, sir," the head of the forensics team reported. "Eleven bodies."

"Impossible," ben Eliahu protested. "Twenty men could not have destroyed that patrol."

"With all due respect, sir, I wouldn't have thought that eight could have put up the fight that these men did."

Major ben Eliahu frowned. That was true enough. Fifteen top men dead plus that many more wounded, an M-1 and a Cobra destroyed. All by eight men in a ruined house. Still, something just did not seem right to him . . .

"I want a concentric search from this location for the rest of the night," he ordered.

The sun slowly sank toward the horizon. Garth took another swallow from his canteen. Conserving water was not a concern—the helicopter would be here tonight. He trusted Korva's word a lot further than he had ever trusted Amar's. If Korva said the helicopter would be here tonight, it would be if the captain had to fly it in himself.

They had marched all night, pausing long enough to watch the two firefights to the west. Wyrth had apparently done quite well. They had thought him defeated after the first battle. Then the second had begun and Wyrth had apparently bagged himself a helicopter, or some other aircraft. Garth would recommend him for a posthumous commendation when he made it back to Nicaragua. Wyrth had certainly upheld the honor of the Morvir in this world.

Soon, the sun sank below the horizon and the temperature began to drop. Good. Now they no longer had to fear discovery by satellite. It was time to get out from under cover and proceed to the transport site . . .

Chapter
-------- Eighteen ------------

ALEXANDER PULLED INTO Escuintla a couple of hours after Steve's . . . attack. From what the kid had said, the alien sorcerer had contacted him through his sister's mind— to give him a phone number, of all things.

Alexander glanced in the rear-view mirror. Steve was stretched out in the back seat. The incident had really shaken the kid up. Alexander hoped he was going to be okay. Of course, he'd made it through worse already . . .

"We're here, Steve," he said. Steve sat up, groaning a little at the effort in the moving Jeep.

"I've been thinking," he said, "let's push on into Guatemala City. That way we can check into a real hotel with a phone and base our operation out of there for now."

"Operation?"

"Yes," Steve replied. "We're going to get my sister back."

"How?"

"I'll have a better idea of that after I've talked with Belevairn."

"I cannot thank you enough for the safe return of my granddaughter, Mister Williams," Don Estefan said. "Ask anything of me, and it is yours."

"That's right generous of you, Don Estefan," Williams said. "I have two things in mind that I think you'll approve of."

"Name them," Estefan replied.

"I want some new equipment for my men," Williams said, handing a list across the desk. "Stuff that we'll be needin' for that assault on the Morvir camp."

"Of course," Estefan agreed, scanning the list. "What else?"

"I want to be in on the plannin' of that attack," Williams said. "I've been there. So far as I know, I'm the only merc that has, in fact. I want to have input on that as your liaison to the commander."

"Done. You want . . . nothing else, *señor*?"

"Nope. I told you when I hired on with you, Don, that, except for expenses and pay for my men, all I wanted was a crack at the Morvir."

"That you shall certainly have," Estefan agreed. "Will you also handle the negotiations with this . . . Colonel Anderson for me?"

Colonel Anderson was the one man Williams knew of who could probably raise a force large enough to tackle the Morvir camp. Mind you, he would just about have to hire every merc in the world to do it, but he could probably do it if he had the money. Don Estefan was supplying that.

"Be happy to," Williams replied.

"*Bien!* I have booked a flight for two to Guatemala, if you want to take one of your men. Colonel Anderson is waiting to meet my representative at the Guatemala Hilton."

"When do I leave?"

"In four hours."

"What about the monkey?" Williams asked.

"What about it?" Don Estefan asked, looking at Williams intently.

"If possible, it might be good for Anderson to see it," Williams said. "It would help my credibility when I warn him about them."

"*Sí*, I understand," Estefan replied, nodding. "Will a videotape be sufficient?"

"Yeah, that should do."

Steve sighed as he dropped the luggage on the floor and collapsed onto the bed in his room of the suite. A real bed with a *real* mattress. However, before he could enjoy his one stay in a luxury hotel, he had a phone call to make.

He got up and went out into the sitting room of the suite. Robert just about had the tap hooked into the suite's telephone. Steve wondered if the photographer had ever considered going to work for the CIA. He certainly seemed to enjoy this kind of thing.

"Ready to tape?" he asked. Alexander wanted a taped record of his telephone conversation with Belevairn and Steve thought that sounded like a good idea, too.

"Just about," Robert said, connecting an alligator clip into the phone's wiring.

"There," the photographer said, "that should have it. Ready to call?"

"Yep," Steve said, picking up the phone. He dialed the operator.

"Guatemala Hilton," answered the operator.

"This is Steve Wilkinson in room twelve-oh-three," Steve said. That was another advantage of calling from the hotel. English-speaking operators.

"I need to make an international call to a mobile unit," he continued. He gave the operator the number and waited. These international calls seemed to take forever. Finally, Steve heard the ring at the other end.

"Korva here," a male voice said. Steve blinked in surprise. He was speaking in Morvan.

"I need to speak with Lord Belevairn," Steve said, also in Morvan.

"Master Wilkinson?"

"That is correct."

"I was told to expect your call. Hold on a moment."

Great, Steve thought. *You can't even call a Dread Lord without getting put on hold.*

"Greetings, Master Wilkinson." The rasp of Belevairn's voice was even worse over long distance. "I take it you received my message?"

"I wouldn't be calling if I hadn't, now would I?" Steve replied, switching to English. "Do you mind if we don't speak Morvan? It gives me one hell of a headache. Probably something to do with how I learned it." Not to mention that a conversation in Morvan would be useless on tape.

"Not at all," Belevairn agreed, also switching to English.

"She had best be all right, Belevairn," Steve said, "or I'll make sure you burn real slow."

"She is quite well, I assure you."

"Yeah, well your assurances don't mean a whole lot to me," Steve retorted. "I want to talk to her."

"That is not possible at this time."

"Why not?"

"She is still recovering from the ritual," Belevairn replied. "She will likely sleep until morning."

That sounded reasonable. Now that Steve's own version of Belevairn had been evicted, he had a more difficult time accessing the information from Belevairn's sorcerous training.

"Well, then," Steve said, "I guess I will call you back in the morning."

"Wait!"

"What?"

"Do you not wish to know the details of the exchange?"

"I haven't decided how the exchange is going to work yet," Steve replied.

"*You* haven't decided?" Belevairn said. "As I recall, I have *your* sister. We will make the exchange . . ."

"No, Belevairn," Steve interrupted, "we won't. We do this my way, or we don't do it at all, and you can take my sister back to Daryna instead of me. Won't she be pleased with that?"

"I . . . see."

"Good. Don't worry, I will give you whatever oaths you want to insure my cooperation. I just want to make certain that my sister *is* released and on her way home *before* I surrender to you. I will call you at ten tomorrow."

"Very well," Belevairn agreed. Steve could almost feel the Dread Lord's anger over the telephone. It was obvious that Belevairn had not expected to be dictated to when he held the upper hand.

"Oh, and Lord Belevairn?"

"Yes, *Master* Wilkinson?"

"Answer the phone yourself, this time. I hate being on hold."

Mike Williams paid the cabbie and stepped out in front of the Guatemala Hilton. He was moving up in the world. His new affiliation with Don Estefan was proving to be quite profitable indeed.

He walked into the lobby and verified that his reserved room was waiting for him. He had opted not to bring anyone with him. No need for it, really, and it saved the Don a little money.

He checked into his single room and deposited his bags in the closet. He picked up the phone and dialed Anderson's room. The phone rang once.

"Hello?"

"Colonel Anderson?" Williams asked. "This is Lieutenant Williams." A promotion seemed in order, now that he was serving as Don Estefan's liaison officer.

"Yes?" The colonel was playing it cool. Williams couldn't blame him, really.

"I'm here on behalf of Julio Estefan to negotiate a service contract. When would be convenient for us to meet?"

"I'm free now, Lieutenant," Anderson replied. "Care to meet me in the bar for a drink?"

"Excellent, sir. I'm wearing civvies—a short-sleeved cotton print with gray slacks."

"I'll look for you."

"Very good, sir." Williams hung up the phone. So far, so good.

"Damn, Steve," Alexander said. "I couldn't believe the way you talked to that guy! Are you trying to get Tammy killed?"

"No," Steve replied as he pushed the elevator call button. "Exactly the opposite. I had to change who was in control of the situation, and I accomplished that. And now, I need a drink."

"I'll bet," Robert agreed. "It's not even *my* sister, and I could use a drink after listening in on that call."

"I hope the bar is still open," Steve said.

"It's only ten, Steve," Alexander replied.

"Really?" Steve shook his head. "It's been a *long* day. I would have sworn it was after eleven."

They walked into the bar. There were several people sitting around various tables, talking and drinking. One beer, and then upstairs to collapse onto that wonderful bed that he'd spent about two minutes on, sounded exquisite.

They ordered drinks from the waitress. Steve's eyes lingered for a little while on her as she left for the bar. He smiled, remembering another waitress, a barmaid more accurately, a world away. He still hadn't quite forgiven Arthwyr ap Madawc for bribing her to kiss him.

"Enjoying the view, Steve?" Alexander asked, smiling.

"Remembering something, actually," Steve replied.

"Must be some memory."

"You could say that, I suppose," Steve said. The waitress returned with their drinks and the three of them settled back to relax, drinking and chatting. Alexander told a few stories about girls he'd run into in Nam. Eventually, Steve found himself telling Dick and Robert about Arthwyr's little prank with Rea.

"And, of course, this woman had never even *seen* a toothbrush," Steve added.

"This Arthur sounds like quite a character," Alexander noted, laughing. "Did he make it out all right?"

"Yeah," Steve replied. "Yeah, he did. Born to hang, that one."

Steve took another sip from his second beer, listening to snippets of the various conversations around him. Some were in English, some in incomprehensible Spanish.

" . . . Morvir won't know what hit them . . ."

Steve sat up with a start, sloshing a little of his beer onto the table. Ignoring Alexander's startled response, Steve looked in the direction he thought that small piece of conversation had come from.

Two men sat at a nearby table, one older, about forty, gray at the temples, and the other about thirty, dark-haired.

Both had very short haircuts and were clean-shaven. Military? Or mercenaries? Steve had no way of knowing. They looked American.

He stood up and walked over toward the table. The two men seated at the table saw him immediately and stood up as he approached. Their expressions were guarded.

"The Morvir won't know *who* hit them?" Steve asked.

The two men exchanged a glance. Steve had heard right—his question had just hit home.

"I'm afraid we don't know what you're . . ." the younger man began.

"Bullshit," Steve replied. "I heard that comment *quite* clearly. If someone is planning a hit on the Morvir, then I want in. Or at least a little information."

"We'll talk more later," the younger man said to the older. "I can handle this." The older man nodded and left.

"Tell your friends to stay put," the younger man said to Steve.

Steve glanced back at Dick and Robert, who were getting up from the table, and shook his head. They stopped and sat back down.

"Would you care to sit down before we attract the attention of hotel security?" the stranger asked.

"Sure," Steve replied, pulling out the opposite chair.

"Okay, kid," the mercenary began, "who are you?"

"Steve Wilkinson," Steve replied. "From New York."

"You a merc?"

"No."

"I didn't think so. You're not one of them, either."

"That should be obvious," Steve agreed.

"So then, what's your beef with the Morvir?"

"They've got my sister."

"I sure hope she's ugly," the mercenary said.

"No," Steve replied, "I'm afraid she's not. I've got a picture."

"I don't need to see it, for Christ's sake," the guy said when Steve started to reach for his wallet.

"Suppose I believe you," he continued. "What do you want?"

"I thought we might start by trading information," Steve said. "You're a mercenary, right?"

"Might be," he said. "Why should I?"

"Because I know a lot about these people," Steve said.

"Like what?"

Good question. The apparent validity of Steve's information would depend on what this man himself knew. What should he mention? The *goremka*—not likely. Belevairn would keep that well concealed. What, besides the Morvir, could Belevairn have brought with him? Steve blinked at an unexpected thought. There *was* one possibility . . .

"I don't suppose," Steve said, "that you've run into anything *besides* the Morvir, have you?"

"I've run into a lot of things."

"No, these would be with the Morvir," Steve elaborated. "Probably in the jungle around their camp."

The mercenary straightened in his chair. Apparently Steve had hit paydirt. Would Belevairn have actually brought *galdir* with him?

"Yes, I have run into something around the camp," the mercenary said. "Why don't you tell me what it was?"

Steve exhaled. All or nothing.

"They look a lot like baboons," Steve began, "but they're a hell of a lot smarter. They can use tools and simple weapons—spears usually."

"Yeah, I caught one of them," the mercenary said.

"Shit!" Steve said. "They've even brought *galdir* with them, then."

"Gawl-deer?"

"Yeah, that's what they call the ape-men," Steve said. "Can we take this conversation somewhere more private?"

"Sounds like a good idea to me," the mercenary said. "Mike Williams, by the way."

"Nice to meet you, Mister Williams," Steve said, shaking his hand. "*Real* nice to meet you."

"Wait just a damned minute!" Williams objected. "Are you trying to tell me the Morvir come from another planet?"

"More like another dimension," Steve corrected. "An alternate Earth."

"Now I've fuckin' heard everything! You've got a screw loose, kid. Maybe more than one."

"Do you think the *galdir* came from Earth?"

"I don't know *where* those damned things came from."

"What about that language?" Steve asked, gesturing at the tape recorder. "Have you ever heard it before?"

"No, but there're a whole lot of languages I've never heard before."

"Look," Steve said, "either you can believe me, or you can walk out the door, but I could sure use your help getting my sister out of there."

Williams sat back in the sitting-room chair. The kid did know about the monkey-men, the gawl-deer or whatever it was he called them. And Williams had recognized Captain Korva's voice on the tape. Apparently the Morvir took this kid seriously. Very seriously, if they had gone to the trouble of kidnapping Steve's sister from Albany.

"All right, I believe you," Williams said, "but you've got to come up with another story, kid. I know things that make it believable, kind of. Other people won't."

"I don't think I'm going to be telling it to too many other people."

"Yeah," Williams agreed. "Are you serious about surrendering yourself to them?"

"I don't have much choice, do I?"

"Not if you want your sister back, apparently. So, what do you want from me?"

"What do you know about their camp?" Steve asked.

"Kid, I've been there."

"You have?"

"Yeah, ransoming Don Estefan's granddaughter out of that hellhole."

"And now he wants to hit them back?"

"Right."

"Okay, so what am I walking into?"

"Hell," Williams replied. "The camp is centered around some ancient Aztec or Mayan pyramid. The Morvir have a few Quonset huts and lots of tent-houses set up around it."

"How many of them are there?"

"Over a thousand of the Morvir . . ." Williams began.

"A thousand!"

"Yep. Not to mention a tank and an APC and God only knows how many of those gawl-deer."

"Anything else?"

"There are almost as many camp slaves as there are Morvir," Williams added. "All of them women. And this Lord Belevairn, he calls himself Don Espantoso, is a real psycho. They're sacrificing people at the top of that pyramid, like they were really the Aztecs or something."

Steve nodded. That was where Belevairn was getting his Power. The pyramid itself was probably a source of some Power, and Belevairn was rejuvenating it with human sacrifice.

"So," Steve said, "how would you make the exchange?"

"It's going to be tricky," Williams said, "but you seem to have this guy over a barrel. Have him fly your sister into the airport here, with an escort of Morvir. Make the exchange at the airport. You put her on a plane and then you can do whatever you want. Might be a good idea to have a few men hidden around as backup in case they try anything funny."

"Can you arrange that?"

"Piece of cake. Can you pay for it?"

"How much?"

"Bodyguard work? One day? Probably a couple thousand per man."

"Two *thousand*!"

"It wouldn't be quite so high, except the Morvir are involved," Williams explained.

"I could afford to hire a few men," Steve said. "How many do you think?"

"I dunno. We can work it this way—five hundred per man plus an additional two thousand if the Morvir try anything. How many could you afford that way?"

"Assuming the Morvir try something, about four." Ten thousand would eat almost half of his money. Plane fare for three, after that, would probably leave him with less than ten thousand. Oh, well, he wasn't going to need it after this.

"Okay," Williams said, "so you tell Belevairn to only send two Morvir with her. Tell him that if any more than that show up, the deal's off."

"When?"

"Day after tomorrow," Williams said. "I can have the men lined up by then, easy."

"Good. I want to get this over with."

"Got a question for you," Williams said.

"What?"

"Are you really going to go with them once your sister's on that plane?"

"If I don't, Belevairn will just grab her again," Steve replied. "Yeah, I'm going to go with them."

Williams shook his head. "It's been nice knowing you, kid."

Steve watched the clock. Five minutes until ten. Close enough, especially by the time the call went through. He picked up the phone and dialed the operator. Robert, Alexander and Williams listened in over the tap.

"Korva here," answered the Morvan captain.

"Give me Belevairn," Steve said, in English.

"Hold a moment," Korva replied.

Steve waited. He shouldn't have made that final crack yesterday about being on hold. He had to wait twice as long today.

"Greetings, Master Wilkinson," Belevairn said, in English.

"Let me talk to Tam." Steve waited while the phone was handed over.

"H-hello?" Tam's voice said.

"Tam?"

"Steve?" she said, excitement creeping into her voice. "Steve, is that you?"

"Yes, Tam—it's me. Have they hurt you?"

"Steve, don't try to rescue me! They'll kill you!"

"Tam, have they hurt you?"

"No," Tam replied, her voice shaking. "I'm all right."

"Good. We're going to get you out of there."

"No, Steve! They'll . . ." Tam was cut off as Belevairn took the phone away from her.

"Take her back to her cell," Steve heard Belevairn say in Morvan before he came back on the phone.

"So help me God, if you've hurt her . . ."

"As she has already assured you, she has not been harmed," Belevairn interrupted, "so your empty threats are not necessary."

"All right, then," Steve said coolly, "let's discuss the exchange. I want you to . . ."

"No," Belevairn replied. "I am not going to allow you to dictate the terms of the exchange. You are in no position to make demands."

"I see. In that case, say hello to Daryna for me." Steve hung up the telephone.

"Damn!" Steve said, once certain that the connection was broken.

"Good job," Williams said. "You can't let him get the upper hand. And you sure can't let him know how steamed he's got you."

"Thanks. Shit!"

"He'll cave," Williams assured him. "This guy wants you bad—he's gone to too much trouble to fuck it up now."

"How sure are you of that?" Alexander asked.

"I've worked these things before," Williams replied. "The kid is doing it right. A kidnapper always wants something. You have to use that against them."

"Unless they decide to cut their losses and run," Alexander noted.

"This guy's not in that position," Williams said. "He doesn't have to worry about getting caught. And, from what Steve said, he's under a hell of a lot of pressure to deliver. He'll deal."

"He'd better," Steve said, picking up the phone.

"You sure you're ready?" Williams asked.

"Yep. Here goes round two."

The phone was answered on the first ring.

"Belevairn here."

"Wilkinson," Steve replied. Belevairn had even answered in English.

"Are you *mad*?"

"Do I have to spell it out for you?" Steve asked. "You have my sister. If I agree to make the exchange your way, she is as good as dead. If that's the case, I might as well keep coming after your ass, mister. We do the exchange my way, or I write my sister off and I make you pay, you son of a bitch. Do you understand me?"

There was a long pause while Belevairn considered.

"Yes," he finally replied. "I understand your position."

"Good," Steve said. "Now—do you remember the Mound?"

"Yes . . . ?"

"You offered to give me information if I swore by Mortos's name and my fealty to Erelvar to release you. If we make the exchange my way, I will swear those oaths to guarantee my cooperation. If that is not acceptable to you, then you might as well kill Tam now—and then you had best start writing your obituary."

"Let me hear your plan," Belevairn grudgingly agreed.

"It's simple," Steve replied. "I am in Guatemala City. You have my sister flown here with two Morvir. Have her arrive tomorrow afternoon. I will meet them at the airport with her ticket to America. Once she is on that plane, I will surrender to the Morvir who were escorting her."

"And what is to prevent you from simply boarding that plane with her?" Belevairn asked.

"Three things," Steve answered. "One, you will have my sworn word. That seemed to mean *something* to you in Ohio."

"Go on . . ."

"Two, the Morvir escorting her shouldn't have too much difficulty preventing that. Three, I know exactly how easy it is for you to grab her all over again if I double-cross you."

"True," Belevairn agreed. "Very well, we will proceed with your plan. If I may have your oaths . . . ?"

"One thing," Steve added.

"What?"

"I said two Morvir, and I *meant* two Morvir. If any more than that show up, the exchange is off, and you know I can spot them."

"Agreed. Your oaths . . . ?"

"Very well," Steve said, "I swear in Mortos's name and by my oath of service to Lord Erelvar that I shall not violate this agreement unless it is first violated by you or your agents."

"Well stated," Belevairn acknowledged. "Contact me again in two hours, and I shall have the arrival times for you."

"Very well," Steve replied. "Two hours." He returned the phone to its cradle, breathing a ragged sigh.

"Can I have a nervous breakdown now?" he asked of no one in particular.

"Sure," Williams answered. "For about an hour and a half. You did real good, kid. Now, if you'll excuse me, I have to go finish that meeting you interrupted last night and then line up your bodyguards for tomorrow."

"Thanks, Mike," Steve said. "Thanks loads."

"Anytime," Williams replied, shaking Steve's hand. "Those bastards got my brother—I'll help screw 'em any chance I get."

Williams left the room, and Steve collapsed back into the chair by the phone.

"What about us?" Alexander asked, once Williams had left.

"I'm going to be buying tickets back to America for you two as well," Steve replied. "Looks like this is the end of the story, anyway, and I'm going to be counting on you to get Tam back home safe."

"Yeah," Alexander agreed. He didn't sound overly happy. "We won't let you down, Steve."

"Thanks, Dick. I'm counting on you."

Chapter
-------- Nineteen -------------

GARTH STOOD AT attention at the head of his platoon as dawn broke over the camp. The other four platoons of the company flanked him, two on each side. Of the five platoons that had arrived a month ago, his had taken the heaviest damage.

"Company, atten-tion!" Korva's aide, Lieutenant Orlas, barked. Garth snapped to attention and heard his men do the same behind him.

Captain Korva walked up to address the company.

"Company, parade rest!" he commanded, and the men shifted from attention into the slightly more relaxed stance.

"Your month of service here has ended," Korva began. "All of you have served well and upheld the reputation of the Morvir in this world. I am pleased to now select from among your platoon commanders the man who will command your company.

"The platoon formerly commanded by this man will be divided among the remaining four platoons to bring them to full strength. Ordinarily, any excess above four platoons would be removed to fill miscellaneous positions."

Garth already knew this. That was where the men on the tank crews had come from. A company was uniformly four platoons. The fifth was to absorb casualties . . .

"In your case, however, this company has sustained severe casualties," Korva continued. Garth did not react, but felt his face flush with shame. His platoon was the source of most of those casualties.

"However," Korva went on, "this company has also done more to enhance the reputation of the Morvir than any other before it. So, I am pleased to announce that Lieutenant Garth is hereby promoted to captain and placed in command of Jared Company."

Garth blinked in surprise. Captain? After his miserable showing in the West Bank?

"Lieutenant Garth, front and center!"

Garth came to attention and marched up to Captain Korva, saluting.

"Lieutenant Garth reporting as ordered, sir!" he said. Korva returned his salute and, as Garth stood at attention, removed his lieutenant's bars and replaced them with the insignia of captain.

"Congratulations, Captain," Korva said, *sotto voce*.

"Thank you, sir," Garth replied.

"Captain Garth," Korva said, "assume command of your company."

Garth saluted and marched to a position at the head of the company. Once in position, he relaxed into parade rest.

"Lieutenant Ulan is hereby promoted to Lieutenant Aide of Jared Company," Korva continued. "Lieutenant Ulan, front and center!"

Garth watched as Korva went through essentially the same procedure with Ulan. So, Ulan was to be his aide. That was acceptable. Garth watched on in detachment. He had not expected to receive command of the company. However, his platoon *had* seen the heaviest fighting.

He almost smiled when Sergeant Dalin was promoted to lieutenant and given command of Ulan's platoon. Dalin was still going to be his problem, not some platoon commander's. That would leave his company with two sergeants to bust back to corporal. Not a pleasant task.

"For meritorious service in the Mistress's army," Korva began, "Sergeant Wyrth is posthumously commissioned as a lieutenant of the Morvan Special Forces."

Garth smiled, as Korva continued the posthumous awards. He had learned from Captain Korva that Wyrth had killed twice as many Israeli soldiers as he had men before destroying an M-1 and a Cobra. He had become a credit to the Morvan Special Forces. Unfortunately, because of Amar's treachery, Garth would no longer have his resources to draw upon.

"Captain Garth," Korva said, once the promotions were finished, "once your company has been reorganized and dismissed, you and Lieutenant Dalin are to report to my office."

"Yes, sir," Garth replied. "Company, atten-tion!" Garth saluted as Captain Korva left.

Alexander stood at the window, watching dawn break over the city of Guatemala. He had not been able to sleep very well last night. Nightmares had plagued his sleep all night long.

It was the jungle, partially. Waking up old memories—memories he'd buried long ago and half a world away.

But that was only part of the reason. Today, Alexander was going to send a friend off to his death. Was going to put him on a plane and wave goodbye as he flew away to die.

Steve may have sworn an oath to cooperate with the Morvir, but Alexander hadn't. If it was the last thing he did, he was going to find some way to get Steve out of this . . .

It had taken a little over an hour for Garth and Ulan to reorganize the company. They were still a few men short, but those would be replaced with raw recruits back in Delgroth. No single platoon was more than three men short, however, so this should not be a problem.

Lieutenant Dalin opened the door to Korva's office and Garth entered.

"Captain Garth and Lieutenant Dalin reporting as ordered, sir!" he said, saluting.

"At ease, Captain—Lieutenant," Korva replied.

"You wanted to see us, sir?" Garth asked.

"Yes, Captain," Korva replied. "I wanted to let you know that we haven't had any luck tracking down Amar and his men yet."

"I see, sir."

"Don't worry—we *will* find him. It's a shame you won't be here to handle that mission, once we do."

"Yes, sir. I would very much like to be."

"I'm sure you would," Korva agreed, nodding. "However, I didn't call you in here just to brief you on our efforts to locate Amar."

"Sir?"

"I have one last mission for Jared Company," Korva explained.

A mission? They were only three days from the big exchange. The camp had been preparing for it for a week now.

"Which platoon, sir?" Garth asked.

"No platoon, Garth," Korva replied. "Just you and Lieutenant Dalin . . ."

"Okay," Steve said, "here are your tickets back to America." He handed Richard and Robert their tickets.

"Dick, I want to you carry Tam's ticket and passport along with the rest of my money. I won't be needing it where I'm going."

"Yeah, right," Alexander replied flatly.

"Hey," Steve said, "don't be so glum. I'll be okay."

"Yeah, right," Alexander replied.

"Here are the keys to the Jeep. Once the exchange has been made and I'm gone, give these to Mike Williams. He can best dispose of what's in the Jeep."

"Sure, kid."

"I can't believe you're this upset at losing your story," Steve said. Alexander looked up, his expression first shocked, then angry.

"Losing . . . ?" he began. "Dammit, you son of a bitch, I'm not upset at losing a story! I've still got my story— I'm upset at having to send a friend off to die!"

"Oh," Steve said. "I'm . . . sorry, Dick. That was . . . well, I'm sorry."

"Yeah. Me too."

"Anyway," Steve said after an uncomfortable pause, "promise me you'll get Tam back home, safe and sound."

"Done. Is there any chance at all that you'll come out of this alive?"

"I doubt it," Steve replied. "I suppose that anything's possible, though."

"How much longer?"

"The Morvir's flight should arrive in about an hour. Your flight out is scheduled for two hours after that."

"What are you going to do with the time?"

"Talk with Tam," Steve replied. "Try to explain what's going on. I could use those pictures that Robert has with him . . ."

"No problem," Robert replied.

"Thanks," Steve said. "Let's go grab a bite to eat while we wait."

Garth glanced out the window of the airplane as they approached the city of Guatemala. He was still mesmerized with the experience of flight. He had been flown everywhere for the last month, usually in helicopters. The few jets he'd flown in had been transports without windows. This flight had been different.

The jet had taken them above the clouds. It had been incredible to watch the cloud envelop them like a thick, autumn fog and then, as they rose above it, to form into what appeared to be solid, snow-covered hills far below them. Even the Dread Lords, mounted on the *goremkir*, had never witnessed that sight.

Now the city of Guatemala lay below them as the airplane made its landing approach. Garth glanced at their prisoner, seated between Dalin and himself. Her reddish-blonde hair and brownish-green eyes made her look almost Olvan—would have if she'd been taller.

She had not spoken during their flight, or during the trip into La Cruz, for that matter. Like Maria, she was being released to further the cause of the Morvir on this world. What they were receiving in exchange was infinitely more valuable than the three hundred thousand American dollars that had been paid for Maria.

Tamara was being ransomed in exchange for her brother,

the Dreamer. The one man who, according to prophecy, could cause the destruction of the Morvir and possibly even the Mistress. Once he surrendered himself to Garth and Dalin, which Lord Belevairn assured them he would do without resistance, those prophecies would be defeated.

Garth was anxious to meet the man who had caused their defeat on the Plains of Blood five years ago. It was said that he had defeated two Morvir in battle before he had been captured and killed by Lord Belevairn. Somehow, instead of dying, he had returned to the world of his birth to live again.

Garth shook his head. Such was the stuff of sorcery, and beyond the concerns of a warrior such as himself. He had been ordered to bring this man back to the camp, and that was what he would do.

Tammy could hardly believe that she was going to be released. It was all beginning to seem like a nightmare that she'd had a lifetime ago.

She was dressed in the clothes that she had been wearing when she was kidnapped. At least they weren't making her go home in one of those sack dresses. She glanced out the window as the plane banked to the left, looking at the buildings of the city of Guatemala. She had always wanted to travel, but this wasn't quite what she'd had in mind.

Tammy hoped that Rosita would be all right. She closed her eyes tightly against the memory of the women the man in the gold mask had killed. It had been two days, and she could still taste the blood in her mouth. Surely it was just her imagination . . .

"Are you well?" the guard in charge asked.

"Just motion sickness," Tammy lied. "I'll be fine."

He nodded and went back to looking out the window. The plane dropped toward the runway and Tammy saw the ground rise into view beside the plane. There was a hard bump and the screech of the landing gear on the runway and they were down.

She was going to meet Steve here, and he was going to take her home. Then, after she had thanked him for rescuing her, she was going to kill him for getting her into this mess. What did he think he was doing, getting involved with people like this?

They taxied to the terminal and soon the passengers were debarking. Tammy started to rise, but the guard in charge grabbed her arm before she was even half an inch off her seat.

"We will wait for the other passengers," he said. "Then we will debark."

"Yeah, sure," Tammy agreed. He removed his hand from her arm. Boy, would she be glad to lose these jerks.

The last of the passengers passed their seat. The other guard got up; he was in the aisle seat. The head guard motioned for Tammy to get up. She got up and he followed her into the aisle.

She was going to go home . . .

Steve watched the departing passengers eagerly. There was no sign of Tam, so far. Then someone who stood half a head taller and twice as broad as the other passengers emerged from the walkway. That, in combination with his dark complexion, identified his origins.

"That's a Morva," Steve said, nodding in the direction of the man who had just emerged. The man's eyes met Steve's, and Steve nodded once. He received an answering nod.

"Big enough, isn't he?" Alexander observed.

"The Mistress likes them big, strong and stupid," Steve said.

"Yeah, I know girls like that," Robert added.

Then Steve saw Tam, followed by another Morva. No one else followed them off the airplane. Tammy was looking about, searching for him.

She finally spotted him.

"Steve!" she shouted, running from between her guards to literally jump into his arms. Steve caught her easily, something he could never have done before, and swung her around in a circle before tossing her up in the air once and catching her.

"Whoa!" Tam said. "Putting on some muscles there, big brother! I bet those college girls like that!"

"Are you okay, Tam?" Steve asked, placing his hands on her cheeks and tilting her face up to look at him.

"I'm a *lot* better, now!" she replied. "A whole lot better."

"Master Wilkinson?" one of the Morvir interrupted, in Morvan.

"What?"

"Are you prepared to surrender to us?"

"Once my sister is on her flight out, yes," Steve replied. "That flight leaves in two hours. Until then, I am going to spend that time with her, not you."

"We have been instructed not to allow you out of our sight."

"Fine, then you can tag along at a distance," Steve replied. "However, my agreement with Belevairn was that I would not surrender to you until she was safely on the plane."

"Very well," the Morva agreed. "However, if you attempt to escape, I have orders to kill both you and your sister."

"Regardless of the fact that you will then, yourself, be killed."

"That is correct."

"You're Morvan, all right."

"Yes. Our return flight leaves in one hour and fifteen minutes," the guard said. "You will surrender to us then. You may spend the intervening time with your sister."

"I said that I would not surrender to you until Tam's flight leaves."

"We cannot change our flight," the Morvan said. "You will depart with us at that time, or we will be forced to kill both of you. Your sister will be safe at the departure gate. I assure you, we have no interest in her."

"Thank you *so* much," Steve replied. "All right, we'll do it your way. Now get lost."

The Morvir walked away, to stand about twenty paces away.

"Where did you learn their language?" Tam asked.

"Tam, honey," Steve said, "let's find someplace and get you something to eat. I've got a lot to tell you."

It was almost an hour later when Steve finished telling Tam everything.

"Steve," Tammy said, "that's insane."

"I don't blame you for not believing it . . ." Steve began.

"No, wait a minute," Tammy said. "What's even more insane is that I do believe you. Steve, when you came out of that coma you were . . . different. And what I've seen . . ."

Tammy fell silent, remembering. The horse monster, the sacrifices, the blood. All of it supported Steve's story. Not to mention the pictures these newspaper people had of him fighting that horse thing. She laughed.

"What is it, Tam?" Steve asked.

"I just remembered," she replied, giggling. "I told one of the girls in the camp that you were no knight in shining armor. I guess I was wrong."

"Surprise, surprise," Steve said, smiling.

"Steve," Tammy asked, "are you really going to go with these . . . monsters?"

"I have to."

"No, we're in an airport. We can all just walk onto the plane and shoot them the bird while we do it!"

"No, Tam," Steve said. "We can't do that. They told me that they have orders to kill us both if we try that."

"But they can't do that here . . ."

"Yes, Tam, they can." Steve leaned forward. "Tam, they've been told to do that, and they'll do it. And yes, they know that they'll be killed for doing it. They don't care—they're Morvir."

"But, Steve, they'll kill you."

"Probably," Steve agreed. "But better me than you, Tam. Now, we need to get you to your gate before they take me away. Once you're behind the metal detectors, *don't* come back out here. They could send someone else in to grab you again."

"O-okay," Tam said, her voice trembling.

"Hey, don't worry," Steve told her. "I'll be all right. I seem to have this stupid lucky streak . . ."

"I hope so," Tam said. Then she stood up and threw her arms around him.

"I love you, big brother."

"I love you too, Tam."

They walked toward the metal detectors, and the Morvir followed them. They caught up with them at the detectors.

"I cannot allow you to accompany your sister through the gate," the Morva in charge said.

"Yeah, I figured as much," Steve said.

"We've got to part here, kid," Steve said, turning to Tam. "You take care. And tell Mom and Dad goodbye for me."

"Okay."

Steve kissed her on the cheek. Then he turned to Alexander.

"You make sure she gets home safe," Steve said.

"Will do, kid."

"Thanks."

Steve watched as Tam and her two escorts passed through the metal detectors. Mission accomplished. One of the Morvir started to take him by the arm. Steve jerked loose.

"I'll walk on my own, thank you," Steve said.

"Let's go."

Alexander watched as Steve and the two Morvir boarded the plane that would take them back to Nicaragua. He waited for it to start taxiing away from the terminal. The original plan was that Steve was going to wait for them to be in the air before he left. This changed things. In fact . . .

"Robert," he said.

"Yeah, Dick?"

"Here's the money and Tam's ticket," he said. "You make *damn* sure she makes it home."

"Huh? Where the hell are *you* going?"

"To catch Williams," Alexander replied. "I'm going to make damn sure that, when Williams's men hit that camp, there's one person there whose goal is to get Steve's butt out of there."

Alexander left the gate, looking through the crowds for Williams. He had seen the mercenary several times during their stay at the airport.

Alexander spotted him heading for one of the exits.

"Williams!" he shouted. The mercenary stopped and turned around. Alexander waved and hurried to catch up with him.

"They took him, right?" Williams asked.

"Yeah."

"And the girl's safe at the gate, right?"

"Yeah."

"So what's up?"

"Take me with you."

"We don't need a war correspondent," Williams said, turning to go. "Thanks."

"I was in Nam," Alexander said, grabbing Williams by the arm. "One hundred and first Airborne. You can use me."

"Why?" Williams asked.

"They've got a friend of mine, and I want to be there when they get hit."

Williams studied Alexander's face for a minute. Apparently he was satisfied with whatever he saw.

"Okay," he said, "you're on my squad. But you better pull your weight, old man."

"Don't worry," Alexander replied. "First, though, there are some things that we have got to get out of Steve's Jeep."

Chapter
-------- Twenty ------------

THE MORVAN CAMP was huge. Williams had been correct—there were easily a thousand men here. The pyramid dominated the center of the camp. Steve tried to reach out and feel the Power, but he could not. Apparently that ability had been lost when Belevairn was exorcised from him. It was just as well, he supposed.

Even so, he could sense a feeling of evil from the stone structure. It was obvious why Belevairn had chosen this place for his base of operations. In a world starved of the Power, he had a ready supply of it. Just add blood . . .

The Morvan captain helped him down from the jeep, Steve's feet were shackled together with a short length of chain. His wrists were also shackled with a chain connected to the chain between his ankles. These people weren't taking any chances with him.

The captain gave him a shove, and Steve started hobbling in the direction of the pyramid. A figure in black with a golden mask was approaching from the pyramid. Belevairn, coming to gloat.

"Greetings, Master Wilkinson," he said. "How nice that you could join us."

"Go to Hell, *malvera*," Steve said. He heard a gasp from beside him. The insult meant dog-lover, and it was almost impossible for a Morvan not to show a reaction to it. Belevairn was no exception.

The force of the backhand blow knocked Steve about three feet. For a moment, his vision blackened and small lights danced in the blackness. He felt two pair of hands drag him to his feet.

The camp, and Belevairn, slowly came back into focus. He was being supported between his captors. Belevairn grabbed Steve by the throat and lifted him from his feet.

"You are mine, Dreamer," he said. "I would advise you to remember that."

"Daryna . . . might   disagree . . . with . . . you," Steve choked out.

"Oh, I shan't kill you," Belevairn replied. "That honor is hers. But I can make your stay here very unpleasant."

Steve managed to spit. Belevairn howled in rage as he dropped Steve to wipe the spittle from his mask. Steve fell onto the ground, and one of the Morvir kicked him in the stomach. Steve involuntarily doubled around his stomach, heaving. Fortunately, he had not eaten since leaving Guatemala.

"Take him to his cell," Belevairn commanded. "I shall deal with him later."

The cell was spacious. It was one of the chambers in the pyramid. A mattress had been placed on a stone ledge to serve as a bed, and someone had actually installed a light bulb in the ceiling.

So, this was how it would end. Tomorrow was the new moon—no doubt Belevairn had plans for him. Something on the wall by the bed caught Steve's eye. Someone had scratched the letters T and W into the wall by the bed. Tam.

He smiled, tracing the letters with his finger. At least she was safe now. He had accomplished that much. He might not be able to save Quarin or the Northern Kingdoms, but at least Tam was out of this mess . . .

Belevairn had returned to brag about his plans. The Dragon was about to be turned loose on the plains. A dragon with armor like unto burnished bronze and which spits smoke and fire from its mouth. A tank.

For the last six months Belevairn had been training an army on the battlefields of Earth. Tomorrow night, he was taking the bulk of that army back with him. Lord Erelvar would never know what hit him, much less be able to defeat them.

Steve sighed. He had failed. The prophecy was quite clear on the consequences of his failure. That world was going to be destroyed, unless he could figure some way out of this. Short of a miracle, though, that wasn't going to happen.

Belevairn stood atop the pyramid. Soon it would be midnight. He would have preferred to make the exchange at noon, but circumstances had prevented his doing so.

The *kaivir* brought the first sacrifice to the altar. Belevairn raised his knife—it was time.

The truck bounced along what passed for the road that led to the Morvan camp. Alexander sat in the back with the other members of Williams's squad. He'd taken a little ribbing about the sword he wore on his back, but not much.

It had been a long, long time since he'd sat in the back of a truck, uniformed and armed for a night attack. Williams's squad was not going to participate in the initial strike. Lieutenant Williams had turned out to be Don Estefan's liaison to the mercenary commander, Colonel Anderson. He would be going in once the attack was well in progress.

That was fine with Alexander. It had been a long time since Nam and, from what he'd heard, the Morvir were worse opponents than the Cong had ever been. Otherwise, by the time Alexander would have been able to get his combat reflexes back, he would have probably been dead.

The truck stopped and Williams slid open the rear window.

"Okay," he said, "we're in position. Now we just gotta wait for it to go down."

Garth stood at the head of his company. On his way to Earth, he had ridden in one of the trucks. On his trip back home, he was going to march through the tunnel between worlds. The trucks would be loaded with supplies. Even if that had not been the case, there were nowhere near enough trucks to transport five companies.

The tunnel opened, first as a pinpoint of light, rapidly widening until they could all see the Burning Hills at the far end. It was daytime on the other side of the tunnel. Garth's stomach tightened. He hated having to deal with sorcery. The thought of marching his company through a tunnel held open only by the will of the *kaivir* terrified him.

What would happen if something went wrong? Would he and his men be stranded between worlds forever? Would they simply die? These were questions that Garth was not certain he wanted an answer to.

The tank was the first to proceed through the tunnel to the Burning Hills, followed by the armored personnel carrier and then the two ammunition transports followed by a fuel truck. Finally, the twenty-five truckloads of supplies passed through the tunnel.

After the training company arrived in its trucks, it would be time to march the companies through. Garth called his company to attention. He was *not* going to enjoy this.

The three Cobras flew through the night over the jungle in staggered formation. Their orders were to go in, hit the target for thirty seconds and depart. Colonel Anderson did not want a repetition of the incident with the Israeli helicopters.

They were observing radio silence during the approach. Precisely one mile from the target, the lead helicopter cut its navigation lights. The other two followed suit. No abort command had been received—they were going in.

Belevairn watched as the last company marched into the interdimensional tunnel. He trembled with the exertion of maintaining the portal. As they approached the other end, their passage became more swift as they came to match the time rate of Delgroth. Once the last man stepped out of the tunnel, Belevairn allowed the portal to begin its collapse.

The new company had formed up, and Korva was giving them their introductory briefing. This was the seventh company. Only five more, and then all training would be moved to the Burning Hills. Each of the Twelve would then have one experienced company to draw upon. Belevairn's own company would remain on Earth to continue to conduct operations here.

Once he had recovered from the ritual, he would take the Dreamer to Delgroth with him on the *goremka*. Daryna would be extremely pleased . . .

The sound of helicopters reached him, interrupting his musings. Korva apparently heard them as well a few seconds later. They were definitely getting closer. What was happening?

Three trails of fire answered that question. Korva had already raised the alarm and was dispersing the new company, but it was too late. The three missiles struck among the new arrivals. Indeed, that had probably been their target.

The lights of the helicopters came on, floodlights panning the camp as the machine guns began to strafe the tents and Quonset huts. Belevairn hurried down the steps of the pyramid. He must get to the Dreamer's cell and summon the *goremka*. Curse the luck! Who was attacking them?

"Flash grenades!" Lieutenant Olaf shouted to his platoon. "Charge!"

Colonel Anderson was hoping that the flash grenades would neutralize the ape-men guarding the perimeter long enough for the mercenaries to penetrate the camp.

Their total force was only three hundred strong. If they were going to defeat the Morvir, even after the boys in the helicopters had had their fun, they were going to need every single man they could get into the camp.

Steve heard the muted rumbling inside his cell. Surely that couldn't be thunder? Another rumble penetrated the stone cell—Steve could actually feel the vibration through the stone.

That could only mean that Williams's attack was going down tonight. Steve laughed. This *could* be the miracle he'd been hoping for.

The stone door to his cell began to open. Steve rose from the bed as Belevairn and the guard hurried in.

"Don Estefan sends his regards, I see," Steve said.

"What?" Belevairn asked.

"Don Estefan," Steve replied. "I ran into the men he'd hired for this attack while I was in Guatemala."

"You knew?"

"That it was coming, yes. I just didn't know when. Did the attack interrupt your transfer?"

"No," Belevairn replied. "It did not." He handed the guard a pair of handcuffs.

"Manacle him," Belevairn ordered.

Steve held his arms out, hands together as the Morva approached, careful to maintain a resigned expression.

"Turn around," the guard ordered, "and put your hands behind your back."

Steve sighed, placed his hands behind his back and began to turn. Halfway through the turn he spun and kicked straight back, slamming the Morva into the wall behind him. He spun, slamming the heel of his open hand into the Morva's nose as the man rebounded from the wall.

Belevairn tried to tackle him. Steve caught the sorcerer by the arm and threw himself to the ground, using Belevairn's momentum to hurl the Dread Lord against the opposite wall. Unfortunately, the impact would not render Belevairn unconscious as it would have a normal man.

There was no way that Steve could defeat Belevairn unarmed. He ran out through the open door into the corridor. Which way had the exit been? To the left—Steve turned and ran down the corridor and out onto the steps of the pyramid.

The camp was embroiled in battle and, from what he could see, the Morvir were not having an easy time of it. All the seasoned troops had departed for Delgroth, except for Korva's company, which had probably been sleeping. It looked like the new recruits had been iced at the start.

Steve ran down the steps of the pyramid. He had to find a weapon capable of killing Belevairn.

Alexander fired a burst from his AK-47, killing the Morva who had run from between the tents. It had not taken as long as Alexander had thought it would for the old reflexes to kick in. The jungle, the heat, the sounds of battle brought it all back to him.

Things were not quite working out as had been planned. Instead of driving in on the mop-up, the battle in the camp was still raging when Williams's squad had arrived. As a result, Williams's squad found itself in heavy combat.

Anderson had expected these Morvir to roll over and die too easily. Just because a Morvan was mortally wounded did not mean that he couldn't fight up to the moment he dropped. In fact, that's exactly what these bastards were doing.

Alexander had to make it to the pyramid. If Steve was still in the camp, that was where they would be holding him. The only problem was that there was a cleared perimeter at least a hundred feet across surrounding the base of the pyramid. How was he going to cross that without getting shot?

A lone figure raced down the stairs and out across the cleared zone. Steve? Whoever it was had not been armed. Alexander ran to intercept that man.

Steve made it to the cover of the tents. *Nothing like being an unarmed man in the middle of World War Three*, he thought. Still, there were enough corpses around—he ought to be able to find something to use to defend himself.

Finding something that would kill Belevairn, though, was another matter. He would need a flamethrower, or maybe some incendiary grenades. The only problem with that was that he would also need someone to show him how to use them.

He found a machine gun by one of the bodies. Okay, so how did the damned thing work? One lever released the clip; after a little fumbling he was able to get that clipped back into place. Another must be the safety. So, he would guess that the last one was the single-shot selector. Of course, that was assuming that this particular gun even *had* a single-shot selector.

Chances were it would have been set for automatic. He pushed the lever in the opposite direction. Hopefully, it was now set for single-shot use. He doubted that he could handle the weapon at full automatic. Now he had to work on finding something that could kill Belevairn . . .

Someone rounded the corner of the tent. Steve brought the rifle up and pulled the trigger. Nothing happened—the trigger was jammed. Great—he'd found the safety.

"Steve?" a familiar voice asked.

"Dick?" Steve asked. "What the *hell* are you doing here? Where's Tam?"

"She's safe," Alexander assured him. "Robert flew with her to the States. I joined up with Williams. I wanted one person to be here who was looking out for your ass."

"Well, you almost just got yours shot off," Steve said.

"Do you know how to use this thing?"

"Apparently not. What I thought was the single-shot switch was apparently the safety."

"Lucky for me. Here, let me show you." Alexander ran over the basic operation of the gun for him.

"Got it?" he asked.

"I think so," Steve replied. "Now I have to find a flamethrower, or some incendiary grenades or something to use on Belevairn."

"How about this?" Alexander asked, drawing Steve's sword from its scabbard on his back.

"Dick, I love you!"

"Hey," Alexander said. "Let's keep this professional."

"Give me the scabbard." The consecrated sword ought to have *some* effect on Belevairn.

"Right. Hold on." It took a few seconds for Alexander to remove the scabbard. Meanwhile the battle raged around them, punctuated with bursts of gunfire and explosions. Steve fastened the sword to his belt.

"Now what?" Alexander asked.

"I've got to find Belevairn," Steve replied. "He's still in the pyramid."

"I'm going with you," Alexander said. "Buddy system."

"Right," Steve replied, starting to get up. Alexander grabbed his arm.

"Wait until I'm in position to cover you," Alexander said. "You're new to gun battles, aren't you?"

"They're definitely not the same as cavalry charges," Steve agreed.

"Okay. When you get to the pyramid, you get down and cover me while I cross."

"Got it," Steve acknowledged.

"Go!"

Steve sprinted across the cleared space around the pyramid, expecting to get nailed by a bullet at any second. He reached the steps of the pyramid safely, however. Once there, he turned and knelt down on the steps.

Alexander followed a few seconds after Steve had settled on the steps. So far, so good.

"There's an entrance halfway up the steps," Steve said. "It might be guarded."

"Okay," Alexander said. "We go up the steps, real slow. Stop short of that landing."

"Right," Steve agreed. Together they slowly climbed the steps, hunched over to make smaller targets. This was not the Richard Alexander that Steve had known before. This man was a warrior—with all of a warrior's instincts.

Alexander held out a hand, calling a stop several feet short of the landing. He advanced half the remaining distance, practically sitting on the steps. Then he straightened, rising above the level of the landing to aim his rifle at the doorway.

He did not fire. After a second he glanced back down at Steve and motioned, with his head, for Steve to advance. Steve joined him.

"You go on in," Alexander told him. "I'll cover you from here."

"Right."

Steve ran up to the door and stopped beside it, his back

to the wall. He spun around through the doorway, aiming the rifle through it. The corridor was empty. He motioned for Alexander to join him.

Together they advanced into the pyramid. They came to the entrance to Steve's cell. It was still open. They entered cautiously.

The Morvan guard was still on the floor. Alexander looked down at the body—its pistol was missing.

"Did *you* kill this guy?" he asked Steve.

"Yeah," Steve replied. "Caught him by surprise."

"Unarmed? Not bad, kid."

They advanced further into the pyramid. They came to an intersection, as another corridor branched to the left.

"Which way?" Steve asked.

"Right-hand rule," Alexander said.

"Huh?"

"Keep your right hand on the wall," Alexander replied. "Figuratively speaking, that is. When you want to get back where you started you turn around and keep your left hand on the wall."

"Figuratively speaking."

"Right. Let's go."

Alexander passed the side corridor quickly, turning to cover the hallway as he passed it. Steve jerked back as Alexander fired a burst down the hallway.

"Then again," he said from the other side, "we follow the guy I just shot at."

Steve spun around the corner. A Morva lay dead on the floor.

"Don't think we're going to be following him anywhere," Steve noted.

"Still, this is the way."

"Yeah."

"Get his ammo, Steve."

Steve yanked the clip from the Morva's rifle. They pressed on, deeper into the pyramid.

Belevairn hurriedly packed the papers from his desk into his saddlebags. He was going to have to begin all over

again. Actually, he would be able to bring back one of
the experienced companies with him. Korva had said good
things about Garth.

Then he would have to track Wilkinson back down
again. The Mistress was not going to be pleased by
this turn of events. Belevairn only hoped that he could
convince her that he was not at fault for this unexpected
attack.

A burst of automatic gunfire reached his ears. Had the
enemy gained the pyramid? He gathered up the saddlebags,
loaded mainly with American money, and picked up the
pistol he'd taken from the dead guard.

Curse Wilkinson! Only a fool would have had the gall
to attack an armed guard barehanded.

He stepped out of his office, face to face with Wilkinson
and another man. Wilkinson's companion fired just as
Belevairn did. The burst of gunfire knocked Belevairn to
the floor, but his shot hit the mercenary.

Belevairn reached for the fallen pistol as Wilkinson fired,
not at him, but at the pistol. The bullets sent it skidding
down the corridor even as they reduced it to scrap.

"Well done, Wilkinson," Belevairn said. "But your weapon will not harm me."

"No, you're right, Belevairn," Wilkinson replied, smiling. "It won't." With that, he simply discarded the rifle,
tossing it behind him. Belevairn noticed the sword that
hung at Wilkinson's side as he reached to draw it.

"But this *will*," the Dreamer informed him.

Belevairn drew his own sword. Wilkinson was correct.
Belevairn could feel the Power in the blade that the *rega*
held. How had he managed to obtain an empowered sword
in this world? For that matter, how had he managed to
smuggle it into the camp?

Wilkinson stepped forward, swinging the sword down
in an overhead strike. Belevairn lifted his own sword to
parry the blow and then snapped it around in a horizontal
strike toward Wilkinson's neck. Wilkinson brought his own
sword across to block the blow. The strength of Belevairn's
strike rocked the young *rega* to the side.

Belevairn pulled his blade back and thrust forward, hoping to catch Wilkinson off balance. Wilkinson parried the thrust easily, responding with one of his own more quickly than Belevairn could counter.

Belevairn's chest burned like fire as the consecrated blade pierced it to the hilt. He found himself staring into Wilkinson's eyes, inches from his own.

"For Caradoc!" Wilkinson whispered between clenched teeth. "And for Richard." Darkness obscured Belevairn's vision as he slid, backwards, off the blade.

For a moment, Steve simply stood and stared at the body of his fallen enemy. Movement down the corridor caught his eye. Steve dropped, instinctively, into a fighting posture as the *goremka* walked forward. It stepped forward and nuzzled the body of the fallen sorcerer.

"You have slain my master, Templar," the *goremka* said. Steve blinked in surprise. He had not realized the monsters could talk!

"You have my thanks," it continued. Before Steve's eyes it began to fade.

"Hold, *Ragavale*!" Steve cried. The *goremka* was his only possible means of reaching Quarin. It could not be allowed to escape.

The *goremka's* form resolidified.

"You have spoken my name, Templar."

Steve took a deep breath.

"By the Power of your name, Ragavale," he began, "and by the Power of the Almighty invested in me, I command you to remain in your stall in this pyramid until, at a time of my choosing, you are to deliver me to the destination which your former master, Belevairn, has tonight sent his forces and then to return to the abyss from which you were summoned."

Steve could feel the demon's anger and hatred for him as it fought to free itself of the command. Steve glared at it—he had felt the Power in the words as he spoke them. Ragavale had no choice but to obey.

"Very well, Templar," Ragavale said. "By your own

words is the compact sealed. So be it." The *goremka* vanished. Steve let out a sigh—he needed to check on Richard. Then he needed to figure out what the hell he was going to take with him—literally.

Chapter
-------- Twenty-one -------------

NOTHING MOVED IN the Morvan camp. Anderson's men had left long before morning. In the dawn light, smoke drifted lazily into the sky. A few fires still illuminated the ruined camp, but most had already burned themselves out.

Steve looked out across the camp from atop the pyramid. The methods might be different, but the end result was the same. The Morvan camp looked like the aftermath of many of the battles that he'd been in before—even down to the bodies of the *galdir* that were littered through the camp. A lot of good men had died down there.

Richard was going to make it, though. He had taken a bullet in the shoulder which Anderson's medics had removed. Williams had the reporter set up in Steve's old cell, resting. Thank God it hadn't been any worse. He'd lost far too many friends to the Morvir, as it was. Far too many . . .

"You ready?" a voice behind him asked.

"As ready as I'll ever be," Steve replied.

"Alexander wants to see you off," Williams said.

"Is he up to it?"

"Yeah," Williams replied, "he's a tough old hound."

Steve smiled. "He is that. Has my stuff been packed?"

"Yep, four rocket launchers, your shotgun and ammo. I've got your pistol, complete with silver bullets, and I've also put together a bandoleer of frag grenades. You're all set, kid."

Steve nodded. It was ironic that the Morvir were supplying him with the tools he needed to destroy that tank. The rocket launchers and the grenades were from the Morvan stores. Williams had gone over their operation with him earlier.

"Promise me that you'll see to it that Alexander makes it back to the States," Steve said.

"You got it. Don't worry, we're not going to let him rot down here. He's a good man."

"Let's go."

Williams had indeed gotten all of Steve's gear packed. Somehow, he had even managed to rig a saddle holster for Steve's shotgun. The *goremka* glared at Steve as he inspected the saddlebags.

"Are you really going to ride that thing, Steve?" Alexander's voice said behind him.

"I'm afraid so," Steve replied.

"Why?" Alexander asked.

"Because I have to," Steve said.

"No, Steve, you don't," Alexander insisted. "You've shut them down. No more weapons or supplies are going to be going to the Morvir from Earth. You've killed the only person who knew the way. It's over. Go home—pick your life back up again."

"No—Daryna still knows about Earth. Someone else will find the way here, and it will all start all over again."

"How are you going to stop that?"

"I don't know," Steve said. "I just know that I have to try."

"Well, good luck, kid."

"Thanks. Williams is going to see to it that you make it back to the States."

"Good—it will be nice to get back."

"Yeah. Do you . . . have the tapes I made?" Steve had used Alexander's recorder earlier to record letters to his parents and to Tam.

"You bet," Alexander replied. "I'll make sure they get them."

"Thanks, Dick. Make them understand, if you can."

"I'll do my best."

"That's all I can ask."

Steve turned and looked at the *goremka*. It stamped and snorted, just like any impatient horse. Steve knew better.

"I guess I can't put this off any longer. It's been eight hours here—eighty there. Over three days. God only knows what's happened over there."

"Good luck, Steve."

"Goodbye, Dick."

Steve placed his foot in the stirrup and mounted the *goremka*. It felt good to be in the saddle again, even though he knew it wasn't truly a horse beneath him. It had been a horse at one time, before it had been sacrificed and fashioned into a prison for a demon.

He nudged Ragavale in the ribs, and the *goremka* started forward at a walk. They left the chamber that had been converted into his stall and went through the corridor onto the temple steps.

Belevairn's memories provided him with the command he needed next. Steve goaded Ragavale forward with a kick and then pressed with his knees. The *goremka* climbed into the air.

Steve stopped the *goremka* and turned. It felt for all the world like he was riding on firm ground. Only his eyes told him they were actually hanging in mid-air. The men of Williams's squad had gathered on the landing of the pyramid's steps and were staring up at him.

Steve drew his sword and saluted before turning away. With a triple click of the tongue he commanded the *goremka* to leave reality for the surreality of the Gray Plain.

Alexander watched as Steve vanished into the rift that had formed into the air. He lowered his good arm, the one he had been waving with.

"Kid's got balls," Williams said.

"No doubt of that," Alexander agreed. "No doubt at all."

"Let's get you out of here, old-timer," Williams said, clapping him on the good shoulder. "I know a doc back in the States who can fix that arm up like new—and who *won't* ask questions."

*   *   *

A pile of dust, mixed with a few bits of crumbled bone, lay on the floor of the corridor. Atop it sat a golden mask, set with gems and cast with a demonic visage.

A booted foot scattered the dust as a hand reached down to grasp the mask. The soldier looked at it, admiring the obvious value of the item. Furtively, he stuffed it into his pack. With this he could retire, quit mercenary work and live quite happily for the rest of his life.

However long that might be.

A week later, Alexander arrived at the Wilkinson home. His arm was still in a sling, but that doctor Williams knew had done a great job on it. In another week or two he would have use of it again. He handed the cabbie a fifty.

"Keep it," he said.

"You bet, mac!" the cabbie replied. "Hey, you want me to wait around?"

"No," Alexander said. "Come back in about an hour. No, better make that three."

"You got it."

Alexander walked up the walk to the front porch. Something on the ground by the walk caught his eye. A cloven hoofprint was burned into the ground. It was almost grown over.

He took a deep breath and rang the bell. A woman answered the door.

"Mrs. Wilkinson?" he asked.

"Yes?"

"My name is Richard Alexander, with the *Clarion*," he said. "I'd like to talk with you about your son."

"Can't you reporters leave us alone . . . ?" Mrs. Wilkinson began.

"You don't understand, ma'am," Alexander interrupted. "I knew Steve—your daughter can verify that. I have some taped letters from him."

"Oh. Oh, please . . . come in."

"Thank you, ma'am."

Epilogue

ERELVAR STOOD ON the battlements of the fortress of Quarin looking out over the city that now bore the same name. While he had not intended such when he built this place, Quarin now served as a major trading center. Since it sat at the intersection of four rivers, he should have expected as much.

Erelvar did not mind overly much. The city served as another layer of defense for his fortress. On each corner of the river the city extended for a mile. At that point a stone wall blocked access to the city. Each gate in that wall was a fortress in itself. This was true even on the Olvan side of the river.

Of course, the Olvir had allowed him to expand there for their own reasons. Having a portion of Quarin on their border did not precisely harm their trade either. Unlike the other kingdoms, however, it was not their first concern. The forest, blighted six years ago during the war against the Morvir, had proven permanently damaged. A city prevented the growth of the strange and twisted plants that had begun to appear there.

Erelvar had not thought of that war in some time. Tonight, though, the memory of it weighed on his heart. He had visited Steven's tomb. The ornate monument he had built for his friend had become a site for pilgrims of all faiths to visit. Steven's body was interred in the base of the statue, in state with his armor and sword.

The fact that the Dreamer was interred there would have been enough, in itself, to inspire pilgrimages. Shortly after his friend had been interred there, however, words had appeared, carved into the stone at the base of the statue.

When the land again has need of it, this Sword shall live again.

Erelvar knew that the prophecies had not been fulfilled at the time of Steven's death. The Dragon had not appeared. For the last six years, Erelvar had awaited that appearance. Now, however, he was beginning to wonder if that event would occur in his lifetime. There was but one Dreamer, but there had been many Champions of Mortos. That duty might fall to another, after him.

He allowed his gaze to lift from the city, out onto the moonlit plains. Why had his thoughts turned to these things tonight? Was this melancholy, nostalgic mood born of resentment that he might not be present for the final defeat of the Mistress? If so, that was naught but vanity.

An odd, rumbling sound reached his ears. He cast about, trying to locate the source of the sound. It seemed to be coming from the north, from the Plains of Blood.

In the moonlight, he saw it as it topped a rise. Its armor was like unto burnished bronze, and its eyes glowed with a steady, white light. The Dragon had arrived . . .